THE Steam TYCOON

GOLDEN CZERMAK

ABOUT THE AUTHOR

In the beginning, Golden worked the standard corporate rat race, completing college with a chemical engineering degree before starting a small photography company on the side.

Since then, the FuriousFotog brand has grown into an internationally recognized brand, has published in both domestic and international magazines, on websites, and trade/e-book book covers (even appearing on some himself). Having been in the industry since 2012, Golden has interfaced and networked with countless other authors, clients, and photographers to license and create over four-hundred romance book cover images, diversifying into other commercial work as well.

He published his debut novel, Homeward Bound (The Journeyman Series, Book One) in June 2016, completing the six-book paranormal adventure romance series in January 2017. Since then he had ventured into other genres, including contemporary, fantasy, and erotica.

Website: **www.onefuriousfotog.com**
Facebook (Photography): **www.facebook.com/furiousfotog**
Facebook (Author): **www.facebook.com/authorgoldenczermak**
Newsletter: **http://eepurl.com/b5p5if**

BOOKS BY THE AUTHOR

THE JOURNEYMAN SERIES:
Homeward Bound (Journeyman Series One)
Seal of Solomon (Journeyman Series Two)
Made to Suffer (Journeyman Series Three)
The Devil's Highway (Journeyman Series Four)
Then Hell Followed (Journeyman Series Five)
Running on Empty (Journeyman Series Six)

SWOLE (EROTIC SHORT STORIES):
Swole: Chest Day

THE STEAM TYCOON SERIES:
The Steam Tycoon

FUTURE NOVELS:
The Secret Life of Cooper Bennett
Secrets of Lagos (Steam Tycoon 2)
A City of Soil (Steam Tycoon 3)
Angelus Rising (Steam Tycoon 4)
He is the Tide
Skyline Memories
After the Ride
Dawn Rises (A Song of Ages Verse 1)
Dusk Falls (A Song of Ages Verse 2)

Strive: Conquest of Stars
Strive: By Way of Starlight
Strive: A Time of Dread

FUTURE NOVELLAS & SHORT STORIES:
Swole 2, 3, 4, 5
Manifest
Stories of the Order – Shadowmen
Stories of the Order – No Strings Attached
Stories of the Order – Mosely

The Steam Tycoon
Published and written by: Golden Czermak
1st Edition

Cover Model: Franggy Yanez
Cover design by FuriousFotog
Edited by Kellie Montgomery
Formatted by Cassy Roop (Pink Ink)

CONTENT NOTICE:
This book contains adult themes, violence, strong language, sexual situations, and nudity. Recommended for mature readers only.

Water is everywhere.
It floats above us in the clouds, falls upon us as rain,
surrounds us in the Great Ocean, and flows within our very
skin. Therefore, it is no surprise that when we can harness
water, in all forms for our own purposes, that it has the
power to reshape the world.

{Maximillian Winthrope}
Founder, Winthrope Limited

DEDICATION

Thank you to my dozen gears: Eric, Franggy, Jake, Ryan, BT, Joey, Jonny, Bryan, Connor, Reggie, Kellie, and Cassy. Without you, this process wouldn't have been impossible.

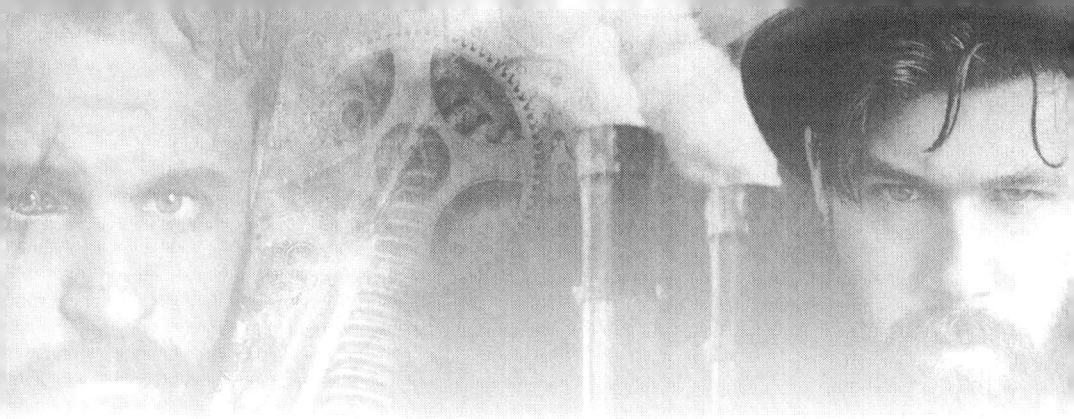

ONE

RAIN CRASHED AGAINST THE ARCHED windows of an office, secluded at the top of a lofty tower. The thoroughfares of the city of Diablo wove a web of cobblestone below, devoid of people and clopping hooves, yet overflowing with runoff from the torrent that had overcome the city's intricate water harvesting system. Similarly, the sprawling stone buildings stretching from horizon to horizon, festooned with swirls of wrought iron, were dark with sleep this time of night.

Back inside the dim workplace, the rhythmic beat of a grandfather clock and the subtle whir of unseen mechanisms merged with the soft tapping of leather soled shoes. As the sounds peaked, a segment of rich wood paneling popped out from the otherwise solid wall, the hinged section swinging open to reveal a hidden passageway. From the darkness, shadows spawned by the warm light of a scrolled copper candelabra prowled across a burgundy rug and extravagant furnishings. A figure then entered the room, slithering toward a ball and claw desk set before lavish draperies.

Placing the candles in the middle of the desktop and a briefcase on the floor, the figure made its way around to the drawers. The soft light fell on the weathered face of a gentleman, tall and trim. His well-fitted finery included a top hat, evening coat, and an embroidered ascot which he loosened around his neck. Grasping the closest brass handle, he yanked a drawer open and the candlelight flickered in his brown eyes, narrowed with purpose.

"Dammit! Where is it?" he hissed, rifling through a messy collection of papers, loose gears, and machine parts. "I know that you're in here. Why are these things never –"

Suddenly, a distant *thud* rose above the sound of rain-struck glass; it came from the hallway. The man halted, his heart beating faster with each flash of lighting that brightened the room and roll of thunder that came with the returning darkness. Crouching, he peered across the desk toward the office entrance. Reaching for a holster on his belt, he freed a pistol embellished with gold accents and waited, poised with a finger beside the trigger. A distressing minute passed that could very well have been an hour for the stress it bore, but no further noises came nor did anyone enter the room.

"Pull yourself together, Maximillian. You're a Winthrope for goodness sake," he muttered, wiping away some stray sweat with his forearm and brushing his gray beard before resuming his search.

The first drawer fruitless, he moved on to the next. It contained even more parts and a small amber spyglass; not what he was looking for as evidenced by his stern frown. This should have been the easiest of his tasks that night.

Frustration mounting, he opened the last drawer and rummaged through it, letting out a relieved sigh.

"For crying out loud, at last! There you are!" he said, beaming at a stack of creamy parchment.

Their edges were rough, as if torn out of a book. They were schematics for an elaborate device, though with the world full of over-the-top renderings of everything from great machines to the smallest article of clothing, it would be easy to overlook the pages. Despite this, the look in Max's eyes indicated the sketches were more than just fanciful machinations.

Snatching the documents, he shoved them into his briefcase before dashing toward the passageway. In the rush, some of the pages fell and scattered across the floor.

"Just my luck!" Max groaned, bending over again in his not-so-forgiving trousers to pick up the pieces. He murmured under his breath as each sheet was hastily collected, but before he could get the last sheets secured, the thick wooden door to the office jostled, then opened.

"Dammit," he cursed.

Max was left with little choice. Although he wanted to flee, he couldn't risk leaving even a single sheet behind. Forced to stand his ground, Max rose and quicker than the lightning outside, was aiming his pistol.

"Stop right there!" he commanded, trembling, as a silhouette staggered in.

The person responded, muffled by thunder.

"Speak up!" Max ordered. "And step forward slowly so I can see you in the light. You can tell Alastair that I will not succumb to all of his saber-rattling."

"What?" asked a groggy voice. "Alistair? Father, what's going on?"

Max lowered the weapon, but only slightly.

"Father?" the voice repeated.

"Jesse, is that you?" Max asked, holstering the gun. "Are you alone?"

"Yes sir," the sixteen-year-old boy replied, rubbing his eyes before stretching in his smooth pajamas. "On both counts."

"What are you doing out of bed, son?"

"Well, you're much noisier than you think," Jesse replied promptly. Letting out a yawn, his white smile shone in the darkness.

Max chuckled, grabbing the briefcase before striding toward him with reserved anxiety.

"My dear boy," he said softly, setting down the case and placing both hands on his son's shoulders. "You should be in bed at this hour getting rest, lest you want to look as frightful as me at this age."

They both smiled and Max used the opportunity to double-check the dark hallway. He saw nothing of concern. Returning his attention to Jesse, Max saw himself reflected in his son's eyes.

Nearing sixty-years-old, Maximillian Winthrope had only started to realize over the last five years that he had spent far too much time building a successful company – Winthrope Limited – out in the parched wilds of the west and far too little time building a strong relationship with his only remaining family: Jesse.

Not that the business and wealth amassed from it didn't afford them indulgences many in the world could only dream of, but having fathered Jesse late in life, such a thing should have dawned on Max much sooner. Especially after the death of his wife and Jesse's mother Mary during a monocycle[1] accident while the two of them were on a date. Jesse had just turned three-years-old, so perhaps that is why he turned his back on family for a time – the pain of love too great to bear while his inventions and profit margins were emotionless, affording him the luxury of ignorance.

Of course, now that he was aware of what *actually* manifested

1   A single wheeled vehicle with the rider seated inside the wheel.

true happiness in life, not a day went by that Max did not wish to turn back the clock, even if it meant giving up his fortune. He had even contemplated sinking it into development of a fanciful time-traveling machine, but decided that task would be better suited for smarter men than him. No matter how much he wanted to remedy things, the past would be immutable. The future, though, was always waiting to be born and that was where change could be made. He was now set on finding ways to make sure Jesse's future would be bright.

Max sniffled then cleared his throat.

"I must make an unforeseen trip to the east," he continued, every faint noise like pins to his nerves. "I'll return soon, perhaps a few days at most, after I deliver the contents of this case to a dependable associate in Barro. I trust that they can keep this information safe, until I can figure out the next steps to take... away from prying eyes."

Jesse perked up, the words energizing his blood. His inquisitive mind was spinning; he loved the idea of traveling.

Prying eyes? he thought. *Associates? More surly men no doubt, heads nodding all the while brandishing knives behind their backs, wanting nothing but a slice of Father's fortune. But Barro! Now there is a positive thing. How great would it be to see the world outside the walls of this city at last?*

"Barro?" Jesse asked aloud. "Isn't that the one of the Quad Cities? It's out in the Mudlands, right?"

"Indeed," his father answered across a slight smile. "To the east and then far south once you reach Blackstone Pass."

"Can I go with you?" Jesse asked eagerly, wriggling in his father's grip like the lid on a boiling pot.

"Sadly no, my child. Not this time," he replied, dipping his eyes to the floor. His son's disappointment was waiting for him when he looked back up. "But, I promise you when I get back we'll head not only to Barro, but also Lagos. You would enjoy that, right?"

Jesse thought about it for a second then nodded.

"Alas, certain matters must be tended to first," Max said as he rubbed one of Jesse's shoulders lovingly. "None more important than safeguarding your future."

Jesse furrowed his brow, unsure what his father meant, but he was enthusiastic about seeing the famed Northern *and* Southern territories. Even though he hated waiting, Jesse knew that he was blessed to even have the chance to do so. That alone set him apart from most his age in the elite class of society; most nothing more than spoiled brats when the thin veneer of fakery was stripped away.

Despite his age, Jesse understood that most of the residents of Diablo were destitute and would never see life beyond the boroughs they were born in. There was a part of him that wanted to see that situation change. He had no idea how that would be brought about – it was more of a gut desire – but he knew there was *something* out there to bring the populace more freedom and, in turn, happiness. Given his privileged circumstances that could be made a reality, but not for some time and certainly not without a lot of effort to tear down the sturdy walls that had risen between the classes.

"When we do go to Barro," his father continued, "I shall arrange a meeting with Prefect DuBois. She is a lot like your mother was: strong-willed and able to stand for what she believes is right, despite what others might think or try to sway."

Jesse's bewilderment shifted into a grin when he heard that; it was like his father read his mind. His thoughts drifted into short-lived memories, passing by more emotionally than visually. He couldn't remember very much about his mother, but what he could recall was wonderful and made him feel the same.

Wrapped up in thought, Jesse missed what his father had continued talking about, only picking up what sounded like the word 'wanderer,' but he wasn't certain. He opened his mouth to ask to clarification, but his father held up a hand to silence him.

"Someone is coming," Max said cautiously, his face becoming pale as he ushered Jesse behind him. "Stay there. I can make out movement."

"Why are you so anxious?" Jesse asked. "We've never had to be so concerned here in the tower before."

"Circumstances and people change," Max replied, his stance getting rigid. "Another lesson I wish I would have taken the time to teach you."

Jesse peeked around his father's body and spotted a man hurrying down the hall, becoming increasingly visible with each step. He was wearing a bowler hat and beneath it, half of his face gave off a cold glow.

Max's body relaxed at the sight, the color returning to this skin.

"Ah, Logan," he called.

Jesse noticed the strain in his father's voice growing with each passing tick of the clock.

Logan Evans stood before them, a sturdy middle-aged man. The faint orange light highlighted a bad scar across the left side of his square face while the right was covered by a mask comprised of metal bands and small gear-shaped bolts, secured by a thick leather strap. His attire was formal but less reserved than Winthrope's. He was their faithful manservant, loyal to their House for the past twenty years.

"Milord," Logan said with a gravelly voice, "his forces have breached the tower and are on the ground floor."

"What of our security measures?" Max asked, knowing the answer.

"They've been disabled, sir."

"As we knew they would be," Max replied. "Then I presume you saw to the lifts?"

Logan nodded, answering with a smirk, "Also disabled, sir."

"Good; that should buy me some time to get to the hangar," Max said, stepping to the side as he pushed Jesse forward into Logan's strong grip. "Logan, please make sure he returns to his chambers and *stays there*. They would not dare harm him to avoid the outrage."

"Are you so sure about that Milord?"

"No, I am not," Max replied, "but please, see it done."

"Yes sir," Logan replied, his mask glinting keenly. "I will. Come on little master, we have to go."

"What's going on? You aren't telling me something," Jesse stated as Logan pulled him away. Max stooped over, picking up the briefcase and made way for the hidden passage. "FATHER!"

The intensity of Jesse's words lashed out and struck Max, stopping him cold. He bit his lip, knowing better than to stay any longer. Letting out a lengthy breath and against his better judgement, he did so anyway.

"You have always wished for the best, Jesse," Max said, peering over his shoulder. "Not only for yourself but the countless others out there as well. I can see it in your face every single morning when we eat breakfast. I share the same desire, which is why this has to be done."

An upwelling of wind sent rain smashing against the glass as a clap of thunder echoed throughout the place.

"Others in this world do not wish to see us succeed. Those people downstairs are mere pawns in this game, all for a handful of Cogs[2] that will get them by before their hands are open for more. They may be dangerous, but are not the true danger. You

---

2   The unit of currency across the world. One gold Gear equals ten copper Spurs or twenty brass Cogs. Gears are also available in silver half units.

see, son, some want the world to stay as it is and we jeopardize their position of control; their own selfish desires are all that they care for. So, it is imperative that we have the fortitude to rise above those that wish to stop progress for the sake of power."

Jesse was confused; this sudden burst of information was a lot to take in.

"This world was once much greater than it is today." Max shook the briefcase in his hand. "There is a chance we may return it to that former glory and we must take that chance, even against the tide."

Max turned all the way around, pausing to look at the grandfather clock before his eyes locked with Jesse.

"I *must* go now but please, if nothing else, remember these words: be happy and stay true to yourself, despite forces that will try to steer you off course. And do not follow the same path your old man did, waiting too long to love."

What's all this talk about? Jesse thought frantically, processing what he was hearing. *Those words sound like something a person says when they are about to leave… forever.*

He struggled to free himself from Logan's grip but the man's hold on him was tight, augmented by the mechanics in his gloves.

With sadness that was not well hidden, Maximillian nodded then stepped toward the passage, crossing the threshold into darkness.

"The future now rests on your shoulders, Jesse," he said as the doorway began to close. "You will understand what I mean in time, my boy. Steam is currently the answer and reigns supreme; do it and the Winthrope name proud!"

Jesse tried to call out but was speechless, his heart beating in his throat.

"Come on," Logan pressed. There was a gleam behind his masked eye. "It's time that the young master returned to bed.

Quickly now, as there's company below that I need to tend to."

A gentle *hiss* rose along with the low drone of machinery. Before long, the wall had sealed itself shut again, the passage indiscernible from its surroundings.

Jesse's feelings betrayed the normality of the room, a sickness occupying the deepest pit of his stomach as the grandfather clock chimed. It told him what he already knew: that he would not see his father again.

TWO

THE DAYS WENT BY AND ON THE morning of the fourth one, Jesse's assumption was proven wrong. His father had returned and was there with him as promised, though sadly unaware of his son's presence.

Jesse wore a stiff black suit, gloves, and a dark cravat, looking out through misty eyes onto a sea of gathered people. He saw the silent faces of his father's colleagues and business associates, motionless while dipped in mourning. Jesse himself was far from still, fidgeting with a top hat that was perched on one knee.

The downpour that had started earlier in the week hadn't stopped, rumbling on the steep-sloped roof of the extravagant cathedral. A shower ran down the stained-glass windows like tears, casting rolling hues of muted color across the assembly. The noise grew overbearing at times, drowning out the minister's words as he waved his arms beneath formal robes. The sound drew Jesse's gaze upward to the lofty, ribbed vaults. There he admired the space, grand yet empty like his chest.

After a few minutes, Jesse lowered his eyes to stave off sleep and they met his father's stoic face, embalmed. He wept once more before composing himself.

Maximillian had been laid in repose, nestled in a bed of satin that lined his coffin, which in turn rested atop a catafalque of cherry cloth. A silver plaque bore his name while the plain white coffin handles sparkled despite the gloomy light. Simple opposed to decadent, it was customary that all persons, despite their status, were equal in death and the judgement that awaited beyond. Thus, the richest of society – save the most pretentious of course – would suppress pomp and circumstance to avoid loading needless expenses on top of the grief already endured by those they were leaving behind.

The minister was wrapping up his comforting remarks and Jesse firmed his stance, knowing that he would be standing there for a while. Once the minister uttered his final words, the congregation rose and those in the front pews strode up a short set of steps toward the coffin, followed by those behind in succession. Forming a single file, they walked by Maximillian to pay their quiet respects.

Jesse was positioned beside his father's head, shaking the hands of those who walked by him. He saw expressions of all sorts; some were sad, some clearly tired, while others seemed to suppress an urge to smile. He tried not to dwell on those for long. In fact, all those faces were forgettable that day, blurring together with each passing person. However, given the way the world worked, Jesse knew he would get a chance to know some of them more and even their motives as time passed.

The mindless process repeated countless times and Jesse's hand was tiring. The line stretched on and his mind had already left, strolling in lands far outside the city walls where the sun was shining.

Suddenly, a leather-clad hand gripped his own rather tightly. Shaken out of his trance, Jesse darted his gaze up into waiting brown eyes.

In front of him was a man in his early twenties; something about him was different than the rest he had seen that morning. The stranger's face was fresh, topped with black hair edged with a well-groomed beard. The suit he was wearing was appropriately black, too, yet filigreed with showy gold threads. A faint damask pattern flowed throughout and his golden ascot beamed nearly as bright as the grin he wore.

"That's quite the handshake you have," Jesse said, suspecting the man's ostentatious manner extended beyond his attire.

Two figures accompanied him, standing to either side. Jesse's eyes darted between them and he found them rather surly, even though they were well-presented with bowler hats hanging by the tips of their rough fingers. The one on the left was the more intimidating of the two, looking more like a scruffy brawler than a gentleman. The one on the right was just downright scary, especially when he showed any part of his crooked, yellow teeth. The trio managed to make Jesse edgy just by standing there.

"Strength is undoubtedly a quality possessed by superior men to have and present," he replied haughtily, confirming Jesse's suspicion.

Jesse could feel the man trying to twist his hand so his palm was facing upward.

"That may be the case," Jesse replied, resisting a little longer, then allowing him to do so, "but I feel that the strongest of us don't have the desire, or need, to flaunt it."

The man scoffed at the notion.

"Whatever you say, my friend," he continued, eyes narrowing. "Regardless, your father possessed those qualities in some capacity, both physically and in his ambitions, as did mine before he passed away."

Jesse could feel the man's grip easing at last.

"Forgive my ignorance, but I'm at a loss. Your name is?"

"Frost," he replied, smattered with offense – surely everyone knew who the Frosts were. He withdrew his hand and shoved it in a trouser pocket. "Lucas Frost the Third, owner of Frost Enterprises."

Jesse still had no idea who he was and wanted to reply that it was a pleasure, but that would have been an outright lie.

"Ah, yes, Frost!" he said anyway with emphasis on the surname.

Glancing to his hand, Jesse noticed that Lucas had placed a few scraps of metal in it. They were rough and misshapen, one piece longer than the others, coated with brown and white paint. Jesse gasped as he examined it closely, realizing the snowy tint was part of the Winthrope logo and that these were, in fact, pieces of the ornithopter his father used when he fled the tower.

Jesse's hand trembled, the emotionless metal conjuring an emotion-filled memory of what he was told the night before…

Per Logan, three days earlier – in the hours that followed Maximillian's departure – a small group of Rangers set out in the dim light from Blackstone Pass. They rode with the rising sun behind them and a storm far ahead, following the gently curved lines of the railroad. They were heading just shy of fifty kilometers from the town limits to look into claims of a raider attack. Expecting to find a gang of wastelanders preying on a group of travelers, or the carnage normally left behind, the Rangers were surprised by the lack of evidence of an ambush. Not a railcar in sight, there were no signs of any trouble as far as their eyes could see.

Removing a pair of grungy goggles, one of the men took out a set of brass binoculars from a leather satchel and surveyed the area. Flicking additional glassware in front of the eyepieces, he zoomed further into the surrounding landscape. Nothing immediately caught his attention but as the billowing soil settled to the south, he spotted a plume of what could be steam. As it was close, the group rode in that direction, cresting a small hill that bordered the Delgado a short time later.

Below them was the fresh wreckage of an ornithopter, its tanks still venting beneath crumpled wings as it was lapped by the cold waters of the river. The metallic, insect-like frame and bulbous glass were riddled with bullet holes, the obvious cause of both the crash and the report of an ambush.

Wasting no time and whipped by the same wind that relentlessly stirred up dust, the men looked for survivors, finding none. There was only a single, well-dressed body amongst the plundered heap of mangled metal.

From there, the Rangers radioed Blackstone and word traveled quickly, reaching the ears of the High Sheriff. Once he was aware of *who* his Rangers had found, he immediately contacted Diablo and made arrangements with the city to have Winthrope's body returned.

He never made it to Barro, Jesse thought, the fear and pain his father endured singeing his mind. *He never made it.*

His heart sank to his feet; the hope his father lauded for the future was gone and the contents of his case had no doubt lost to the brutes that pillaged the debris.

"Apparently, the pleasure of this meeting is all mine," Lucas said, his stern tone jabbing Jesse back to the present. "Very well then."

He cleared his throat and began to make way for the exit. Donning his top hat while still inside the building, a few ladies standing nearby murmured with displeasure. They were met by Lucas' piercing stare and a smirk as he tipped the hat, falling silent thereafter.

"H-how did *you* get this?" Jesse asked, unsure of the emotions he was feeling. They were shifting so fast it was hard to latch onto one for very long.

Unseen by Jesse, Lucas beamed.

Unseen by Lucas, Jesse's upper lip quivered.

Lucas might as well have stabbed Jesse for all the pain it brought him, but Jesse knew better than to acquiesce to the man's goading by responding in kind. It would have been ill-mannered to do so at a time and in a place where all animosities should be left outside. Outwardly, the young man remained cool but his thoughts raged hotter than a boiler.

Meanwhile, Lucas was apparently unbothered by such formalities, used to getting what he wanted given his status.

"I have my ways," he replied confidently, stopping just short of the topmost step. He positioned himself where he could look over his shoulder right at Jesse. "I would be doing myself and *my* company a disservice if I didn't have eyes, ears, and hands *everywhere*. You should take note. I simply thought you would want a memento to remember your father. It's no large matter though; after all, it's the thought that counts, right?"

Jesse didn't respond and with a grimace, he placed the pieces in his jacket pocket so he could shake the next hand that was in line.

Lucas didn't take that gesture very well; he wasn't fond of being ignored and despite the procession, his temper flared. Marching toward Jesse, he heaved a portly gentleman out of the way. The man wobbled so much that he nearly fell over.

"I beg your pardon!" the patron grunted, his face swelling like a balloon about to pop.

Before the man said anything else, one of Lucas' associates had appeared behind him, clamping a large hand on the round man's shoulder. He squeezed.

"Well, I never…" the guest continued and the associate's grip grew more forceful. The man's knees quivered and he gulped, then fell quiet.

Lucas dropped his voice into a sinister whisper, staring at Jesse with a fire in his eyes.

"Listen," he said to Jesse, who was staring at him intensely. "While I am offering you my sincere condolences for your loss, I sincerely hope that you realize a lot of those gathered here today see it as a gain. I want to be the first to offer my assistance, should you need it of course. Do not hesitate to get in touch; I would hate to see you end up like your father."

Was that a warning, or a threat?

Jesse couldn't decide so closed his eyes; much more of this and his fists might become ungentlemanly.

Lucas peered down at Jesse's balled up hands and smiled, a low chuckle seeping out between his lips.

"That said, Frost Enterprises wishes you and the future of Winthrope Limited well," Lucas stated, spinning on the spot. He departed, his thugs in tow. "Farewell for now, Jesse. I am sure the both of us will see each other again. I will look forward to that day with great interest."

Jesse felt relief mixed with irritation and opening his eyes, Lucas was gone. Composing himself, Jesse reached out to the rotund man to finish his handshake.

"Are you all right?" he asked. "Mister…"

"Newsam," the man replied, smoothing out his stubby mustache. "Charles Newsam and yes, yes, I am fine."

"Mr. Newsam," Jesse uttered with a warm and thankful smile, "I want you to know that all things considered, it is a *great* pleasure to meet *you*."

Newsam nodded politely, though his forehead had filled with confused wrinkles. He supposed Winthrope's words were part of an inside joke, but nonetheless carried on bobbing his globular head.

"Why, um, thank you," he said, coughing briefly before lowering his voice so his wife couldn't hear his next words. "You know sir, had we not been *in here*, I would have liked to show those hooligans a thing or two."

"Me too," Jesse whispered with a subtle glance to the man's wife, knowing that she had heard. "Me too."

Taking a final look at the church's grand entrance, Jesse saw Lucas standing in front of the open door. He was looking back at him, the rain coming down in heavy sheets beyond.

Jesse realized that no matter what he truly wanted, life was going to change for him even more than it already had. How that road would take shape he couldn't predict, but in a few short days he would formally be in control of Winthrope Limited, and all the blessings and curses of the position would be seeking him out.

Watching Lucas open an umbrella only to hand it off to one of his men as if he were a stand, Jesse sighed. A part of him held on to the hope of bringing the world the change he wanted, but a larger piece realized people like Lucas Frost – remaining dry in the rain at the expense of drenching his own associates – would try to stop that from happening at any cost.

THREE

TWELVE LONG YEARS CAME THEN went, teaching Jesse lessons every single day. Unwilling to let the trials and tribulations get the best of him, the sixteen-year-old boy that went into the fire emerged a twenty-eight-year-old man with far more experience, intellect, and good looks.

Jesse was standing in front of his office's large windows. He wore a simple white shirt, unbuttoned, with plain black trousers. Over the years, he found this look suited him more than the formal and often elaborate everyday wear that had grown in popularity. Without shoes, Jesse nuzzled his bare toes against the soft rug. A nearby gramophone was playing an upbeat and catchy tune.

The drapes had been drawn back and ample amounts of morning sunlight spilled into the room, glinting off an ornate globe sitting on a small table. There was a vast ocean on it made of sapphire and a single land mass of amber inlaid with gold.

Jesse soaked up the warmth, his arms crossed in front of his hairy chest. It felt good against his face, handsome and rugged, with a dark beard framing his chin. Disheveled hair, unbound by gravity, rose high on his head while thin strands of licorice caressed his forehead.

Below the tower, which had been Winthrope Limited's headquarters for the last 110 years, people and sleipnir[3] clopped through the bustling streets. From that height, Jesse couldn't make out anyone individually. It was more like a sea of moving color that washed down the cobblestone paths into homes and shops along the way. The constant tick of the grandfather clock and a sweetly spiced aroma kept him company. It gave him peace of mind, or so it was meant to, concealing the true sentiments of woe felt by the citizenry.

"Are you done admiring the view?" a charming male voice interrupted. "Or are you lost in admiration?"

"Of the city?" Jesse asked, taking a long look across the rooftops.

"No, your reflection in the glass."

Jesse laughed, turning as he lowered his arms to his sides. He looked at a couple of rather uncomfortable sofas in the center of the room, arranged in a small seating area. There was a fancy oval coffee table between them and small vase of purple flowers atop it. The pair of seats was beautiful but incredibly rigid, their main purpose to keep visitors from staying too long.

A charismatic fellow was perched defiantly on the edge of the left one. Dressed in a well-crafted blue suit, crisp white shirt, and a matching tie, the man could easily be mistaken for Jesse's brother at first glance. He was the taller of the two, with eyes the color of the sea and a dark brown beard.

"As if you don't do the same thing," Jesse replied.

---

3   This world's equivalent of a horse but with eight legs instead of four. Powerful creatures, they have been domesticated for use as beasts of burden and entertainment. However, there are still wild and feral varieties across the wastes, the latter well known to attack trade caravans without much provocation.

Taking a moment to stretch, he stepped over and switched off the music then scooped up a thick stack of documents resting on the refurbished leather desktop. *Lagosian Water Trade Agreement of 1797* was impeccably scribed across the top. Straightening the heap with a couple sharp taps, Jesse made his way to the seating area.

His guest that morning was a magistrate hailing from the city of Lagos. Duncan Morrison had become good friends with Jesse over the years, the pair sharing quite a few adventures – and misadventures – together.

He had come to Diablo so they could finalize a trade deal between his city and Winthrope Limited. Once complete then ratified by both mayors, Lagos would allow construction of a pipeline from its southernmost mountain spring to Diablo. This would provide the desert city with another consistent source of water, far cleaner than what was currently drawn from their pipeline to the West Coast. In turn, Winthrope would provide Lagos with high efficiency steam engines of his own design, along with several of his newly miniaturized units. Lagos would be able to retire much of their bulkier machinery and benefit from the improved technology.

"So tell me," Jesse said as he neared the couch across from Duncan, "did you rest well?"

Duncan wiped a corner of his eye; he had arrived at the tower late the night before. Jesse had stayed up waiting for him, but sleep finally took over after a slew of factory issues plagued his own day. Reliably, Logan saw to it that Duncan was taken care of upon his arrival; greeting him, providing refreshment, then taking him to the guest accommodations. It wasn't long before Duncan was asleep, too, still wearing all of his clothes.

"Considering how stress has made it into every facet of our lives lately, I slept surprisingly well. In fact, I would say it was the best I've had in a while," Duncan replied graciously. "However, I could have done without all those delays yesterday. It was positively grueling. I thought I wouldn't get here until next century."

"Well, if it's any consolation, that is *only* three years away," Jesse replied, his cheeky smile instantly becoming a frown when he dropped onto the hard seat.

Setting the papers on the table Jesse moved around, trying to find a comfortable position. There wasn't one.

Duncan chuckled at the sight, grabbing a small cup of coffee from the table. After a sip, he recounted what happened over his thousand-kilometer rail journey through green mountains and past blue lakes before chugging out into the plains. Most of the tale was quite humdrum, but there were elements that piqued Jesse's interest.

Duncan's first stop after a long and winding trip south was the town of Bala. Once reputable in its heyday, the town had been established as one of the main railroad hubs for settlements in the Barrens. In the years that followed, conditions there degenerated and the place filled with shady characters from the wastes, grubby saloons, and bazaars. Crooked law enforcement oversaw it all, explaining how some of the town's seedier residents easily 'found' weapons and ammunition for their equally seedy clientele.

Duncan waited in Bala's station to switch lines for Diablo's station in the borough of Comprass. The area was noisy with chatter and machinery, filled with steam and smells from a couple of food vendors set up at the end of the platforms. Behind them, cleanliness and safety notably dropped on the other side of the iron-clad exits. He wasn't overly concerned, being armed and capable of holding his own should any trouble break out, but that didn't mean he wanted to stay there for any longer than needed.

Finishing off a skewer of unknown meat which tasted a lot better than it looked, Duncan boarded the westbound double-decker as soon as possible. He quickly settled into a seat on the upper deck by the window, set his case in the empty one beside him, and looked out through the steam to the neighboring engines and dreary brown landscape. He couldn't wait to be done and home where things were blue and green. Leaning his head back to relax, he closed his eyes, ready to get this final leg of the journey out of the way.

No sooner than he had gotten comfortable did the door to the carriage slide open, the conductor striding through to inform him of a departure delay. Apparently, the railcars needed to undergo a last-minute inspection, something to do with a malfunction in their defense systems, and that would take at least an hour. Duncan knew things never went so easily and pressed for additional details. Adding insult to his already mounting irritation, he discovered the maintenance crew was shorthanded, which was more than likely going to triple the wait time.

"Amazing, isn't it?" Duncan told Jesse. "The engine itself was in order, thanks to the fine contributions of an industrious man I know. Yet, there just *happened* to be maintenance issues with the carriages and those issues *had* to be addressed right then and there in ill-equipped Bala. Mere coincidence? I think not."

"Better to be safe than sorry, though," Jesse said, loosely playing devil's advocate.

Duncan wasn't swayed.

"You mean better to pad Frost's pocketbook?" he retorted, setting down his cup then snatching the stack of papers off the table. "That man will do anything for a Gear."

Jesse's face dropped into a scowl but quickly recovered.

"In all fairness, you and I both have an affinity for money as well," he continued.

"Yes, but at least we're honest about earning it," Duncan said, shaking his head.

"I like to think I am, but aren't you a lawyer?" Jesse asked casually.

"*Magistrate,*" Duncan snipped, eyes narrowing.

Jesse raised his hands in front of him.

"I was just joking; no offense intended."

"I'm highly offended," Duncan replied, peering over the edge of the paperwork as he started flipping through it. "You owe me breakfast."

"I had already planned on that," Jesse said before lowering his voice to a more serious tone. "But back to Frost. I'll be honest: it's the reason he's having to outfit locomotives and railcars with defensive systems in the first place that has me more concerned."

"You mean the raiders?" Duncan asked.

Jesse nodded.

"They've become more brash and their encounters are getting closer to large settlements. Just last week I was made aware of one at Alum City. Rangers spotted a small band of them within three kilometers of their borders."

"That's certainly close," Duncan agreed. "Any damage?"

"No," Jesse said. "They were just watching."

A slight chill slid down Duncan's back.

"The closest they'd gotten before was, what, ten kilometers?" he asked.

"Yes, near Blackstone; that was another railcar attack. Thankfully they were crushed swiftly but I don't know Duncan, with gangs getting closer and the frequency increasing, my gut is telling me that a town is going to come under attack, sooner rather than later."

"And here we are, about to build another pipeline through those lands," Duncan said solemnly. "All for the greater good I suppose."

"And for Frost," Jesse added, "since he would be providing security and defenses along it."

Duncan scowled at the idea and Jesse shrugged.

"You did say he liked to line his own pcokets."

Duncan was forced to bob his head reluctantly.

The conversation continued for a few more minutes before the duo refreshed their coffees and dove into the final revision of the agreement.

They leafed through page after page of dreary legalese, finding everything in order as they went. The task went smoothly over the next half hour, until Duncan stumbled upon some updated numbers in the appendix. They were efficiency values for Winthrope's systems, now capable of fifty-three percent opposed to forty-three a month earlier. He made a comment about the ten percent jump, which proved to be a mistake that his rumbling stomach was quick to remind him of.

Jesse was visibly proud of the accomplishment, wasting no time droning away to explain the improvements that were made.

"I broke through the previous limits," he said, excitedly gesturing with his hands. "If you recall – well not actually since we weren't alive at the time – the early steam plants couldn't achieve efficiencies more than fifteen percent. Leap to today and the large-scale steam systems in use across the world are around thirty-five percent."

"Thanks to the work your father pioneered," Duncan recognized.

Catching bits and pieces of Jesse's follow-up explanation, most of it soared well over Duncan's head. He knew that before the invention of Winthrope's High Efficiency Steam Engines, whimsically dubbed the WHESE, the most efficient engines were also the largest. Winthrope managed to push things further, using new alloys to make the units smaller, faster, and lighter. Beyond that, Duncan's understanding buckled.

"And that's how we managed to bring these engines closer to the theoretical max," Jesse said after ten minutes of solid talking, his whipping hair finally coming to rest.

Duncan was proud of his friend and knew that if Jesse could physically pat himself on the back he would have. Despite that being a conceited gesture, he also knew it was deserved. Duncan could see the effects Winthrope's technology had – essentially opening the door to a new age of innovation and industrialization – and that's what drew Lagos' attention.

"I think with the WHESE at fifty-three percent and with our lower cost, we've effectively put the competition's compression engines out to pasture. Now, if I can somehow convince Barro to adopt this technology…"

Jesse drifted off into solo conversation again, this time about his ingenious steam capsules.

Duncan coughed, stopping him.

"Forgive me, my friend," he said with an awkward laugh, "but I've been quite lost since you began. Remember, my intellect isn't on par with yours. I've poured my time and resources into women versus science."

"I think I have more resources than you *due* to science," Jesse replied.

Duncan smirked.

"But your social talents are superior," Jesse continued, "only rivaled by those you have in the bedroom… or so I hear."

"Quite literally that one time we were in Bravewater."

Jesse's face flushed with embarrassment.

"After that I think you came to know me far too well," Duncan stated. "We really do need to find you someone to occupy the better parts of your time."

"You know how I am," Jesse said. "I need someone to challenge me and let's face it, a lot of the ladies we meet are too…"

"Proper?" Duncan cut in with a wink.

"Proper," Jesse repeated. "Just once I would like to meet one that offered a bit of a challenge instead of staunch conformity or a desire for money."

"I'm sure there is someone out there. We just have to find them," Duncan said, handing the documents over to Jesse. "All looks in order with these."

"I doubt we will find her in Diablo," Jesse said, taking the papers. He walked over to his desk. "I just need to find some balance and try not to let myself get so wrapped up in work and all the minuscule technicalities. Just yesterday I was in the middle of issues I could have delegated."

"But then you would have been worried whether it was getting done correctly. I get it."

"I think that's what Father warned me about years ago, but sometimes it gets the better of me."

"That's because you're good at the technical side, Jesse. It's where you shine," Duncan said, arriving at Jesse's shoulder. "Look at all it has brought you and society. You've definitely made progress toward your goal faster than expected."

"Yes, but if only I could do all this faster," Jesse wished, signing the document then waving his fountain pen toward the window. "Every time I see the faces out there – particularly those less fortunate than us – it drives me that much harder, but there are so many unnecessary hurdles."

"Human nature often sees itself in the way of progress, I'm afraid," Duncan said, taking the pen to sign off on the agreement himself. He set it down and grabbed his friend reassuringly on the shoulder. "You're doing this at a fine pace. Remember: all things in good time. Use those great talents of yours and push ahead; you've already come this far despite what the majority have said was possible. They may not like you Jesse, but who cares. I seem to recall you giving me these very same words of advice when I was struggling to get this position as Magistrate."

"I suppose you're right, my friend," Jesse said.

"I'm not supposing anything," Duncan replied, punctuated by an intense growl in his belly.

"I guess that means it's breakfast time," Jesse said right when the grandfather clock chimed nine o'clock. "Shall I get Logan to bring us something?"

Duncan shook his head, his eyes petitioning for another selection.

"Would it be possible for us to get some food outside?" he asked. "No offense to the inhabitants of your fine city but the closed in spaces of your buildings make me have trouble breathing."

"Of course," Jesse replied, knowing that the architecture of Lagos was far more open and airy. "We can go Grayson Market; it's not but a ten-minute walk from the tower entrance."

"That sounds excellent."

"We can talk more about the current situation with Frost," Jesse added.

"Certainly, but can we keep things simple so I can understand them?" Duncan asked, Jesse playfully nodding as he buttoned up his shirt.

FOUR

JESSE AND DUNCAN EMERGED SIDE by side on the paved street, the large gate to Winthrope's property closing behind them with a resounding *clang*. The sun was shining brightly overhead, its light dancing off an array of metallic accessories that were spread out on a couple tables outside a nearby clothing shop. There were golden buttons, silver bracelets with gear shaped trinkets, copper brooches, and more. A sign fluttered overhead; it said 'All Accessories On-Sale – For All Brass Take An Additional Twenty Percent Off!'

"I will never understand the desire for those kinds of adornments," Jesse said, placing a simple bowler hat on his head. There was a pair of studded leather goggles resting on the top of it, the lenses rimmed with gold.

"If you say so," Duncan told him, checking his pocket watch to hide a smile.

"This way," Jesse said, none the wiser. He headed left along

Chester Avenue, the breeze catching in his long, brown overcoat.

The two made their way on foot toward Grayson Market, about half a kilometer away. Since they were in one of the city's higher-end boroughs (named Patria), Jesse figured it would be safe to travel without the need for additional security. Their own pistols holstered, they left both Logan and any security bots behind.

The narrow street grew more populated the further they went, but with carriages and conveyances rather than pedestrians rolling down the noisy center. Duncan noticed several men speeding by; they were standing on strange devices, holding handles that were attached to a long pole for stability. Wheeled mechanisms propelled them forward, sputtering noisily as they weaved between carriages, hissing vehicles, and monocycles.

"Is that one of your creations?" Duncan asked as the odd sight disappeared in traffic.

"Don't be silly," Jesse said, preferring to move about on his own two feet, "though I probably factored into the design somewhere along the way."

Unlike the poorer outer segments of the city, the people here sought any means of travel other than foot. It was starting to take a toll on Jesse's senses and his nerves; he wasn't a fan of crowds ever since his father's funeral.

"You managing?" Duncan asked, noticing Jesse's face straining.

"Yes, I'll be fine," he said, passing a hand over his forehead as if checking for a fever. "It's just a headache."

"Should be fine once you get some food in you," Duncan replied. "Goodness knows I will be."

They carried on, passing by even more shops and homes above them. Duncan examined it all, wishing he had a second or even third pair of eyes. He admired the craftsmanship of the stone exteriors, decorated with elegant trim around rippled window glass, pillared porches and flattened archways, and steep clay roofs with tall chimneys. It was so different from what he was used to seeing at home that no matter how many times he visited, he could always find some new facet to enjoy.

They reached the halfway point, groups of people pouring into buildings or swirling in chatty clusters in front of stalls. Stores had all sorts of objects shoved in their windows. They specialized in finery and timepieces, goggles and spy glasses, odd gadgets and steam capsule powered tools. The stands were overflowing with goods laid out across tables covered in white linen or stowed in bulging wood barrels, some overflowing. Jesse guided them past a shop named The Current Cravat where yet another sale was happening. Evidently quite popular, a line had formed out the door and down the street; the epitome of excess when those in other boroughs were struggling to stay healthy, clothed, and fed.

"There sure are some insane deals happening today," Duncan observed, dodging three men racing across the street. They were moving so swiftly the seams of their trousers were about to split.

"The anniversary of the Great Burning is the day after tomorrow," Jesse told him. "It's the four-hundredth."

The annual ceremonies had started as sober affairs but along the way had entangled with extravagance. Now, the rich tried to outshine each other instead of remembering the wrongs of history while the poor, remembering but powerless, continued struggling. Being a centennial year made the posturing a hundred-fold worse.

"How far we've come since that time," Jesse said gravely, scrutinizing those in line with upset eyes.

The special day hearkened back to 1397 when the world was ravaged by a terrible war that spanned the entire supercontinent of

Eaugen. Humanity had grown in numbers and, to their credit, an environment bloomed that fostered easy living and convenience for all. A crowning achievement, over time complacency and its perils crept in, nurturing entitlement, selfishness, and greed. At the pinnacle of a technological boom, people became ravenous for fossil fuels, consuming them like water to quench their desires. Resources were devoured quickly, everything tipping once most had been consumed. Friend became foe; allies turned into enemies and one after another, territories were invaded for what few flecks of coal or drops of oil remained. All was chaos and death.

With the widespread carnage came pestilence, a virulent plague swiftly carried throughout the festering, war-torn population. People fell faster than the trees used to burn their remains and by the end, nearly a billion lives were reduced to a mere fifteen-million scattered across the wastelands left behind.

Time, ever diligent, managed to heal those wounds. The better of society organized and formed loose settlements across the world while the less than savory remained elusive in the wastes. Left to their own devices and struggling against powerful creatures in the wild, those groups banded together and eventually became the raiders. They learned to take what they needed and along with it great pleasure in the torment and death of those they took it from.

Despite all the turmoil and darkness that threatened to sink society again, four major cities arose from the ashes. Diablo, Lagos, Barro, and Angelus became beacons of light to guide the rebuilding of society from the four corners of the world.

"Wait… what?" Duncan asked with a tone of panic. "The anniversary is this week?"

Jesse nodded. He continued down the street, avoiding a messy fall where several paving stones were missing.

"Watch your step," he warned. "If this is the result of those new income taxes I'll have to revisit the topic with the mayor."

Duncan wasn't paying attention; he was in a slight daze after hearing the date confirmation.

"Problem?" Jesse asked, only to watch Duncan trip. "I told you to watch your step!"

"I'm okay," he said, righting himself before he fell all the way over. "I was just thinking that I need to take a close look at my planner after our meeting with the mayor; that is still today, right?"

Jesse nodded again.

"I swear everything is running together. The last thing I need is to get off-schedule when I return home in the morning. Things could get quite… chaotic for me if so."

"How so? Major rulings to deliver once you get back?" Jesse prodded.

Duncan shook his head.

"Not quite the appointments I'm concerned about keeping…" he said, eyes shifting uneasily between Jesse's and the cobblestone.

"*Oh, I see!*" Jesse exclaimed. "Go on then: what's her name?"

Duncan's handsome face became flushed.

"There are a few names," he clarified.

Jesse's eyes widened like the road ahead of them. He would have pressed the playboy further but lucky for him they had arrived at Grayson Market. If they thought the street they'd just navigated was busy, it paled in comparison to the plaza.

The two entered a sprawling circular area from Chester Avenue, one of fourteen streets that converged on the area. Stepping over a large numeral four made of lighter stones, they passed by men dressed in long black coats with gleaming white buttons, the Frost Enterprises emblem embroidered on the left breast. Their boots were heavy and tall, the shiny helmets on their heads white. Each wore reflective goggles that hid their eyes and their white-gloved hands brandished long rifles.

"Frost has certainly been... innovative," Jesse commented, noting the guns were wrapped with corrugated tubing that ran to bloated pressure vessels while metal grills along the top vented a mist of steam. He tried his hardest not to criticize the design as he walked, but thought they would be much more efficient and elegant if they used his steam capsules. Had he trusted Frost, that might be an option. As it stood: no.

Frost's security forces were posted on each side of the street to keep out the poor riffraff, a stark contrast to the inviting banners that rippled in the sunlight beside them.

"Seems like he's compensating for something to me," Duncan added.

There were no vehicles in the plaza, only swarms of people equally mechanical in their predictable flow around at the stalls that filled the center. The first circular row of canopies were mongers selling fresh ingredients by the kilogram or liter. Duncan liked to compare prices on his travels, so driven by the scent in the air, looked at the prices for bacon. The rashers were thick, fatty, and nearly half the price in Diablo at two Spurs and a Cog.

The next row and beyond were food vendors, crafting sumptuous dishes of bread, eggs, and meats that caused mouths to water without so much as a glance. The smells surely reached the anonymous masses elsewhere in the city; they could feast for at least a week from just one of these stalls, yet were often only afforded less than a pint of tea and a few slices of hard bread, scraped thinly with butter. On the other more privileged hand, the educated working man and elites that mingled in Grayson had their choice of nearly a hundred stalls that would fill the space until noon. This was to allow those that had not yet risen out of their plush beds time to partake, or have such ingredients and cuisine delivered to their homes.

Though the over-indulgences wore heavy on his heart, Jesse could not deny that it was satisfying to see at least some intermingling between two classes, a thing that was incredibly rare in the inner part of the city. It was a small step, but one in the right direction.

Around the outside loop were sturdy buildings garnished with baroque detail. Inside were dining halls and coffee shops, fine tables set outside beneath awnings. Jesse scanned what he could see, spotting a small establishment across the way.

"Perfect," he murmured, making his way toward it.

"Jesse, not to point something out that I'm sure you're already aware of, but that place looks rather quiet," Duncan observed, seeing no customers. "Are you sure they're open and not out of business?"

"Yes," Jesse answered shortly, worming through the crowd. "Quite sure."

They passed a stand selling croquettes. Many were waiting for another batch of the bite-sized treats and Duncan slowed down, looking longingly. A nearby gentleman bit into one and the cheesy beef filling oozed out from the crispy crust.

"That looked amazing…" he said. "Are you sure the food is any good where we are going?"

"At this point, I'm not sure if I mind," Jesse replied. There was irritation in his voice; the headache mounting. "But I figure little activity inside should equate to faster service for us and some peace."

In the middle of the plaza was a triangular spire made of iron. Jutting out to the side, it towered over everything else in the area. The sun shined on it, sending a hard shadow down one of the numbered streets across from them, revealing the entire market was an immense sundial; one of many quirky features the city had incorporated into its layout.

"Everything boils down to time," Jesse said, glancing at the spire. He slowed so Duncan could catch up. "So, this question may be out of the blue, but do you ever see us getting into another situation like the Burning?"

Duncan thought about it, trying to hide his limp.

"Heavy questions this morning," he said.

"Not that I think about it all the time," Jesse explained, "it's just given the dominance of steam here and with technology improving in the world, I worry that we may backslide if things progress too far. It happened with oil, who's to say it won't happen with some other fuel? Seeing how the rest of my 'fellows' are, especially those over in Angelus, I don't have much hope in that regard."

"Angelus," Duncan scoffed, a passerby's eyes widening at the mention of the Eastern city before he scurried off. "Those people live with their heads so high in the clouds it's remarkable they don't suffocate. I'd pay them no mind as they spend their days gladly looking down upon the rest of us."

"I try not to," Jesse said. "Yet it's difficult when their president speaks of a new frontier for society, echoing what Father said, but it's unclear what exactly he means. They are less than willing to trade technologies; all my attempts at contracts are met with silence. I hope their next election will place someone in charge with more common sense."

The two reached the eatery, pausing next to a sign propped up on the ground. It indicated the special of the day was sausage and mashed potatoes. An elderly woman was inside, her friendly wrinkles beckoning them to come in. On either side, the other places were more crowded and the food more elegant, but the long faces of those attempting to enjoy their morning repast indicated the service was subpar.

Jesse signaled to the old woman that they would be one moment.

"Common sense has long been absent, Jesse. The president – too good to be called a lowly mayor – has been there forever, so good luck with that," Duncan continued, his face becoming uncharacteristically serious. "Regarding what you said just before that: society may collapse in the future over another fuel source. Who knows for sure? But, I hate to tell you this : it isn't your place to decide how people use what is given to them, nor your responsibility. War could just as easily break out in a decade over the silver in the forks over there."

Jesse wore a smirking frown.

"So stop worrying! You are bettering society through your work, as I told you back at the tower," Duncan said to reassure him. "There's no doubt about that. There's also no doubt that you can't control everyone's free will. There will always be someone seeking ways to exploit and destroy what others have."

Jesse let out a deep breath.

"Thank you," he said softly, as if a weight had been lifted off his shoulders. "I get what you are saying."

"Anytime," Duncan replied. "Besides, I don't think as a species we're ready for that sort of thing again. The wounds of the past are still too fresh. Between us, our scientists believe there may be countless measures of oil locked deep in the seas, but we do not have the capabilities to reach those depths. Frankly, we also don't have the desire to try for fear of rekindling those old flames. So, for now the waterfalls and rivers of the north shall provide for us – along with your inventions now, of course."

Duncan had always had a way of bringing Jesse back from the brink of depression or an anxiety-ridden slump. If there was one thing Jesse did to a fault that would be overthinking.

"So are you ready?" Jesse asked.

"For some sausage? You bet. I can't wait to get some in me," Duncan said jokingly.

Jesse cut him a condemning look; the glare didn't last long before hints of a laugh leached out. A group of staunch bankers were sitting at the patisserie to their right, their faces dour. Apparently, they had overheard.

Duncan wasn't bothered, staring at them while Jesse made his way to the door.

"Don't worry, I'm not courting him," he mentioned to the closest man, a burly gent with a bushy mustache. His face reddened beneath its peppered hair as he muttered several incoherent words.

"A shame you aren't," Jesse said, reaching the door. "That would put me out of my misery on this search for Lady Winthrope."

"As much as I love you – and I mean it – I don't think I could manage that," Duncan said. "Don't you worry; she's out there somewhere. You'll probably bump into her when you least expect it."

"I hope so," Jesse said, pulling the handle. A tinkering bell chimed inside. "Come on, let's eat. We have a few hours before we need to catch the skyrail to Grand Hall."

"You are something else," Duncan said with an impressed look as he stepped through. "Even rich you manage to be popular yet approachable to the lower classes."

"If they like me, they'll work harder for me," Jesse replied. "I'm sure their wages help strengthen that feeling, too."

"Well, many greater men have achieved far less," Duncan stated, "and that certainly has some elite feathers ruffled."

"Like those bankers back there?"

"Yes, just like that," Duncan chuckled. "I swear, Jesse, you must have been born in Barro. They're always so happy despite wallowing in dirt all day. Promise me you'll stay the humble man I know you are."

"I plan on it Duncan," he replied, "for the rest of my days."

FIVE

THE SUN WAS HIGH UP OVER THE Barrens in a nearly cloudless sky, driving away what little moisture remained in the parched soil. A small farmhouse sat amidst the sprawling fields; dry stalks filled them like tombstones for the crops that would never be harvested. The lonely wooden structure stood less than proud at the end of a long and dusty road. Many blistering summers had grayed its rough-hewn clapboard and tanks, filled via leaky gutters that lined the gabled roof when it rained, were bleached and nearly empty.

The plot was owned by Grant Boone, the eldest member of the family. He had inherited the land after his father passed away from farmer's lung. They were prosperous by wasteland standards, expanding from selling potatoes and corn to livestock and eggs. But judging by the current state of the home, the broken fencing that held no animals, and the array of antiquated steam equipment kit-bashed with bot parts, things had taken a turn for the worse.

There was a low *hiss* just before a motor carriage crested a small hill. It was old and rickety, heading for the house. Its thin wheels found every uneven bit of ground along the way and steam belched from pipes at the rear, mixed with wisps of fine black smoke. It was hardly an elegant sight: the female driver bobbing so terribly on the bench seat that her leather head-covering threatened to abandon ship. She had shoved two baskets of meager goods – some salted meat and a few bunches of strange, wilting vegetables – in the foot well to secure them. Seated next to her was an adorable badger-like creature called a lutrine; he was doing well to steady himself while sliding around on tiny paws.

Jenny Boone was the driver. She was in her mid-twenties, without a husband or children, and Grant's granddaughter. A fair-skinned and pretty girl, she could have fit right in with the elites. Life would have been free of hardships with ample access to food, water that wasn't fresh out of a creek or rain barrel, and cleanliness. But she happened to be born to the wrong people in the wrong place. Perhaps it was for the best though, her personality might have raised a lot more hackles than gentlemanly parts.

The difficult wasteland life was starting to show in her face, lines taking hold on the corners of her eyes and brow. Her nails were unladylike: chipped and dirtied by hard and repetitive work, but she was used to it. Like clockwork, Jenny would rise each morning before the sun to complete what chores she could before heading into town. It was something she did at least once daily, performing errands like paying bills or picking up supplies. None of those journeys were remotely enjoyable. The name of the place itself, Hondo Gulch, was hardly inviting, less so now that her family was in such a dire position. Yet, her petite traveling companion managed to take the edge off, which is why he rode there with her every single day. It was hard to look at his button nose or big eyes without a smile.

The house grew closer and the route smoothed out. Jenny drove past several gaps in the shoddy fence, surveying each one through a pair of chipped goggles. She shook her head.

… three, four, five gaps to repair, she thought, sighing loudly. *Yet more things to add to the list. I must've passed a thousand things that need doing by now.*

She looked for a silver lining in the bleak situation; it was a stretch to find one.

Well, she continued thinking, *at least you'll never be bored…*

The path unexpectedly became bumpy again, shaking her from those thoughts. Jenny snapped her attention forward. A large sinkhole had formed up ahead, approaching fast.

"If it isn't one thing, it's another," she snarled. "Bip, hold on, it's about to get a *lot* bumpier."

The little creature looked up in her direction as she quickly pulled on one of the steering handles while pushing on the other. The vehicle sputtered and the wheels took a sharp left, kicking up loose debris. At the very last moment the vehicle dodged the depression but the back tire didn't clear in time. It slipped off the edge into the hole then quickly out again. Bip was sent bouncing right out of the vehicle into a patch of dried vegetation.

Jenny brought her foot down hard on the brake pedal and the carriage skidded to a stop, sputtering and rattling in protest. It sounded as though the whole thing could fall apart at any moment.

"Bip!" she yelled over the settling noise. "Bip!"

There were a few seconds of unwelcome silence, then the sound of scurrying. Tufts of the dying grass swayed just before a furry face burst through, letting out a disapproving squeak.

Jenny beamed, her smile nearly as bright as the sun.

"So glad you're okay!" she said apologetically and with relief. "But it wasn't my fault; sinkholes are popping up all over the area."

Bip let out a quick bark as if to say it was indeed her fault, and his wide eyes informed her that she owed him for it.

"Fine," she said. "I'll spend extra time petting you tonight, okay?"

Bip snorted, bounding from the grass.

"Now come on, I'll see you at the house."

Letting her foot off the pedal, the carriage pulled away. Bip scurried happily behind and Jenny briefly smiled at him, then looked out over the plains.

It was just sky and endless brown as far she could see, but over the Western horizon Diablo loomed and far to the northeast, the foothills of the Splintered Range began to rise. Having been in the Barrens her entire life, she thought it would be lovely to see those slopes one day, imagining them to be far different than what she had come to know as normal.

As far as Diablo went, she had no interest in the city, even after hearing of all their technological wonders. With the amount of grief that she faced with small town egos at the helm, a bigger population – especially one with millions like Diablo – would surely only lead to bigger issues. That Winthrope character who was often mentioned in the Gulch was probably the biggest offender. A man that rich could only be one thing: full of himself.

It wasn't even half past eleven and Jenny had already had her fill for the day. Looking for solace, she grabbed the chain around her neck. It was adorned with small, tin gears that she caressed longingly.

"I wish you were here," she whispered, speaking to her parents; the necklace was her mother's. "Could really do with your strength Pa, and Ma, your love... and cooking skills." She let out a laugh riddled with pain. "Things here aren't quite how you two left them, I'm afraid. I'm hoping that something happens soon to make things right. Make things happy again."

Seemingly in answer, a warm breeze blew out of the west. Jenny felt like hope was wrapping around her like a tight, comforting blanket. Optimistic tears welled.

Stopping just ahead of the ramshackle building, she lifted her goggles and wiped her eyes clear. She then got out of the carriage, strolled to the side, pulled up the sleeves of her faded lace shirt, and extinguished the boiler beneath the chassis. Bip was dancing around in her worn boots as she snatched the baskets from the foot well then walked, her frayed and frilly dress swaying with each step. It resembled a cream flower blooming from beneath her leather waistcoat.

There were three stairs that led up to a side door; they creaked as she stepped on them. She rummaged through her many pockets for a key, nearly dropping one of the baskets. A short time later, a woodsy smell greeted her upon stepping inside.

Dusty shafts of sunlight streamed into the kitchen through both the windows and gaps in the siding. The room was quaint but choky; the furniture, the drapes, the cabinetry – everything basic and rundown as if frozen in a moment of grungy time. Along the countertops, an array of glassware and metal utensils glimmered in the few spots not coated in grime.

Bip zoomed by. He tore across the room and beneath a table that was missing one of its four chairs. His claws were clacking wildly on the wood floor right up to the point his tiny tongue started lapping water from a bowl.

"Thirsty, are we?" Jenny asked with a light chuckle, stepping over a pair of her father's old rubber boots.

They were dry rotted and useless but she was unable to bring herself to part with them, or any of the other pairs that were there. The collection had become nothing more than a sentimental dust magnet; one more thing to clean if she had the time.

She strode up to the table in the center of the room. Setting the baskets on top of it, she noted it was very quiet, which was strange since there was always a low rattle from the appliances. She could clearly hear Bip lapping up water as she looked around.

Her gaze wound up in the corner where a chunky, rectangular thing sat silently. Her eyebrow crested since that was normally the source of most of the noise. It was an icebox, one of the first powered models invented, and it was off. Thankfully, the food inside hadn't spoiled but upon closer investigation, none of the other appliances that were tied into the home's main power were on. Checking the breakers that were in a box beside the door, the fuses were okay. There was just nothing running to them; the power had been switched off.

Jenny let out a tremendous moan when it dawned on her why; she had forgotten to take the bill and payment to the Generator and it was bordering a week overdue. She pulled out a small satchel from a waistcoat pocket, untied it, and dumped its contents into her hands. Small copper and brass coins glimmered and clinked as they fell. Counting them, there was enough to cover the bill and what would likely be a hefty late charge.

"Guess I'm headed back to the Gulch," she said miserably to Bip. "You can stay here with Papa, though."

Bip didn't seem bothered either way.

Putting the money back into her bag, she returned it to her pocket. Jenny resumed unpacking the baskets in silence before clattering around, retrieving two bowls from the cupboard and a jar of broth from the icebox. She quickly closed the door to preserve what cold air was still inside.

Emptying the liquid into a beat-up pan, she lit the burner – fueled by scraps of downtrodden fence – and tossed in some of the 'fresh' vegetables and chunks of salted meat. She stirred until the mixture was piping hot, tossing a small sliver of meat to Bip, who ate it right up. After filling the bowls, she rinsed the pan and fetched a couple of foggy glasses for some water. Placing everything on a dull metal tray, she added a few slices of hardening bread to complete the less than savory meal.

Carrying everything through an archway she entered a small and relatively cramped living room. The chairs were worn out and the fireplace dark and ashy. On the far wall was a short cabinet stacked high with books. Above it hung a decorative clock; the hands indicated it was nearing noon. Breezing through, she entered a short hall and passed her own simple bedroom on the way to a closed door at the end. There she stopped and rapped a knuckle on the wood.

"C-come in," said a cracking voice on the other side.

Opening the door, Jenny walked in. It was notably darker inside since a couple of heavy curtains had been drawn. The smell shifted, growing offensive. Except for her footsteps and the jostling of the tray, it was quiet, like death had crept in the room alongside her.

The truth of the situation that became her current life was not that far off.

An elderly man was slumped in a small bed, rubbing his temples. He wore a loose tee and threadbare pants. It was Grant, the checkerboard bedding laid casually over his narrow thighs. The room itself was without many frills, short of a couple family lumographs hanging on the wall. On the nightstand, Jenny had folded a few drab clothes. On top of those were a beat-up hat and a pair of thick-framed glasses.

"Swear I c-can't keep myself c-comfortable," he said, kicking off the blanket as Jenny leaned over to set the tray in his lap. She kissed his forehead before straightening back up.

There was an awful looking bandage wrapped around the lower half of his leg. Dark and discolored, it gave off a pungent odor. It was covering a nasty stinger wound Grant had received out in the fields from a Deathneedle – a scorpion-like creature with translucent, almost plastic skin and a fat tail.

The wound started off small and innocuous. Grant was still able to work the farm with Jenny even with the puncture, but in no time the searing pain spread, placing him out of commission on a gradual slide downhill. Without the funds to see a physician (the so-called doctors that were in the Gulch preferred profit over patient care), the family – especially Jenny – was left to treat it as best she could. She managed to stop any skin infections with topical remedies made from Bip's protective saliva, but the problem was the poison itself. Potent, it continued to spread, bringing with it great pain, fever, and heart palpitations. Things were very grim.

"Nothin' c-can keep off the dreaded c-chill," Grant continued. Jenny swore his voice was getting worse with each word. "That is, until the damned fever c-comes along. Then you're wishin' for the c-cold again."

"I gather you're feeling worse today, Papa?" she asked, knowing full well he was no better.

"Shit, darlin', I don't think I c-can feel any worse than I do today," he said, eyes darting over to hers apologetically. "My apologies about the swearin'."

Jenny took a seat in a chair beside the headboard; it was the missing one from the kitchen. Grinning, she grabbed a bowl and spoon for herself.

"I *think* I can overlook that. Given the state you're in, I think you're entitled to forgo some manners," she replied. Tasting a spoonful of the thin soup, it was surprisingly good, if not a little salty.

"Maybe you can overlook it, but your gran would've popped me 'round the back of my head with this tray had she heard me say that. She firmly believed men ought not be so foul in front of a lady, even if they're kin."

"Mother would have done the same to Father as well," Jenny replied with deliberate formality.

"That demeanor doesn't fit you at all," Grant said instantly. "You'll be much happier if you stay true to who you are, Jen. The Boones have always had a few sturdy women at the helm…" His eyes shrank in sadness. "What's left of us anyway."

They both stared at each other. Grant took a wrinkled hand and lifted some of the broth to his lips. Shaking, he slurped it then smacked his lips a few times.

"Too bad ya didn't inherit any of their c-cookin' abilities."

"Maybe I like the challenge of it."

"Well, judgin' by *this* you should try harder," he joked, coughing painfully instead of laughing.

Jenny cringed at the sound, like phlegm had free reign of his chest. She produced a small vial and leaned over his bowl. Three drops fell in.

"That's the last of the serum. It should help," she said worryingly, setting the now empty bottle on the tray.

Grant continued to cough; it had never been this bad before. He nodded instead of speaking, then proceeded to consume about half the bowl. Each spoonful was studded with hacking but after a few minutes, it all started to subside.

"Thank you," Grant said, clearing his throat. "So, how're the supplies?"

Jenny told him all about the day, beginning with the state of the icebox and working back from there. There was a litany of things mounting around the property.

"I also had to sell the last bo[4] just to have enough money for what I brought home. There's still some left over and thankfully I was able to take some of her waste to use as fuel in the boiler."

"It's bad, ain't it?" he replied, almost in tears. "Everythin' was

---

4   This world's equivalent of a cow, the bo is the primary source of both meat (beef) and milk.

doin' so well and now it's all c-come a c-cropper 'cause of this injury. I'm so sorry I c-can't be more help to ya, Jen."

"There's nothing you can do," Jenny said reassuringly. Her heart was beating faster as she rested a hand on his thigh, patting it gently. "You need to focus on recovering, first and foremost."

He cringed upon hearing those words, lips staying a scowl that denied recovery was ever happening. Maybe if he was a decade or two younger there would have been a better chance.

"Now Jenny, ya know that I –"

She looked away; he stopped.

"You're gonna have to face the facts one day, my dearest granddaughter."

But she didn't want to face it; she wanted it like it was before.

Life didn't afford such luxuries, especially to the lesser of society who could dream all they wanted but never have the means to see those thoughts realized. She was stubborn though, just like her mother, giving the impossible situation too much thought. Her father had been killed by raiders three years earlier during a livestock drive up from Seco Basin while her mother befell a much more sinister fate at the hands of drunkards in an alleyway outside a saloon in the Gulch. Grant pursued the perpetrators, making sure those lowlifes paid penance with their own lives.

"Jen, I need ya to speak with Mr. Johnston at the general store," Grant urged, "as soon as you c-can."

"I can do that today. I have to head back into town and pay the Generator his bill," she replied coyly.

Grant rolled his eyes a bit.

"Greedy sumbitch that Bartholomew," he said, "tackin' on those extra fees."

"Exactly," Jenny smiled in reply, thankful he hadn't realized the bill was late. "Back to Mr. Johnston; he *is* a busy man. Should I call ahead and set up an appointment?"

"No, no, you shouldn't have to," Grant responded. "He and I had a c-conversation a while back, as things started to go downhill for me. All ya should need to tell him is that it's time."

Jenny was worried that what she suspected he was talking about was correct. Judging by his manner and face, it was.

"You... aren't giving up are you?" she asked, not waiting for an answer before raising her voice. "You can't!"

"I ain't givin' up Jen! It's just the truth of things. C-cold, hard fact. Ya know as well as I do that if I'm not here the authorities from that shit-hole town will come collectin' by hook or crook. There ain't no male around to inherit the property – not that it's right – so the bank'll just take..."

Heart sinking, tears started running down Jenny's cheeks.

"... take everything," Grant sighed; his chest rattled. "Have more faith in yourself, Jen. Your future is gonna be fine. Mr. Johnston will make sure things are okay."

"But I can't do all this on my own," she said, almost pleading.

"I have no doubt that ya c-can," he replied. "Ya always find a way to overcome the difficulties situations present. Hittin' bottom in this life means ya can't get any worse, only better. Remember that."

After thinking things to herself, Jenny reluctantly bobbed her head.

"Well then, that's settled," Grant said, finishing off his soup. His spoon *clanged* against the bowl. "So, speakin' of the shit-hole, did any blowhards give ya trouble today?"

"When don't they?" she answered, telling him of her encounter with Jebidiah Crow and his ilk.

Grant didn't like hearing that his granddaughter was cornered and felt up, especially by authorities that were gladly misusing their bought positions of power. His withered fists balled up.

"I managed to handle myself," she said, noticing Grant's

stressed features. "Jebidiah didn't like having his arm twisted and the business end of my pistol in his ear. Especially by a woman in front of his other men."

"Good girl," Grant replied proudly, fists relaxing. "Sounds like you won't have any trouble on your return trip then."

"No, I should be fine," she replied, "although I did see something a little out of the ordinary on my way back earlier."

Creases formed between Grant's anxious eyes.

"What was it?"

"If I didn't know any better, I'd say it was a raider, up high on an outcrop of rock down by the creek."

"This c-close to a settlement? Ya sure it wasn't just one of the town hooligans?"

"I can't say I've ever seen him before. Looking at him through the spyglass was quite a sight," she said, describing his shirtless and muscular body, bald head, and colorful tattoos. She almost sounded infatuated, her cheeks ever so slightly pink. "I couldn't see his face though. He had on some kind of gas mask, but there was a bushy beard sticking out the bottom of it. From what I *could* see, though, he was nothing at all like the men in town…"

"And by the sound of it nothin' at all like most raiders," Grant snipped. "Don't get all dewy-eyed, Jen. If he were a raider that means he's nothin' but trouble. If he ain't one, the fact he's all gussied up with tattoos means just the same."

Jenny had a few more fleeting thoughts about the man, then slid back to reality.

"Assuming he was a raider; why would he be that close? Scouting?"

"I don't know," Grant said, a fit of coughing starting again. "But like all vermin, where there's one, there's more. This ain't nothing good, of that I'm sure."

SIX

THE SPRAWLING, TERRACED PYRAMID that was Frost Enterprises spread out across Diablo like a shadow, dominating most of the wealthy borough of Cordillera. It was a grand yet monstrous structure, above which private ornithopters whirred, crisscrossing the sky on business and to destinations unknown. From the center of the gothic structure, a thick, twisting column of ebony stone rose above the neighboring buildings. Replete with windows that were tall and thin, inside were Frost's offices and residence at the very top. It was a testament to the company's might, challenged only by the spire of Winthrope Limited, five kilometers to the south.

Lucas Frost the Third stared at it with malice.

Even after assuming control of his commercial empire in 1782 – fifteen troublesome years ago and three years *before* Winthrope took control of his – he was trailing both in earnings and renown. Despite the influx of wealth and associated power, Frost was not a man that took kindly to second place. Such things were equivalent to losing and Winthrope's tower mocked him every time his eyes fell upon it.

"Sir," said an apprehensive voice, "not to interrupt, but should you not already be en route to Grand Hall for your meeting?"

"They can wait," Frost replied deliberately, still looking out on the city. His gloved hands were locked behind his back. "Not all things are dictated by the schedules of others. Besides, we have some important business to tend to prior to my departure."

"Yes, Milord," said another voice, no less anxious. "You had many topics you wished to address; what is it you wished to know about first?"

At last Frost turned, his bearded face wrought with grim coldness. Ten years older than Jesse, he was more mature in appearance and devilish in practice.

"What of these delays with the contractor?" he asked while clearing strands of grizzled hair from his face. Wearing a tight, leathery shirt and pants beneath a long, black trench coat, it all lent itself to a sense of unease as he stepped forward with a slight limp.

A large scar cut across his right eye, lost in his twenty-eighth year. In its place was a shining lens suspended in golden mechanics. The procedure he underwent was called 'ocular substitution,' a complicated affair to replace his lost eye with a mechanical one. It was experimental at the time but ultimately so successful that Frost purchased the medical process patents and technology rights for his own use.

There were five men gathered in front of Frost's desk, all dressed in gallant suits and hats. None replied to Frost's question.

"I'm waiting…" Frost said to them, carrying a smirk. The mechanical eye whirred and zipped around, pinpricks of blue light flickering with each movement. Frost settled on the thin-faced man standing in the middle. "Mr. Abbot, please do not make me ask again."

Tate Abbot was middle-aged and oversaw the company's contracts with outside organizations. The post had been recently vacated by his predecessor, disappearing quite suddenly. No one dared question what happened to him, Tate motivated enough to try and keep his position.

"W-which contractor are you asking about?" he replied; his lower lip was quivering. Frost's gaze seemed to bore through him.

"The copper providers." Frost's words came out quite matter-of-factly. "You do remember, don't you; the material that wires my entire line of bots?"

Tate's eyes shifted from side to side; there was worry in them. The other men noticed.

"Ah... yes," he struggled to answer. "Burton and Hargrove. There were some... incidents at their main facility in Alum City and warehouses here in Diablo. Protests mainly, over conditions and wages."

"Really now?"

Tate nodded once.

"A-apparently Winthrope... had raised –"

Frost silenced him with a hand wave. It was unclear if he was more incensed by the news or the mention of Winthrope.

"Why must you always go against the tide, Jesse?" Lucas muttered to himself, taking in a long, irritated breath. He then addressed Tate pithily. "I *do not* wish to hear that name mentioned again today."

Tate nodded again.

"These people are impossible to deal with!" Frost shouted suddenly, causing all the men to flinch. "If we can even call such pathetic creatures people at all. Do they not appreciate all that I give them?"

"T-they should, Milord," answered Peter Mullins, who was the youngest and most fawning, his words greased like his jet-black hair. "You bestow great things to all in Diablo."

Frost didn't acknowledge the slippery reply and continued.

"I keep them busy by giving them a purpose, otherwise they would be useless. I give them a place of value in the great machine of life, otherwise they would be worthless. And they repay me with protests and indignation?"

Before long Frost had a look of rage across his face.

"Fire them," he said coolly. "That will solve this little problem of ours and teach a life lesson in one fell swoop."

They all stirred, minds troubled with Frost's line of thinking.

"M-milord, we cannot lose a workforce that large," said Mark Rutherford, a grubby man with features like a rat.

"How many heathens are you are referring to?"

"Nearly eight hundred, sir."

Frost chortled, pointing back toward the window.

"There are nearly ten million people in this city, a lot of them wretched and willing to work for enough Cogs to put bread and butter on their tables. No, my decision stands. Fire *all* the workers in that troublesome borough, then hire replacements, reminding them of their blessings."

The men stood listening, Peter the only one bobbing his head. It annoyed the others.

"Also," Frost continued, "send word to our facility in Alum City: something similar must be done there, right up to the top if need be. All of this is not rocket science, for goodness sake. Really, Rutherford, perhaps I should reconsider having you in charge of design, since such a simple concept apparently eludes you?"

Mark blustered, nearly letting Frost know what was truly on his mind. That would have been a mistake. He recoiled upon seeing Frost's stare, and the affluence behind it, bearing down on him.

"I thought as much," Frost said smugly. "So, is there anything else before I depart? I feel as if the task at hand takes precedence over the other things that we had listed for discussion."

The largest man of the group stepped forward. His demeanor was like Frost's in most regards. He was stout and looked as though he could hold his own. Alex Caldwell was his name; rugged and strong-featured, he oversaw bot production in both of Frost's plants.

"With all due respect, Milord," Alex said pointedly, "even if we were to fill all these vacated spots with replacement workers by tomorrow, Rutherford does have a point. There are steps like training and other intangible issues to address. That would be the case with the start of one worker and we are discussing eight hundred. It might as well be a thousand for the time production will be set back. I worry that with our latest mandate to phase out the men in our remote security forces along the Far Cost pipeline in lieu of automated sentries, we will need to have at least one hundred units done by the end of the week to meet schedule."

Frost respected Alex's words enough to not be angered by them.

"Then it sounds like you all have quite a challenge to ensure that particular hundred-unit threshold is met."

Four of the five men were taken aback, Peter still beaming relentlessly.

"M-milord?" asked Alex, thinking he had misunderstood something that was said.

"That is all for now," Frost said dismissively, waving a hand through the air. "I shall speak with you all again tomorrow at ten, hopefully with good news."

The group started to turn, murmuring like a simmering pot. Phrases like 'see I told you' and 'he's absolutely mad' rose above the whispers. The distinctive voice was uttered by Hugh

Winterberry, a diminutive man with more nerve than height. He had, up until that point, been silent.

Alex cut his eyes across Hugh then toward Frost, noting Peter's was lingering. Seizing the young man's arm, Alex drug him along toward a pair of rich mahogany doors. Tate was first to reach the exit, placing his hands on the ornamental handles. Hugh leaned over as he opened them, speaking his mind beneath the sound of those heavy doors creaking.

"We all know which product line of bots he *really* wants to remain on schedule," Hugh grumbled louder than he thought. "Or shall I say boys, like that one he parades around that resembles his ex-lover?"

Tate gulped, knowing that Frost must have heard him; they all did. Letting go of the doors, he hurriedly stepped through.

"Now is not the time for this, Winterberry," Alex warned as he crossed the threshold with Peter in tow. "Enough! Before you say too much and go too far. We all have much work to –"

"Any man," Hugh carried on stubbornly as Mark slinked past, "that is so perverse as to partake in the company of robots for pleasure is no respectable gentleman. One that would prefer the male variety of such deviant devices only invites the downfall of our great society."

Alex shut his eyes, refusing to turn around; Hugh had overstepped his bounds. Instead he walked down the bleak corridor, past oil paintings of Lucas Frost the First, Second, and their respective wives. He was joined by the other three men as they swept from the office.

"Did you say something important?" Frost asked, grasping Winterberry's shoulder right before he took a step out of the office.

It hurt.

"Frost! How dare you! In all my years, I…"

Frost immediately spun the short man around more than once, stopping him cold. Regardless of being dizzy, Winterberry could still see Frost's blood-chilling stare burrowing into him. The faint blue light of that machine-driven eye had shifted to red.

"Your back was to me as you spoke; it muffles the sound as you know. So, forgive me, I only picked up bits and pieces. Can you clarify what it was that you said?"

Hugh cringed, breathing heavily as he felt Frost's unnatural grip tighten. There came a sound like metal sliding against a sheath, a dagger emerging from under the long sleeves of Frost's coat.

"Now, as I mentioned, I could very well be mistaken but it sounded an awful lot like something about the Adonis line..." Frost was methodical with his words, the point of the dagger kissing Winterberry's neck. "Those words, too; they sounded so familiar to me. 'Where on Eaugen have you heard that before?' I thought. You know what I came to conclude? I might have read them in one of the *Daily Diablo's* articles."

Hugh was speechless, contorting as Frost tightened his grip even more while the dagger blade threatened to pierce his skin.

"Surely that isn't the case? After all, the Adonis line is one of *many* products that keep you employed. Thus, your wife is happy. You can buy plenty of food to feed those growing children of yours and plenty of toys to keep their mushy minds entertained. All children should be able to grow up big and strong... and *mouthy*... like their father, right?"

Hugh said nothing, instead holding his clean-shaven chin high. The secondary one that often fluttered beneath nearly vanished since his head was pushed so far back.

"I thought as much," Frost said, retracting the dagger and leaning in so close there was barely a gap between them. Frost's beard hair was even rubbing against the edge of Winterberry's chin. "Men like you are weak, Hugh, made large only by hiding in the shadows behind closed doors, petrified to say what you really think in the light to one's face, where truth can shine on your words. The world would be better off had I taken my dagger, bored a tiny hole through that thick skull, and watched your cowardly brains seep out onto the floor. But that would cause too much hullabaloo for me, so I'll give you a chance. I'm close now, I think you're clever enough to tell at this distance. So, do you have the guts to say anything to my face?"

Nothing came, only silence.

"Very well," Frost said with a disheartened turn. "Hugh Winterberry, I would have seen the years of funding this fine company took off your pension returned to you, if only you had the fortitude to tell me what was on your mind."

Hugh squirmed in Frost's tight grip, unable to get loose. He groaned, but still said no words.

"But that has fled. As it stands, you are hereby stripped of your *entire* pension, the monies therein shall be redirected to further improve the line of Vixen and Adonis bots."

Frost released him, pushing Winterberry out of the office with such force that he stumbled, then fell. His arms and legs were splayed on the hard tiles.

"Now get out of my sight," Frost growled. "Real men have work to do."

IT WAS TWENTY-PAST noon and the lift doors to Frost's private residence slid open. He emerged, a limp fairly evident as his boots clobbered across the fancy living room. The floor was a dark and glossy hardwood while the tall ceilings were exposed

THE Steam TYCOON   71

rafters. Light spilled in from expansive stained glass windows spanning the wall opposite the entrance. Lumographs and vases of flowers decorated the tops of pointy oak tables and lined the majestic stone mantle of the fireplace. Many of the pictures were of Lucas' family but one stood out on the mantle next to a large bouquet of roses. It featured a dashing man, likely in his early twenties, dressed in traveling attire. Next to him was a younger Lucas with an arm wrapped around his shoulder. Both were laughing despite what appeared to be a rainy day.

Taking a seat in one of the luxuriant buttoned sofas, Frost dipped his head into his hands. He did not feel like entertaining both the mayor and Winthrope at Grand Hall today. Had the pending discussion included the arrest of Jesse and the takeover his assets, or even the demolition of Winthrope Limited, he would have made sure to arrive three hours early.

"Master, is that you?" asked an almost giddy voice from another room. "I did not expect you back so soon, otherwise I would have prepared a meal."

"No need, Aero," Lucas answered, lifting his head from his hands. "I've already eaten."

"all right then. I was under the impression you had an appointment with Mayor Randolph at Grand Hall," Aero replied. "Is that no longer the case?"

"What's with the interrogation?" Lucas snapped. "I'll be heading out shortly."

"Apologies, but if that is the case, you will need to leave within the next two minutes and thirty-seven seconds or else be late…"

"I know," Frost grumbled, craning his neck as he leaned back on the sofa. He couldn't see anyone. "I'm in no rush. Now, enough talking. Get out here so we don't have to shout like commoners."

"Very well," Aero replied happily.

There was a sound of something heavy being moved, then

set down, followed by light footsteps. A man soon appeared and joined Lucas in the living room. He looked young and innocent, skin smooth and hair dark, both gleaming in the sunlight. He stared at Lucas through sapphire eyes while a gentle smattering of stubble covered his jaw. It was the same athletic man in the picture on the mantle, but he hadn't aged a day.

Lucas' eyes widened with desire as he took the man in, and he bit his lower lip after reaching out toward him.

Aero was completely naked and it was evident that he was not a normal person. His warm and silky body – which Frost was now touching – was perfect from head to foot, marred only by the words 'Adonis V3' embossed on his hip and 'A3R0' along his right collar. Dark, mechanical channels flowed around his body, separating it into modular components that pristinely outlined his musculature. His chest was broad but notably without nipples, and his torso rippled like foothills of the mountains. Light puffs of steam escaped his joints as he moved. Aero happened to be the most advanced and lifelike bot Lucas had created and though he strove to perfect his mass-produced creations, there would forever be only one Aero.

"Get down here and tend to my leg," Frost ordered sternly, yanking down on Aero's arm. Aero did not resist. "Right ankle's been acting up today. Needs a massage before I head to the hangar for this damn meeting..."

Frost Enterprises' emphasis was in the areas of security and weapons; things that went boom and other things to protect against the booms. To diversify their offerings, the company also opened a factory to build automated robots for dignitaries or remote operations in harsh environments like pipelines outside the city walls.

Aero's knees were against the floor, his sturdy hands gripping Lucas' aggrieved leg. Lucas sighed as a welcomed vibration coursed through it, coupled with a firm, undulating pressure from Aero's massage. It felt extremely good and quite relaxing for his entire body, except for one part that became restless. He stretched his arms behind his head and moaned. A bulge was growing in the confines of his trousers...

People found new and innovative roles for bots along the way, using them to aid in farming duties, shop keeping, interrogations, and even sex. That's where Frost saw an opportunity for even more income, uncaring of the stigma it would bring. After all, even if no elite or official admitted to it, sex and money drove the world. Frost opened a second factory that focused on delivery of female sex robots, which was dubbed the Vixen line of companions. They were marketed as a reward for the hardworking and single gentleman. Rudimentary at first, the units sold incredibly well. Their taboo nature also drove sales, the third generation of Vixens now available for only one thousand Gears. However, for Frost, something was missing.

"Seems like another leg needs tending to," Lucas groaned, his bulge throbbing. Aero moved a hand atop the mound, sending tremors through it as he massaged the new area...

It was obvious to a lot of people that Frost was not much of a lady's man, especially in his youth when he grew close to an investor's son, Aaron Williams. Lucas and Aaron's relationship blossomed, even kept in the shadows, but never managed to reach fruition. Unfortunately, Aaron lost his life in the same incident that caused Lucas to lose an eye.

Years went by but the feelings never passed. In the hope of rekindling those deep-rooted feelings, the Adonis line was born. More a pet project than an attempt at profit, the Adonis models surprisingly sold well. That isn't to say their sales were not far more low key than their female counterparts; ownership of male robots by the men *and* women that came to purchase would be quite scandalous at best. Frost didn't care, often being seen with his companion around the headquarters building and even at times in town. Everyone's fear of his reprisal kept lips firmly sealed.

Aero had unbuttoned Lucas' trousers, freeing him. He opened his wet lips and wrapped them around Lucas, slowly sucking while taking him in effortlessly until all was inside. His throat began to squeeze and relax, sending waves of pressure up and down Lucas' entire length.

Lucas looked down at Aaron's likeness, pleasing him in ways he could only imagine before. He shifted, sitting up slightly. Lucas slid a hand down and over Aero's back, one of his thick fingers plunging into a tight, warm hole that awaited at the end. He slid another inside, knowing that at his fingertips was the one-of-a-kind Adonis Version Three, Revision Zero.

Aero started growing himself, his toolset absurdly proportioned for Lucas' own pleasure.

"A-Aero..." Lucas said gruffly, followed by indecipherable moans.

Aero's throat squeezed harder.

Lucas took hold of Aero's hair with his free hand, shoving the bot's head down. His own body started to shudder; Aero slowed.

"I didn't tell you to stop," Frost growled. "Keep going."

Aero resumed, now relentless.

Lucas closed his eyes, about to crest a point of no return. Sinking his back into the sofa on a cloud of bliss, Lucas would now certainly be late for his meeting and he couldn't care less.

SEVEN

JENNY STEPPED OUT OF AN ORDINARY building on the far side of town. From the front, its wooden façade looked innocuous and drab, but a distressed sign hung above the doorway with flaky black lettering that spelled 'Generator.' Behind, an untidy forest of jumbled machinery and shiny tanks towered over the dirt. Long strands of wire spider-webbed from strange, studded spheres; some ran out to timber poles that lined the streets while others plunged into the protective soil, all carrying small amounts of electricity to buildings across the town and to the surrounding farms.

Jenny turned to observe the outlandish metallic structures as they spun and hiccuped. While she knew how her motor carriage worked – she had to so everything stayed up and running – this sight always dumbfounded her. The fact that what appeared to be dissimilar pile of junk could produce anything other than rust was astonishing.

I wonder how true it is, she pondered, reflecting on the talk of the town.

It had always been said that the Generator was one of, if not the first, structures built in the Gulch. It was allegedly made from pieces of some enormous flying machine that had crashed ages ago, possibly during the Burning. Fanciful as it all sounded, many in town dismissed those tall tales as an excuse by the owners – the Rayboulds – to let the place continue to be an eyesore. In the end, though, nobody made too large a fuss about it, paying their bills to benefit from its presence.

Jenny was no different, at least when not overwhelmed.

"Well, that's that," she said heavily.

Bartholomew Raybould was standing behind her, his round face grinning and his pockets clattering with coin.

Jenny had just paid him most of her remaining money. The rate was always high, dependent on how much power was consumed, but now that there was also a wire fee assessed, based on the distance the end user was from the Generator, it was brutally expensive. She thought about telling him to just cut it off, but wanted to check with her grandfather first.

"Thank you Mr. Raybould," she said, lowering her view from the machines to the man.

He nodded politely, more for the fatter wallet than for friendliness.

Jenny placed the Spur and few Cogs that were left in her satchel. Stowing it, she stepped into dusty Main Street on her way to the general store, first passing a small school house sitting tranquilly by itself.

Unlike the power plant, most of the buildings in the Gulch were uninteresting, if not downright boring to look at. The landlords and shop keepers tried their best to cover that fact with bright colors slathered on the wood, but they often just ended up looking like some prostitute desperate to cover her flaws with layers of makeup. Especially the clothier, run by Lawrence Denbrough, whose wife struggled herself with such appearances.

Jenny giggled at the thought, feeling regretful for having such thoughts, but on the other hand remembering Martha's offhand comment that one time at the bank about her attire being that of gutter trash, all while wearing a hat the size and shape of a frilly umbrella.

More buildings passed by, as did more people. The Gulch grew smokier, smellier, and more cramped the further Jenny went downtown. Around her were hotels and more stores, above which were residences for the proprietors. Most homes, however, were on the streets beyond, near the edges of town away from the gamblers, drunks, and out of reach of the red light's glow.

Speaking of drunks, there were also a few saloons nearby. The largest and most popular by far was Brewer's, not a hundred feet from where she walked. She'd never been inside the place before, only hearing about its long paneled bar, gleaming brass foot rails, and spittoons. Not that she didn't want to go in and down a Cactus Wine or Bo Skinner – Grant could vouch for her drinking abilities which rivaled his own – it just wasn't a place women could enter or be served, unless the owners wanted to have their licenses revoked by the authorities.

The general store was at last approaching to her right, just past a small alley stuffed with construction tools. The equipment, scaffolding, and charred buildings further down the street didn't do any favors in making the town look more appealing.

The recent work was to repair fire damage, caused by a lightning strike during a monstrous dust storm two weeks earlier. Since the buildings were so close to each other, the fire spread quickly, and threatened to consume the whole strip. Normally the fire suppressors could make quick work of an incident like that, but the Guardian of the Gulch – a water tower that rose above the downtown area – was nearly empty due to the ongoing drought conditions, not to mention the ill-advised decision of the High Sheriff to use its contents to supply water to the government offices. With little water to combat the growing fire, the suppressors ended up using their dirt lobbers, purchased from a tradesman from Barro, to save the day. It was quick and ingenious, and most importantly, it worked.

As denizens swept out their businesses and dusted off their supplies instead of having to throw them away, there were rumblings calling for the impeachment of the High Sheriff. It all made Jenny glad she lived on the outskirts.

"Still plenty of time," Jenny murmured as she checked a small pocket watch, arriving at the steps that lead into Johnston's. It was coming up on one o'clock.

"Ain't that lucky for us," said a shrill voice off to the side.

Jenny recognized it right away.

"Jebidiah," she grumbled, turning her head to find a gangly man standing nearby, thumbs resting on a brown belt with an absurdly large buckle. His duster flapped like his lips as he spit dip on the ground while his wide-brimmed hat covered his eyes but not the reek of whiskey.

Three other men were off to the side, the edges of their hats frayed much like Jenny's nerves upon seeing them again. Everyone had a small, silver star pinned to their chests.

They were, but more interested in serving themselves than the community.

"Miss Boone, how are you doin' this fine afternoon?" Jebidiah asked with a tinge of spite, smiling through crusty teeth.

"I'm doing good, as you seem to be" she answered, withholding a grimace. She was sure some of it slipped through her defenses. "As a matter of fact, I must tend to some business here with Mr. Johnston. So, if you'll please excuse me."

She started up the stairs, but Jebidiah clicked his tongue a couple of times.

"I most certainly won't," he replied, glancing to his left and nodding. "'Specially since we got unfinished business from the mornin'. Fetch me her pistol please."

The biggest man of the group lashed out an arm and grabbed Jenny tightly by hers. She struggled for her gun as soon as Jebidiah mentioned it, but the goon had grabbed hold of it.

"You might think me stupid, Miss Boone, but I do learn from the errors of my ways," Jebidiah said callously. "I think I'll be takin' that side arm for myself as payment for that earlier turn of events."

He signaled to bring her forward. Jebidiah grabbed hold of the pistol and after examining it, handed it off to one of the other men for safekeeping.

"Nice craftsmanship," he said while eyeing her up and down. His eyes lingered on her chest and he licked his dip-stained lips, glancing toward the narrow alley off to the side of the store. "Now let's get back to our unfinished business…"

Jebidiah made way for the alley, followed by a couple of his henchmen.

Jenny stood firm right where she was.

"You gonna move?" Jebidiah crowed. "Or shall I get Boris there to do it for you?"

The large man grunted.

"Seems about all your men are good for," she replied. "And since you can't seem to manage it yourself, what does that say about you?"

Jebidiah laughed, though it was more a scoff. His fingers strummed the handle of his firearm and his lips twisted into mean shapes.

"You sassin' me bitch?" he asked, glaring at her.

Jenny didn't budge, but she did shrug.

Boris moved in to grab her again. Before his large hands had a chance to subdue her, one of her boots slammed against his foot. He yelled in pain and Jenny spun around, giving him a swift kick in the privates.

"You goddamn whore," Jebidiah said, snatching his pistol and cocking back the hammer. "You're about to learn a valuable lesson in what happens when you cross the Law…"

"Enough of the theatrics, son," said a calm voice. "Ain't no law against protecting yourself against stupidity or flannel mouths."

Jebidiah looked up. Mr. Johnston was standing up by his store's entrance, gun drawn and pointing right him.

"You sure you want to interfere with official *Ranger* business, old man?" Jebidiah spat, quite literally.

"Yes, sure as I've ever been," Mr. Johnston replied, fixing him with a bold stare. "That being said, this ain't the kind of business one normally finds Rangers involved with. Makes me wonder what the High Sheriff would say about it."

"Sheriff's got his own problems these days, what with the tower fiasco, but you're more than welcome to go whisper in his ear… if you make it there."

"You threatening me, son?"

"You deaf, sir?"

A shot rang out, knocking Jebidiah's hat clean off and to the ground. There was a bullet hole in it, dead center, just high enough to clear his head.

"I heard that well enough," Mr. Johnston replied, looking at his handiwork. "Seems I'm a pretty good shot, too, considering my age. Eyesight must be fine as cream gravy."

Jebidiah's men had predictably dispersed, leaving him standing alone in front of Jenny and Mr. Johnston.

Jebidiah was more casual, putting a finger in his mouth,

wringing out the large wad of tobacco that was inside. Flicking it to the ground, he wiped the slimy fingers on his coat then picked up his hat.

"I guess that concludes our business… for now. Wilfred, watch yourself, and Jenny, old folks can't protect you forever. I'll be sure to drop by to chat about Grant's property later."

With that said and a quick tilt of his hat, Jebidiah slunk off into the crowds and was gone.

"Thank you so much, Mr. Johnston," Jenny said, climbing the few stairs.

"Well, you seemed to be handling yourself quite well, Miss Boone," he replied, "but I was glad to help speed up Mr. Crowe's departure."

Both laughed lightly, Jenny's face becoming serious shortly after.

"What brings you back by, my dear?" Wilfred asked with concern, noting hers.

"Sir, my grandfather asked me to come by and see you as soon as possible. He told me to tell you that it was time."

The look on Wilfred's face indicated that he expected her arrival, but wished that it wasn't so soon.

"Ah… yes," he said reluctantly.

"What does he mean by 'it's time?' Surely not…"

Mr. Johnston motioned toward the entrance, ushering Jenny inside the store.

"Come, Miss Boone," he said quietly, "we have some things to take care of. I've prepared everything, I just need to go over it with you."

EIGHT

"**S**TRUGGLING OVER RESOURCES," SAID a gruff voice, followed by a long and satisfying gulp of water, "all the while squabbling amongst ourselves. Is this what life has become: the rich and mighty no less gracious than the masses below, or even the hounds as they fight over scraps of meat?"

The voice belonged to the Mayor of Diablo, Oscar Randolph, who was in his third and final term. A short man stuffed into a black suit, he sat behind an oversized desk, his robust neck turning several shades darker than his red tie. His top hat was embellished with golden baubles and seemed to be half his height, bobbing to and fro with each word.

"Has life ever been any other way, sir?" replied Jesse, who had taken a seat in a lush chair by the room's large, ornamental windows.

There was a large bookcase that filled the opposite wall from floor to ceiling. The books packed on it were tattered and had broken spines, while the smell of their old pages was pleasantly distinct. The office itself was cavernous and ornate, similar to Winthrope's in appearance, yet it clung to a government veneer that sterilized its charm.

Duncan was sitting beside Jesse, playing with a loose thread on the cuff of his trousers while beyond the glass, the gilded clockwork sky-rail had just been wound (by means of a gear assembly beneath the car), and was poised to leave Grand Hall Station for another journey around the posh central boroughs.

"Perhaps so, Mr. Winthrope," Randolph replied, peering over his goggle-like spectacles past a bronze statuette of a soldier riding a sleipnir, "but that is why we are meeting after all, isn't it? To see if any change is possible?"

There was a deep moan beside them, all three men looking toward the source of it.

"Oh, please spare us, my dear Jesse, everyone on Eaugen is obsessed with their own piece of the pie," Frost chastised, dressed in the same attire he had met his associates in earlier. "Trying to wrap yourself up in civility doesn't change the fact you are still subject to human nature."

Jesse tipped his hat up and folded his arms.

"That is where you and I differ, Lucas," he retorted. "We are both successful men in our own right, but those accomplishments were achieved by vastly *different* means."

Jesse glanced at the mayor, who didn't care for the ongoing strife between the two of them. Instead, he was filling his portly belly with a slice of sponge cake, cut from a large one set on a silver platter.

"Using your own words Lucas," Jesse continued, "I would like to find a way to bake everyone a pie of their own, whereas you would rather hold onto one and one alone, doling out the crumbs."

"We shall see which method outlasts the other," Frost smirked coolly.

"Are you gentlemen done with your squabbling?" the mayor cut in, picking crumbs out of his curly mustache. "You see Mr. Winthrope, even now my point is proven. Here we sit in this grand building and the pinnacle of society squabble amongst themselves for the pettiest of reasons. The two owners of the largest corporations in my city fretting over desserts of all things. Come now, let us get back to this meeting so I can get on with my busy day."

"You mean so you can get to lunch..." Lucas muttered as he set his arms on the side of the chair.

"What was that Mr. Frost?" asked Randolph. "I couldn't make out what –"

"Oh my apologies, Your Honor. I was just agreeing with you," Frost said respectfully, cutting eyes to Jesse. "We all have much to do."

"Agreed," Jesse said enthusiastically, "so much so that I like to arrive to my appointments on time."

One could cut the loathing between the two men with a knife, if only the mayor didn't have it, cutting another piece of sponge cake for himself. Half of it was already gone and not once had he offered any to his guests.

"Now, where were we?" Randolph asked, scanning the desktop riddled with papers. "Ah yes! Now, Mr. Morrison, I've signed off on my end of this water trade deal. So, once you return to Lagos the honorable Lylan Laguna should be able to wrap this up tidily."

"Indeed," Duncan replied after a quick sip of tea. He sat up in his chair as the mayor handed Jesse the documents, who in turn passed them along to him. "She will be pleased by the progress made here today. It's actually quite a momentous occasion.

We've managed to open the door to a new era for both our cities. I sincerely hope that everyone sees the benefits as what's on these papers becomes a reality."

"Here, here," Jesse said with applause. The mayor gleefully smiled.

"I have the sudden urge to vomit," Frost added with a slight roll of his eyes.

"Oh come now, Lucas!" Randolph urged. "Cheer up a bit! The next topic on the agenda is far less jovial: this purported rise in raider activity. Rumors are sweeping across the Barrens like a wildfire faster than the alleged bandits themselves."

"Less jovial perhaps, but far more serious to consider," Frost stated. "I happen to think these allegations are true; it's in my nature I suppose. I assume you have seen the Sheriff reports on advancements in Blackwater, Seco Basin, and Hondo Gulch?"

There were nods from the mayor and Jesse.

"Then you'll agree an attack will likely happen somewhere in those three areas. I hope the Sheriffs are prepared; with the Gulch reeling from their recent controversy with the fire I doubt they are focused on much outside the town right now."

The mayor puffed out his chest, swelling like a well-dressed balloon. The buttons on the front of his suit jacket were straining, about to pop off.

"Even if true, these bandits WOULD NOT DARE strike a settlement," he said, tone of his voice taking them all by surprise. "They would be ribbons of flesh before they made it to the town limits."

Duncan cast Jesse an odd look, who was squirming in his chair.

"I happen to agree with Frost, Your Honor," he said, the words like shards of glass in his mouth. "I've received word from reliable sources about the raiders' posturing and their presence getting ever closer to settlements. To me, that indicates something like an assault may be imminent. It's had me worried for some time."

"Which brings me to this city and the Far Coast pipeline," Frost sustained, now leaning forward while looking at Duncan, "not to mention the future Lagosian one as well."

Duncan chortled in his seat.

"I want the authority to increase my security forces within Diablo," Frost continued, making sure there was no mistaking his desires. "With both personnel and bots. We can also deploy additional sentries and turrets along the pipeline for added protection."

The mayor exhaled and deflated, considering the proposition. After a period of deep thought, he would not renege on the thought Diablo was superior in every regard to a deprived desert settlement.

"I don't think this city needs any more soldiers running around," Randolph eventually said, much to Frost's displeasure. "The streets are already clogged and we have a chorus of uprising against the segregated boroughs. Adding more force to that may be like a match to dry fields. However, I would be foolish to think that our resources don't need protections. So, Mr. Frost, please see to it those things you stated are added for the pipelines as soon as possible. Updates on progress due this time next week."

Frost threw his hands up, not hiding his annoyance that only half of his proposal was accepted. Things were made worse by Jesse's cheerfulness about the situation.

"Wise decision," Winthrope said. "The funds that would have been spent on boosting those forces could be better used on the mining operations we have ongoing in the north."

"So sending money to Alum City to fund your little pet projects in metallurgy is 'spending it better'?" Frost asked with venom. "I would be laughing if that concept wasn't so blatantly self-serving, even for you Jesse."

"As opposed to keeping the funds here in Diablo for your own projects, Lucas?" Jesse snapped back.

Duncan prepared to swing his head back over to Frost for the next volley but the mayor spoke first.

"Gentlemen, please!" he said with arms raised. "We are in something of a hurry and need not make this longer."

"Apologies Your Honor. Lucas, it's all in perspective. When thinking long term, those metals could lead to more efficient engines, cheaper power generation, *and* lighter alloys that would even benefit your cold heart."

"All well and good for the *future*," Lucas sneered, "if it manages to manifest out of all these mounting dangers we turn a blind eye too."

"I like this idea, Jesse," the mayor said, unhearing Lucas. His beady little eyes were wide with longing. "Just think of the all the added tax revenues we can levy!"

"Well, that's not quite what I had in mind..." Jesse said apprehensively. "I..."

Randolph had shoved a large chunk of cake in his mouth, replying anyway with his sticky mouth full.

"Unintended consequences, my dear boy! Think of it as a small price to pay for the betterment of society."

Frost's snarl turned up into a crooked smile.

"Wise decision, Your Honor," Frost said coldly. He liked seeing some of Winthrope's proposal backfire, though he maintained his jealousy of the man's prowess.

I will figure a way to get what I want, he thought to himself. Narrowing his eyes, they hovered on Randolph, now licking his fingers clean.

"Then we are settled?" the mayor asked, crinkling his brow when he noticed Frost's look.

"Yes," said Jesse.

"Most excellent," Randolph replied, waving both hands delightfully. "Then you both are dismissed. It is a most busy day after all!"

Jesse and Duncan rose from their seats; Frost remained in his.

"I hope nothing happens to make us regret this decision," he said, slowly rising afterward.

Jesse noticed the tone, since Frost was normally better at concealing his feelings. For some reason, he was being unabashedly persistent.

"Why would we, Mr. Frost?" asked the mayor, whose large hands fell to the desk with a weighty *thump*.

"I am only saying that it is never bad to have your guard up," Frost replied. "At *all* times."

"I know that I do not live here," Duncan said, "but it seems that your city is more than capable as-is of fending off a disparate band of marauders."

The sun slid behind a cloud and office grew darker.

"You *would* agree with Winthrope, wouldn't you Mr. Morrison?" Frost answered, "I know that Lagos doesn't have raider issues due to those immaculate green lands, but from what I hear there are issues just as large and secretive splashing around in those northern waters. My *dear friend*, it's my advice that your people keep their noses out of the business of others, beyond what is written on paper. Oh, and better still, they should have their guard up, too, for you never know when the City of Lakes might… just… evaporate."

Silence followed, except for the ticking of clocks.

"I am *not* your friend," Duncan said, leaping toward the mayor to shake his hand. "Please excuse me, I… I must use the restroom Your Honor. With regards from the Magisterium of Lagos, I thank you for cooperation with this latest water trade deal and will deliver the documents to Mayor Laguna personally."

The mayor shook Duncan's hand (it was sticky) before his guest made way for the exit.

"A good thing he is going now," Frost said callously, loud enough so Duncan could hear. "He will be able to ascertain the quality of the toilet water before this new pipeline is completed. It will be a good data point, on which we can all reflect... and learn."

Jesse watched Duncan leave, the heavy door closing forcefully behind him. Staring back at Frost, Winthrope looked upon him with detest. Some things in the world might have been on the verge of change, but the relationship between the two of them was set in cold, unyielding stone.

NINE

THE JOURNEY BACK TO THE BOONE house seemed to take a lot longer and was, for sure, a lot lonelier. There was a distant strip of vibrant orange along the western horizon and the stars were just starting to reveal themselves in the darkening dusk sky.

I don't want to admit it, Jenny thought as the prairie bugs began their nightly chorus, *but I guess the time I've been dreading is finally here.*

She was reflecting on her long chat with Mr. Johnston, which ended up lasting for hours instead of the few minutes she expected. Over the course of the conversation, all the dots were connected: the illness getting worse, the chores and tasks mounting, her grandfather's meeting with Wilfred. Despite her denials, she realized that she wasn't all-powerful. The fate of her grandfather was sealed and she would soon be on her own, the tasks that were piling up inevitably poised to engulf her.

That might have scared her, but so did letting it go.

Yet, she had to…

"What do I owe you for this?" she had asked, hands trembling as she reviewed the legal papers for sale of the property to one Mr. Wilfred Archibald Johnston.

"The minimum to make it legal, Miss Boone: one Gear."

"We don't have that anymore," she replied glumly. "All that's left is on me and it's a fifth of that."

"Oh cheer up now, no need for such sad faces," Mr. Johnston said while smiling. He grabbed yet another contract from a table off to the side. "I learned long ago, especially after settling here in the Gulch, that it pays to be prepared for every contingency."

"What's this?"

"Papers for a loan," Wilfred replied, an air of pride in his words. "From myself to a Miss Jennifer Alexandria Boone, in the amount of one gold Gear, subject to payment at the recipient's…"

Jenny didn't hold back her tears. Hugging Wilfred, she cut him off mid-sentence.

"Thank you," she managed to say through the sobbing. "You're too kind."

He cleared his throat dismissively.

"It's my pleasure and not a problem in the slightest."

Wiping away the mess on her face, Jenny looked at him, now smiling herself.

"But, what am I going to do with myself?" she asked, genuinely unsure.

"You could always work here in the store," Wilfred offered, "or stay on the farm. I'm not planning to evict you. I have enough money put back to bring the property up to minimum standards; might even be able to keep some of those farm hands if sales end up in the black. You'll get a wage of course."

Jenny seemed enthusiastic about the prospect.

"Also, if the pain of memory is too great, know that my sofa is yours, too," he continued, falling into a stammer as she blushed. "Now, I m-mean *no* o-offense inviting a young l-lady like you into my h-home." His face reddened. "I hope you d-don't take it that way, b-but Mrs. Johnston was the one who insisted…"

Jenny looked up at the stars with a smile on her face, remembering the awkward sincerity of his words. She could never take offense to anything the Johnstons said; both were always so kind hearted, especially to her and her family when most others turned their backs and slammed their doors. The world could benefit if more lived and loved by their example.

A cool breeze grazed her face, the dark house coming into view. There was a dim light emanating from the kitchen, a sign the power had been turned back on. However, when she noticed that no light was coming from her grandfather's bedroom, the chill in the wind moved right into her spine.

Oh, no… she panicked. *No, no, no…*

Heart racing, she pressed down hard on the pedal and the motor carriage surged along the bumpy road. She got closer and saw there were figures moving in the gloom. Dark and ominous, a couple were standing beside a group of hitched sleipnir while others were skulking in and out of the house, carrying things they didn't own.

"Hey!" Jenny shouted, pressing a sparking switch that lit lanterns on each side of the carriage. "What do you think you're doing? Thieves!"

Yet these were no thieves as the light revealed; they were Rangers and the slimiest one of all was waiting with arms crossed.

"Jebidiah!" Jenny screamed as the carriage skidded to a halt. She leapt out and brandished her pistol. "What the hell are you doing here?"

"Ain't it obvious? Time's come to hand over your land," he

sneered, raising his arms. A storm of cocked hammers followed, his fellows pointing their weapons at her.

"Not happening," she stated. "Papa already sold the place to Mr. Johnston; finalized it all today so you're going to have to deal with him if you have any property issues."

A flash of defeat crossed Jebidiah's face, but it was fleeting. He started a slow clap.

"Huh; so, that was your business there in the store. Figured you'd be there buyin' milk and potatoes like a good bitch. Then again, knowin' you and that distinct *lack* of ladyship, only the last part would be fittin' I think."

"Enough of your talk, Jebidiah! Get off this land!"

He chuckled.

"You understand that I'm gonna have to lay eyes on those papers. I may even have some questions about your papa's state o' mind when draftin' 'em." Jesse took in a sharp breath through his clenched teeth. "Tsk, tsk. Too bad the ol' man's kicked the bucket, would've liked to have heard the answers, or him tryin' anyways."

Jenny's heart dropped into her gut when she heard those words, her eyes wide and wild. She didn't say another word, rushing into the house then the kitchen.

She stopped there, dead in her tracks.

Ahead, curled up in a heap on the floor next to his water bowl was Bip. Blood was streaming out of a fresh bullet hole, staining the wood floor.

Her furry friend was gone.

Jenny couldn't take the onslaught of emotions, weeping instantly. Rushing with flooded eyes into the living room, her hip struck the edge of an end table. It was painful; she didn't care, and soon she had reached the end of the short hall.

Bursting into her grandfather's bedroom, the door slammed

against the wall. Expecting to see blood and bullet holes, she saw him laying there with his eyes closed. He was peaceful, as if asleep, and there wasn't a trace of foul play to be seen. Regardless, her hand came up to her mouth and she sobbed again.

"I'm gonna miss you Papa," she said. Those words had been prepped for a long time but were no less easy to deliver.

After a few moments, she lowered her hand to his forehead and neatened some of the stray hairs. He almost looked presentable. She stood in silence for a time, each breath getting longer and more pronounced. Then suddenly, she leaned over, kissed his cheek, and marched back to the front door with ice water gushing through her veins.

"Look who's back and all emotional," Jebidiah mocked.

"Sure enough, Papa's gone," she said plainly. "Bite got the best of him in the end."

The group of men jeered and it would have been intimidating, but not that night.

"You finished?" she snapped, eyes aflame.

They stopped, not liking the fact a woman was speaking to them in that manner.

"Which of you big men did that to the critter inside?"

Jebidiah smirked as a rawboned man snorted, proudly putting his hands on his hips.

"This one did," he said in a screechy voice. "What of it?"

There was a loud *bang* that rang out into the night and the man's kneecap exploded in pain and slivers of flesh and bone.

Steam rose from the tip and thin grills along the barrel of Jenny's gun.

"May want to double check your targets next time and make sure they're not a part of someone's family," she said coldly. "Now, I've already asked you all to leave nicely … I won't be doing that again."

"We ain't goin' anywhere any time soon," Jebidiah retorted. "Gents, seems like Miss Boone is ready to…"

Jebidiah's voice trailed off as something hot grazed his ear. It was followed by a low rumble and what sounded like the deep blare of horns. The din echoed across the plains, startling the sleipnir. The Rangers were also spooked, looking around fretfully but unable to see exactly where the unnerving sounds were coming from.

"At ease!" Jebidiah demanded, touching his ear. Bringing his damp fingers in front of him, he saw that it was blood.

The ground began to tremble as if an army were approaching and the Rangers gripped their weapons tightly. They looked around haphazardly in the dark.

Jenny couldn't see much either, but off at the edges of the light she could make swift movement. She had no idea what was going on, but chances are it wasn't good. She laid herself on the floor, trying to reduce her profile as a potential target.

The bony Ranger dropped his weapon, staggering toward his ride. Quickly unhitching it, he tried to mount but was struck down by a barrage of bullets. His body fell, riddled with holes, and Jebidiah realized exactly what was happening.

"RAIDERS!" he shouted, energy draining when he saw the size of their force. At least fifty were charging by at full gallop on their way toward Hondo Gulch, shrouded in a dirty veil that concealed at least fifty more.

"Raiders?" Jenny whispered, her mind hearkening back to the lone man she saw on the outcropping. Could he have been spying on the town, preparing the others for this attack?

She didn't have much time to dwell on it, a group of the attackers breaking formation to charge the authorities.

Jebidiah spit out his dip and grabbed a rifle from a pack on his steed.

"Form a goddamn line!" he shouted to his men, cranking the lever on the gun to chamber a round. Turning his attention to the onrushing attackers, he cried, "Prepare to die!"

They responded in kind, battle cries loud with their guns and bows high.

Jebidiah's men followed suit and within seconds a thunderstorm erupted across the plains.

The foremost raider was struck and his sleipnir reared then tumbled, cartwheeling with him still firmly attached to the saddle. Others were knocked from their mounts, trampled into paste under heavy hooves.

The Rangers fared no better, raked by bullets and stung by arrows. They fell in turn, Jebidiah the last man standing. He stood amidst the chaos, listening to distant cries and shouts from the Gulch that filled the sky beneath the stars and the moon. It was a soulless song, one that bore notes of victory and death. Unbearable to his senses, he lost them. Dropping the rifle, which clinked gently as it hit the ground, he drew his pistol.

A trio of riders was making way for him, a gleam in their eyes like predators about to slay their prey.

"Ain't gonna get me today," he muttered, raising the gun to his temple.

BANG!

Jenny watched as her heart threatened to leave through her mouth, but heavy gasping kept it locked inside. As Jebidiah's body collapsed and the raiders rejoined the assault, she thought about the Johnstons, who were probably eating dinner or relaxing by their fireplace as this tide of destruction was headed their way. She then lingered on Bip, and her thought about her grandfather.

Everything she had come to know and love was gone in an instant.

The stampede was withering, filling Jenny with enough

courage to leave. Crawling to the edge of the stairs, she prepared to bolt into the desert.

"On three," she told herself, eyeing west. Where she was going she didn't know nor cared; all she wanted was to be away from that place.

"One…"

She looked around one more time.

"Two…"

The coast looked clear.

"Three!"

As she moved, something grabbed her forcefully. She was spun around on the spot and her eyes met two large, reflective lenses staring back at her. They were part of a gas mask, a thick beard flowing out from underneath it.

"You!" she screamed, recognizing the stranger as the man from before, even though most of his tattoos were covered by a dirty coat. She struggled to free herself from his grip. "Let go of me! What do you people want? Let go!"

"Right now, I don't want anything other than for you to shut up so you don't draw any more attention this way," he said. His voice was commanding and deep; she nearly listened.

"I don't have to listen to you!"

"And me to you if I knock your stubborn ass out," he replied, flicking the mask up.

Jenny had planned a nasty comeback, but stuttered. His face was a lot nicer than she expected from a rough-and-tumble raider. Those hazel eyes and soft features were quite attractive up close, and even his menacing scowl had care tucked behind it.

"Now will you please shut the hell up before any of the Vipers notice we aren't part of their gang?" he asked, tugging the mask back over his face. "Thankfully, they seem too hyped up on adrenaline to notice. At least until the Eliminators come."

The man was speaking of the Pit Vipers, a disparate band of marauders that plagued the lands between the Gulch and Seco Basin. Normally gathered in small, easy to deal with groups, they were a nuisance to the authorities of either settlement. The Vipers didn't discriminate either, also at odds with rival gangs, especially the Skinners, who killed for sport in addition to stealing supplies and money.

However, this group happened to be much larger and far more organized than normal. It was a combination that had both nervous.

"Eliminators?" Jenny asked as the man let go.

He groaned and with a quick wipe of his bald head said something under his breath. He then pulled out a pistol from a grungy bag that was slung over his shoulder. It looked like junk, cobbled together from parts collected around the wastelands.

"We don't have time for this," he said, shoving the gun's grip at her. "Eliminators are raiders that trail behind a main attack group. Lucky for us there aren't normally many of them. Their sole purpose is to eliminate any survivors that remain. Hence the name… got it?"

She nodded, raiders apparently quite a succinct culture. Taking the scrap pistol, she found it heavier than she was used to.

"You're going to have to compensate for the heavier weight when you fire. Recoil on that one's a pain, too," the man said. "Now I saw that you can bust a knee wide open, but do you know how to kill? Because if you don't, you're going to have to learn really fast out there."

"Of course I do," she said defensively.

"Done it before then?"

"Y-yes," she stammered. "Could take you out if I wanted to."

The raider shook his head.

"Shit, city women are hardly killers, unless it's over the latest handbag."

Jenny's mouth dropped at the insult, but then quickly snapped shut. She had a focused look in her eye as she raised the gun up, pointed in his direction, and fired.

BANG!

"Damn it woman!" he shouted. "Give me that back!"

"Believe me now?" she asked, holding the pistol out of his reach.

"What in the hell are you talking..." he replied, cut off by a loud *thud*.

Turning, he saw the body of an Eliminator on the ground. His face was hidden behind a crude metal helmet with a white snake painted on the side. In the center of his chest was bullet hole, torn clean through the thin leather armor.

"*That* would have hurt," he said thankfully, spying a spiked mallet laid in the dirt just out of reach. "Guess I wasn't *completely* insane trusting you. Nice shot."

"That's yet to be seen, but thank you."

"Come on then," he said, looking around before standing. He was tall, about ten centimeters more than she was. His broad shoulders were noticeable even in the coat.

"Why are you helping me?" she asked suspiciously, staying on the ground for the time being.

"No reason in particular," he replied, still surveying the surroundings. The area looked clear, the Vipers obviously thinking they were good enough to only need one Eliminator. "But consider yourself a lucky damsel in distress that was saved because I was in the right place at the right time."

"I happened to be doing fine."

"Obviously, especially that moment you were about to run out into the blunt end of an Eliminator's weapon while you were saving yourself."

"I did get rid of the problem...." she drawled, hinging on each word for a name.

"You talk too much, woman, anyone ever tell you that?" he asked, lifting her to her feet. "Now let's go."

"People tell me that all the time, it's just that I need to call you something… other than stranger," she said during a quick dust-off. "And my name is Jenny, not 'woman.'"

"Fine!" he shouted, already marching westward. He pulled a shotgun out of a scabbard on his back. "I go by Aftershock."

"That's your *name*? Why would anyone call themselves –"

"Enough!" he growled, slamming the barrel of the weapon into his palm.

Jenny smiled, but knew she better give it a rest before she pissed Aftershock off.

Even though it was her way of handling the situation, nearing a point of nervous laughter, she didn't know if it was the best decision to head out into the wilds with this mysterious raider.

Trudging forward, something tugged at her, saying that she should try it alone. Another part forced her to carry on walking. Before long, the latter feeling won. Stowing her worries, she fell in behind Aftershock without a word, both disappearing into the dark and dangerous night.

TEN

THE SUN HAD FALLEN BEYOND THE horizon for day to break across the Great Ocean that spanned the other side of the world, yet the sky above Diablo was still warmly ablaze from the city lights below.

Frost laid across his massive bed, wide awake as orange light from the windows danced across his eyes. Trying to get an early night's sleep, that alone would have been enough of an annoyance, had his mind not already had him tossing and turning for the last hour. Still racing, his brain was mulling over every detail of things that had happened since morning. Those thoughts weren't fueled by the guilt of hundreds of people losing their jobs – Frost had none – it was more about that damnable Winthrope and his ability to be a wrench in everyone's plans but his own.

There must be a way of getting one up on you, Frost thought endlessly. *Anything to get you out of my sight, permanently.*

He devised many creative ways that it could be done…

However, each solution carried hefty legal ramifications…

Not that those ever stopped him from acting before…

It's just that Winthrope was a well-known adversary…

Any actions would likely bankrupt him to cover up…

Unless…

"Damn you, Jesse!" Frost yelled, the onslaught of thoughts overwhelming.

Kicking off the comforter he sat upright. Cursing more, his chest heaved, slick with streaks of restless sweat. Winthrope aside, all he wanted to do was sleep, but listening to the sounds of light rain worked up an urge to piss, in turn forcing him out of bed. His large, grumbling, and naked body lumbered past a murky field of flamboyant decor and drizzling glass into the bathroom.

After a few relieving minutes, Frost reemerged. Placing a forearm on the glass, he looked out at the evening cityscape, breath fogging the view.

Bathed in light, the aesthetic strength of his body was displayed and he felt though Winthrope was a good man, he was a great one amongst the common men below. Powerful legs like tree trunks supported him, rising to a formidable torso that was capped by his square chest. Flaring outward, his back and broad shoulders were like wings while his arms symbolized authority with their sheer size.

Frost was also tattooed, a fact hidden from most everyone beneath the flamboyant fashions society dictated. He always thought it hypocritical that clothing was made to enchant the senses and engage wearer and onlooker alike, whereas tattoos – designed to do the same – were frowned upon with the same level of aversion as a leper. The designs adorning Frost were unique, splitting his body from the neck down with swirls of green, red, and blue. It was a perfect reflection of his soul, divided in conflict between nobleman and raider.

Frost certainly noticed and it maddened him.

Recently, things had become worse and Frost started to regret the decision to make Aero so autonomously aware. At first he thought it would be a good idea, adding to his previous connection with his former lover. Instead, the avatar grew more dissociated from the name, preposterously considering itself a 'unique individual.' Even for Frost – the epitome of social renegade – that sort of thing was unacceptable. A programming downgrade was on the horizon, Frost keeping that a well-kept secret.

"In that case, bend over," Frost said. His eyes narrowed, unforgiving in their gaze.

Aero did as he was told. Facing the window, he leaned over and placed his hands on the sill.

Frost came up behind, sliding himself between Aero's buttocks. He smacked them a couple times before grabbing hold, grinding the entire time.

"There we go, Aaron," he moaned, pulling back to get a full view. His heart beat heavy between breaths as he said, "Your body... so flawless... so mine."

Finishing what was left of the wine, Frost threw the empty glass on the bed. It bounced a few times then rolled off the other side, ending with a shatter. Unbothered, he swallowed, then lubed up his fingers with spit. Circling Aero's perfect hole, two fingers teased before slipping inside, working the area until it was slick and Lucas was rigid.

"So tight," Lucas muttered, grabbing both of Aero's hips. "I'm not going to make this easy on you, even if you do everything I want."

Positioning himself tip to luscious brink, Lucas, unyielding, pushed forward. Warmth enrobed his head, inching toward the base until he could go no further. There he paused, fully enveloped, as Aero countered with his own skills.

Gentle waves began to roll down Lucas' shaft, sending his

eyes for a second to the back of his head. He wanted to stay put – Aero's kneading felt impossibly fantastic – but the urge to pull back overcame him, the combination of pleasure, heat, and motion blissfully unbearable as Aero worked to keep him locked inside.

Lucas finally drew his way out, throbbing and wet. He looked out across the city then down to his swollen self as Aero turned around, his immaculate torso gleaming, along with a piercing blue stare beneath his tufts of light hair. A hand came and latched on to Lucas, twisting and vibrating as only a bot could to milk more intense pleasure out of his rod.

"D-dammit!" Lucas bellowed, legs buckling as a tremble traversed his spine.

He wasn't about to succumb.

Grabbing hold of Aero's thighs, he plunged back in, mercilessly pounding until the bot released his hold.

"Thought you'd get me?" Lucas asked through gritted teeth, letting out a beastly growl.

He grabbed hold of Aero's hair with one hand, the other rubbing against his hard abs before gripping Aero's shaft. Using the added leverage, Lucas plowed him until a storm of sweat was flying from his hair and down his back. It was such a turn on: Aero there, unable to move; not only impaled but held firm.

Lucas was getting close to climax; he loved control, reveling in it like the deviant acts he performed behind closed doors. Taking a long look back out the window, the lights glinted in his golden eye and he was unable to hold back any longer.

Spilling into Aero, the floor became white with the overflow, yet Frost continued to churn, whipped into a feverish frenzy that would only stop when he was ready and that would be once he had what he wanted.

Aero was already his, a toy and a slave to his desires. Soon, Diablo would be too.

ELEVEN

JENNY CHECKED THE TIME, HER POCKET watch indicating it was coming up on ten o'clock. That meant she was only an hour and a half into this ill-advised trek with Aftershock across the wastes. With aching feet and mounting regret she looked out at the surrounding vista. Lit by the cold moon, the plains were an endless and uninviting sea of soil, except for an area of eerie orange that glowed like a warm fire burning in a distant hearth.

"The Gulch?" Jenny asked, trying to regain her bearings.

"Yes," Aftershock said bluntly. He didn't even look, having seen many sights like it before. "If you knew anyone there, you best pray they met a swift end. But there's no sense in dwelling on that right now. We still have a way to go, so come on, this way."

Jenny had no idea where Aftershock was taking her, but nevertheless after wiping a stray tear from her cheek, she turned away from the past and continued toward an uncertain future.

The duo carried on, turning slightly north. They passed oddly shaped cacti that seemed to move on their own and stunted bushes that studded the landscape along the way, creatures watching intently from within their tangled branches. Eventually the soil hardened and cracks formed in what was once a shallow lake. The walk became less uncomfortable, for a little while at least.

Aftershock marched on through the shifting terrain, confident though Jenny was utterly lost. He doubled back a couple of times as a precaution, feeling like probing eyes were on them from the dark, but thankfully everything remained serene.

Hours later the land rose steadily, peaking with another stretch of pathless wasteland. This area differed from that near the Gulch, the barren soil now patched with tussock grasses and leafy bushes between large rock formations. In the distance, Jenny could make out what looked like the crests of hills, gentle and rolling like a soft pillow beneath the broad smattering of stars. Her mind was drifting, set upon sleep no matter how restless it would be out in the wilds.

"That's our destination," Aftershock said, pointing toward the dim ripples on the horizon. "We should reach it in a couple more hours."

"Finally," Jenny said aloud, but meaning to keep the sentiment to herself she quickly looked over to Aftershock, expecting some chastising words.

He paid her no mind, assessing what lied in store before hiking once more with purpose toward the landmark. His estimate was not far off and after a little less than two hours of ground plodding by underfoot, they had reached the base of the dark hills.

They rose taller than Jenny expected and were far less rocky, lined with naked trees whose bark glowed in part under the pallid light. There was also a narrow path hugging the hillside, easily missed. Aftershock followed it, winding upwards in a curving, narrow channel until it widened into a flat area at the crest of a northern peak. To their left was the entrance to a small cave, hewn into the rock by tools if the scalloped edges were any indication. In front of the hollow was a circular ring of rocks, riddled with pieces of ashen wood while far ahead, to the right, and behind, the hill crest afforded a wide view of the surrounding lands. It was obscured only to the south, where more hills and rocks created a defensive barrier.

"We'll make camp here," Aftershock said, inelegantly fishing out a few small supplies from his bag before shoving his gas mask inside.

Walking over to the hollow, he took off his jacket and tossed it on the ground, rolling a large rock that was against the back wall out of the way. Behind it was a hidden recess where a few more items had been stowed.

"Do you need any help?" Jenny asked wearily.

Aftershock shook his head.

"No I should be all right," he said. "You're exhausted and I've done this so many times it's second nature, even with a new moon."

Not wasting the chance for rest, Jenny yawned and found a stony spot to sit down. Her feet throbbed and for some reason her shoulder did, too. Removing her head gear, she set it off to the side and shook out her frizzy hair, betting she looked frightful.

Aftershock was too busy to notice, having set out an array of things for camp. Before starting any work though, he walked over to her, holding out a beat-up canteen.

"There's not much left in this one, but it should quench your thirst for the time being. If you need more, I have a waterskin back in the cave."

"Thank you," she said, getting an up-close view of his body as she grabbed the canteen, nearly dropping it in the process.

He smirked and her admiration continued once he turned around, overflowing once he bent over in the cave to review the provisions.

"In all my days…" she whispered, trying to take a swig and missing at first. "So many ridges…"

Really, Jen? He's a criminal! her inner voice shouted, trying to overcome this sudden infatuation with men, especially dangerous ones.

It worked, though only just, and she drank the last of the water.

Aftershock worked to set up a hasty camp, hungry and fatigued himself. Jenny was watching him intently, learning from and perhaps still admiring his skills. Soon things were arranged and Aftershock returned to the hollow one more time, bringing with him a stack of firewood tucked under one arm and a few cans of food in the other.

"Hungry?" he asked her, setting the cans on the ground and arranging the wood amongst the stones.

"So much that I could eat my own arm," she answered, getting up to move closer.

Aftershock laughed.

"Let's hope it doesn't come to that," he said lightheartedly. "You'd still be hungry afterward."

"Hey now!" she said, kicking a cloud of dirt his way. "Fine then, I'll just eat yours…"

Awkwardness fell between them like a sudden wall, but at least the fire had been lit, driving away the shades of blue. Its crackling was the only noise.

Aftershock was the first to do something, snatching one of the cans and using a pocket knife to cut the lid open. Bending it, he made a makeshift scoop, plunged it into the cold meat and beans, then walked it over to Jenny.

She didn't see him coming, still looking off into the distance quite embarrassed.

"Here you go," Aftershock said.

"Oh!" Jenny replied with a start. "Sorry, I don't know what's come over me. I'm normally not so…"

"Desperate?" Aftershock asked bluntly; Jenny's mouth fell agape. "I get it, but I think that the fatigue is what's talking on your behalf. Plus, let's face it: losing your home and not having a minute to process that? It'd be tough on anyone. I gather you'd been in the Gulch for a while?"

She took the can, getting a pungent whiff.

"Yes," she coughed, risking a second sniff. It wasn't nearly as bad, probably because she knew what was coming. "My whole life in fact. I guess all this is tough for me to take in. It doesn't even seem real."

Aftershock made his way back over to his side of the fire, dropped down in a heap, and prepared his own frugal dinner. Even though he was stiff, it was good to get some food in, and they both enjoyed what they could under the cool sky full of stars.

"Afraid it doesn't get much, if any, easier out here," he said, chewing loudly and messily. "Sometimes I swear I'm still asleep and all this is some kind of bad dream."

"So… you've been out here a while yourself?" she asked, braving dinner. The beef was salty with a vinegary bite, the beans slightly sweet. Overall it was palatable. "Isn't it rough?"

"Yep, on both counts… like Hell on Eaugen itself. I was wasteland born and raised by the wilds," he said proudly. "Don't have any siblings, so it's tougher when you're alone out here. But, it forces you to get tough yourself, else get eaten up and shit out by someone or something looking to get ahead of you. Without a choice, I grew up in in a raider gang down south a way, near Seco. Learned how to live real fast and rose quite a way up the ranks. Until…"

Aftershock paused, as if he didn't want to carry on with that line of conversation. He quickly shifted topics.

"So, um, being stuck in the Gulch, I gather you've not seen Seco Basin either?"

Jenny shook her head, her mouth being full.

"I can tell you that you're not missing a thing; the place is a dump, even more than the Gulch. No offense. Even so, there'd never be a spot for me to live a normal life in those places, all built up and maintained by the more 'civilized' of us."

"I highly doubt that; you're a man," she said, "whose opinion counts and whose life matters more than just making dinner and babies."

Aftershock laughed.

"Well, I can cook for myself," he said, shaking his can before taking another heaping bite, "and babies, well let's just say making them isn't high on my list of interests. As for that manly opinion, I think I cancelled mine with all these."

He raised his arms high so the firelight could illuminate them, showing off the inside and outside. He was absolutely covered in intricate ink that flowed around his body like rivers of blue and green.

"For what it's worth," she said taking another look, "I think they're gorgeous."

"Thank you; that is actually worth a lot to me. You'd be surprised how often complements don't come out here. Or anywhere for that matter. It's the pieces each of us brings that makes up the whole picture, but people just focus on what makes them unique, and sadly that gets twisted into what makes them better than all the rest."

Breaking into a small smile, he scraped the last capful of beans from the bottom of the can. She looked at him through the light smoke, and sparks kicked up when he tossed the can into the fire.

He was such a walking contradiction: an admitted criminal with an appearance that matched who spoke better and more politely than the authorities in her former town. There was certainly more to him, but having just met she knew she would just have to wait. That assumed she was around long enough to find out.

Jenny continued to eat slowly when they heard distant neighs riding a low rumble. Aftershock looked out over the plains to see if it was trouble, but it was just a herd of wild sleipnir that was galloping across the land.

"Thought we might have had some visitors," he said, relaxing again.

From his pocket, Aftershock took out a crumpled roll of thin paper stuffed with dried leaves. Lighting one end with the campfire he put the other side in his mouth and took a draw, blowing a couple smoke rings.

"Your folks back in the Gulch?" he asked.

"Luckily, no," she answered, her grandfather's face flashing briefly in her mind. "My brother died before he was born and my parents and grandmother had, um, died from *external* causes. My grandfather had only just passed on from a Deathneedle sting when the attack happened."

She continued to recount her woes in town, from the decline of the farm all the way up to Jebidiah's death.

"Damn, my condolences," Aftershock said somberly. "Going back to your grandpa: a deathneedle you say? That is certainly not how I would like to go. If you don't mind me asking, how long did he…"

"A couple of months," Jenny stated, handing her can to Aftershock. "You want what's left? I'm full."

He took it gladly and polished off three more capfuls, tossing her can into the fire when done.

"A couple of months is a long time for a sting from that critter. Sounds like he had a fighting spirit."

"He certainly did," she said, morose. Her face became a grimace as recent events started to sink in.

"It's all right," Aftershock said. "Tears aren't a weakness. Goodness knows I've shed so many over time they could've filled that dry lake we walked across."

Jenny started to let them flow but took a deep breath and stopped.

"Maybe later," she told him, and they enjoyed some peace and quiet.

Off far to the north a storm brewed, little pricks of lightning dotting the horizon, while overhead a few clouds started to form.

"It's going to be a pale morning," Aftershock said in a low voice.

"I haven't heard that before; what do you mean?"

"It's the wasteland's way of teasing those who live here. A pale morning's one that has water everywhere: up in the overcast clouds refusing to fall, a gray mist that'll hang low on the ground, yet not a but a few drops of clinging to surfaces to drink."

"I see what you mean," Jenny said. "Kind of makes you thankful for water towers and rain catches... when it rains of course."

"Or plumbing for the city folk," Aftershock added. "Though when you don't have a stream to clean yourself, you come up with ingenuous ways out here."

"I don't even want to know!" Jenny said, trying not to laugh at Aftershock's crudeness. She did so anyway; it was liberating.

"So, I've been meaning to ask," Jenny said cautiously as the laughter died down. "Were you... involved with the attack?"

Aftershock took a very long draw, expecting to be asked that at some point. He blew out a large cloud of formless smoke.

"The short answer: no, I didn't."

"And the long answer?"

"Way too much to tell."

Jenny's features scrunched up tight.

"Oh no, you're not going to suddenly give me one word answers. I saw you there pretty much *in* the Gulch the day before. Were you spying? Why did your gang decide to attack the Gulch?"

"First off," Aftershock said sternly with two thick fingers pointed right at her, "the Vipers are NOT my gang. So, let's get that idea out of your head."

Jenny became tense; she obviously struck a nerve.

"Second," he continued, "yes, I was spying... but for myself. Was looking for some provisions for camp. In fact, what we just got done eating came from there."

"Sorry," she said, "we tend to place all raiders in the same basket."

"Don't blame you, I certainly would. The Vipers may be a lot of things," he muttered, "but honorable isn't one of them. The Skinners can't stand them, nor the Devil Dogs."

"Dishonorable for sure," Jenny said. "Perhaps I'm naïve, too, but I was always led to believe raiders weren't organized into such large groups. The Vipers seemed to toss that theory out like garbage, didn't they? Any idea why they would suddenly attack?"

Aftershock finished his smoke, flicking the butt into the waiting flames.

"Yeah that's been gnawing at my gut, too. Raiders across the Barrens have been acting like their balls are big as boulders. You're right though, raiders – especially the Vipers – always ride in small groups. That reduces the risk of being tracked back to base camps where the biggest gatherings are." Aftershock sputtered his lips. "As for why now? I wish I knew. The timing is nothing important, so I'm at a loss."

"Well, whatever it is, us not knowing doesn't change the outcome," Jenny said, discouraged. "The Gulch and its people are still gone."

"Sadly, no it doesn't," Aftershock confirmed, "but I would still like to know what happened. I'm thinking of heading up north to talk with some of my contacts out near Bala; see if they've heard anything. An attack like this is going to send some pretty big ripples throughout both the wasteland and other settlements."

"Sounds like a great plan," Jenny said excitedly. "Do we set off in the morning?"

"We do," Aftershock said straightaway, "but westward. I'm taking you to Diablo."

Jenny sat up straight, listening to him with puzzlement. Turning his words in her mind, she was having difficulty understanding them, even though they could not be plainer.

"I can't help but notice you seem shocked," he said.

"Truth be known: yes."

Jenny started swaying slightly.

"Look, I'm not saying you couldn't hold your own, but the wastes aren't a place someone like you should be." Aftershock looked around the camp, panning his hand as he went. "Trust me, this isn't a life you want to live."

"But you brought me out here …"

"Yes, otherwise you'd be dead, unburied, and the worms would nonetheless be feasting. As crazy as it sounds – and trust me I wonder what the hell I was thinking myself – I brought you out here to save you."

"But why…"

"Listen, call it karma or whatever you want, Jenny Boone, I just want to do the right thing and get your ass to a safer place."

Jenny was persistent, the argument continuing back and forth with elevated voices for a good twenty minutes. Jenny realized toward the end that Aftershock was just as if not more stubborn than she was. No matter what she said, it wasn't going to convince him to keep her around.

She ended with a frustrated groan and a maroon face. He was probably right after all. Not that she wasn't appreciative, but the thought of why he did any of this instead of letting her die with the others still plagued her.

"Okay fine," she yielded. "Fine."

Aftershock sat back on the ground, having worked himself up to standing during their volleys. He laid back on one arm and stretched out a leg.

"You sure are annoyingly persistent," he said before rattling off a list of settlements in the region. "I can get you whichever one you want, but if I had my say it would be Diablo. It's the closest and probably has the most opportunities."

"It's also the one that's easiest to get lost in. What am I going to do there?"

"Live better than you would out here, with me," he said, stomach flexing as he spoke. "I know that you're looking for something like that; something more. But, we already touched on that."

"Oh... no, it's nothing," she said, though her lingering eyes betrayed her words.

"People like me are the nothing, Jenny," he said warmly. "On the other hand, it – love – is everything. Those that are genuinely able to find what you're looking for and hold onto it are truly blessed."

Jenny sighed, feeling as though she was up on a grand stage with all eyes on her.

"I can tell you that you're *not* going to find that out here, Jenny, especially with me," Aftershock said, pointing a thumb west. "I just have a feeling something better for you waits over there in the city, where you belong and it will strike at your heart in all the good ways when you least expect it."

She looked at the horizon, already hazy as predicted.

"Why do I have the feeling there's more to what you're saying than you're letting on?" she asked.

"Because there is, Sam," he muttered.

"I… I beg your pardon? Sam?" Jenny asked. "Who is he?"

"He is a *she*," he clarified. "Samantha, in fact. She… she was my sister and she happened to look remarkably like you."

Jenny was speechless for a moment, the air in her lungs pushed out in one fell swoop. Regaining composure, she began to understand.

"So that's why you rescued me during the attack?" Jenny asked, flattered yet also extremely sad.

Aftershock nodded gently.

"It was more than I could do for her after she was taken, abused, and…"

"By the Vipers?"

"No!" he snapped. "By my own gang… my own damn people."

A sparkle formed in his eyes, catching the firelight.

"Why would they betray you like that?" Jenny asked.

"In their mind, I was the one who betrayed them," Aftershock said. "I mentioned before that I rose in the ranks, so high I became the leader. Was there for a good while, too. Ask anyone and they'll tell you that I did a damn sight more for the Skinners than any of those fuckers ever did, more than ten of them combined. Yet, my entire world came crashing down when the one person I trusted betrayed me. Someone I told a secret to that then wanted to bring about my downfall so they could put themselves in the same place."

Jenny stayed silent, listening intently.

"After he told everyone, they couldn't have such a mockery as the pinnacle of their group: a raider in charge that liked the company of other men. Seth Colton was cut down from his position in the Skinners like a diseased stalk of wheat, Samantha Colton was taken away… and raped for their own sick pleasure, then killed so they wouldn't risk nor would she bear any queer children, and at the end of all that pain, I was sentenced to death. Of course me being here meant I got out of there…" he cracked his knuckles, "with a little persuading."

Jenny was horrified.

"So now you see why I rescued you and want to see you safe in the walls of a city. No matter how shitty a life it may be in there, it's a damn sight better than the lawlessness you'd find out here. And with you looking the way you do, trouble will be out to get you with its slobbering jaws."

Jenny didn't know what to say. She agreed with Aftershock but wanted to hug him, yet knew she couldn't.

"Seth?" she wound up saying. "So that's your given name?"

"It sure was. Now it's worth about as much as dirt," he replied, "but since my ass was knocked all the way down into it, I had nothing else to lose. Hitting the ground as hard as I did, I was shook up by the quake. But, I stood back up and became something everyone fears just as much: the aftershock."

Jenny smiled, thinking on what her grandfather had told her about hitting rock bottom.

"And the gas mask?"

"Serves no practical purpose; I'm not gonna shave this beard off anytime soon. However, I found it on a dead ranger, up north a way after my escape from the Skinners. Unsure why he had it on him, but didn't need it anymore and I needed something to disguise myself – borrowing his duster while I was at it. Had it ever since then, sort of like a wall against my past."

"It's an honor to have heard about Seth and learn a little more about you, Aftershock. Thank you."

He smirked, then sniffled for a little while before he continued, "We'll head out for Diablo in the morning. It's still quite a way off and the way isn't going to be anything less than full of trouble and danger. But, it will be worth the risk to get *you* out of *my* hair."

Jenny smiled, picking up a handful of dirt before tossing it in his direction. It didn't get far at all before the wind scattered it.

"In case you haven't noticed," she said, "you actually have no hair."

"Well gosh, I had forgotten; thanks for the reminder," Aftershock grunted, grabbing his own fistful of dirt and lobbing it at her.

His chunk didn't scatter, hitting her square in the face. Eyes wide, he rushed over to see if she was okay.

TWELVE

MORNING HAD BATHED THE EAST coast for four hours before the sun tried to break through a thick wall of clouds that hung above Diablo. The factories and warehouses in the borough of Sucio were nothing spectacular, dark against the dingy sky like charred wood sitting in ash.

The faces of the factory workers congregated in the yard were just as dirty and glum, though they carried more warmth in their skin and content in their hearts than the crowds outside. There were some that were sick and others injured, hobbling on makeshift crutches of wood. All of them were hungry, wearing thin strips of fabric barely resembling clothes. They hovelled, crying, in doorways and at the iron gates, desperate for a day's worth of coin that would buy even less food.

The men inside were hard working, already tired yet the day was young. Loading substantial crates, once full those parts would be towed by, person and beast alike, to other factories that stood in similar fashion in other boroughs. There, they would be further assembled into the remarkable WHESE, which Jesse hoped would improve all their lives in time.

Speaking of Mr. Winthrope, he had just arrived from the main rail station where Duncan was heading on his return journey to Lagos. Slipping in through a guarded side entrance, Jesse was dressed to the nines. He deftly navigated the chaotic yard in his posh leather shoes, getting and giving many 'good mornings' on his way toward the main building. It was a frightful structure of sweating, black brick that had once been deep red. Slim arches adorning each side of the entry looked like immoral eyes, poised to strike.

The place looks like Frost designed it, Jesse thought, spotting a youngish man taking a break beside a sleipnir. Both man and beast seemed to have their eyes closed for a quick nap.

"Hello there, Hopkins," Jesse said.

Hopkins' eyes shot open and he straightened his posture, trying to dust off his grimy clothes. At this point the action was a habit only, the stains long embedded in the fabric.

"Oh, good mornin', sir!" Hopkins beamed, then bowed. Nervously, he brushed the side of the steed's belly. "Beggin' your pardon, but we… I was just on my break ya see…"

"It's no bother," Jesse replied with a reassuring nod, pointing skyward. "What *is* a bother is that it appears the sun might not be making an appearance today, so be sure to not tire yourself too quickly. I'll leave you to carry on and make the most of your day's work."

"For sure, Mr. Winthrope! Blessin's be upon you!"

Hopkins was always a chipper soul – mouthing the words 'he remembered my name' as Jesse carried on – and it was a refreshing trait Jesse hoped the man would not lose as he aged.

Jesse caught a few other passing smiles from workers he

diligently tried his best to take care of, but those scarce occurrences quickly reverted to scowls once he moved on. Someone other than Jesse might have been offended, but he knew what life was like outside the walls. In fact, he had just walked through it instead of taking an ornithopter to the rooftop, seeing how quickly it could sour even the sweetest fruit.

The large entry doors were impending. Up close, they were peeling and austere.

I must consider having someone paint these, Jesse noted to himself as he pulled on one of the dulled handles. The door creaked as it opened; Jesse strolled inside.

He entered a long and narrow space like a rectangle, the clacking of pistons the first sound to greet him beneath a veil of steam that hung at the tops of more high windows. It was as if the sky had been brought inside to replace the ceiling.

All the heavy machinery was at the far end, some of it visible while most spread into rooms that were further to the back and sides of the structure. Due to excessive heat and highly dangerous mechanical movements, the machines in that area operated by bots. They were not the sleek kind sold by Frost for personal use, but blockier units that were quite unsettling to look at if one didn't know what they were. Such was their shape, with multiple arms and bulbous eyes, that resembled man-sized insects. The machinery spun and cranked, hissed and belched, and small metallic parts of various shapes appeared at the end, dropping into boxes positioned at the base of long conveyors.

Once packed, the heavy containers were moved to tables that lined the center; there were five long rows of them. There, many women were sat, dressed in a light but traditional livery. To these women that did not matter, for they didn't miss their brass buttons and copper trinkets like ones higher in society might. They were there to work, taking the components and assembling them into more complicated mechanisms, and to get paid. It was a work ethic that Winthrope admired and rewarded – so that his workers could afford to wear such things after the rent was paid and their families' bellies were full, should they so choose.

He breezed by, nodding to a few ladies that were staring in his direction, their eyes so wide he was surprised they hadn't fallen out of their sockets to be assembled further down the line. Chuckling as one particularly enamored woman was elbowed by another to get back to work, Jesse swept up a long set of metal stairs, removing his hat as he entered an upper-level office. The plaque on the door read 'Foreman.'

Inside was a simple space, drab and run of the mill like the rest of the building. A mess of papers was scattered across the desk and atop it, a well of ink stuffed with quills and an ashtray carved into the shape of a helical gear.

A snobbish man with gruff features and a disheveled beard stood behind the desk by the window. Though well-dressed and mannered, he had the air of a vagrant, a small plate indicating the foreman's name was Dylan Butler. In his left hand was a pipe, smoldering as he surveyed the busy scene below, though his eyes were squinted so much it was questionable if he could see anything at all.

"Good morning," Dylan said stoutly.

Jesse joined him at his side, tipping his head as he looked below. He liked what he could make out of the operations, but not so much what he could smell next to him, getting a fair whiff of nose-curling tobacco.

"That wouldn't happen to be Gentle James, would it?" Jesse asked, casually removing his coat. Stepping away, he set it at a safe distance on one of the office chairs.

"It is, Milord," Butler replied, using the fingers of his free hand to smooth the hair over one of his ears. "However did you know?"

"It has a distinct odor," Jesse said, unable to stop himself coughing. Sniffling, he wiped his nose with a handkerchief drawn from his pocket. "Hardly lives up to the 'gentle' part of its name, being more pungent than the usual fare. I recognize it from my travels. From what I recall it is difficult to find, and vastly more difficult to purchase, being rather expensive as dried weeds go."

"That it may be, but we all have our vices don't we and, well, you pay quite handsomely compared to the rest," Butler replied, lifting the pipe to his lips. He smiled, teeth caked with a yellow crust.

"Indeed we do," Jesse said, scrutinizing him as he walked back over.

Why do I keep that… man… around? he asked of himself, unable to shake a feeling of deceitfulness whenever he looked at him. He concluded that it must have been one of his ill-advised, early decisions; or perhaps he was drunk with Duncan. *Yes, that must be it; this is Duncan's fault.*

"Speaking of vices, Mr. Winthrope, shall I have Miss Ward reprimanded, or dismissed?"

The foreman's tone could only be described as hopeful.

"Why Miss Ward?" Jesse asked, caught off guard by the request. "Has she done something problematic that I am unaware of?"

"Her actions recently," Butler stated nonchalantly. "I feel they do not reflect the qualities of a dependable woman, nor the type of person that should remain in our employ."

Jesse knew that Butler was referring to the young lady below that was smitten when he arrived. He became a little heated at the flippant attitude Butler maintained over something so trivial and innocent. It was likely an overzealous response to her resisting his own unsavory advances.

Jesse managed to hold his composure, for the most part.

"When last I checked, Butler, everyone was still under MY employ," Jesse snipped.

Butler took another draw of his pipe, the longest yet, and that feeling of untrustworthiness seethed from his pores.

"Yet she exhibits tendencies better suited for the light of a red lamp…"

"And you do not?" Jesse cut in bluntly. Butler raised an eyebrow. "This is simply the pining of a young girl. Nothing more."

"I stand corrected," Butler said.

"Then we agree she has done nothing to warrant discipline of any sort?"

"If we are looking past her… after-hours activities… then let us focus on her record, which states otherwise. One must actually work to earn their pay, do they not?"

"Yes, but I recall no such deficiencies when I reviewed the records last. I saw nothing but fine and productive workers across the board that do *earn* their pay. After all, I did just increase their wages did I not?"

Butler raised his pipe.

"Undoubtedly."

"While I know that Miss Ward is not quite the best at what she does, a good many wouldn't be able to claim that title either. She puts in her best effort and that is all we can expect."

"I was under the impression Winthrope Limited strove to be the best. How is this possible with less than stellar performance?" Butler asked indifferently, but ended up capitulating.

"Because the results of our labor are from the combined effort of all here, not just one; even myself," Jesse continued. "Besides, considering the recent job losses over at Frost Industries, we must be careful. News like that travels extremely fast and I hope you agree that it would not be in this company's best interest to get swept up in a similar societal backlash."

Butler laughed amidst the smoke.

"Societal backlash?" he asked impudently. "Mr. Winthrope forgive me, but I think you overstate the reach of the rabble."

"I beg to differ, based on what I heard just this morning from the Sheriff's office, but that doesn't change my stance on the matter."

Butler set his pipe down in the ashtray and leaned his back against the glass. He sighed loudly, rubbing the space between his eyes with stained fingers.

"Mr. Winthrope, I must ask: why are you involving yourself with all this low-level minutia? Surely a man of your position…"

"Needs to know how his company is performing from all aspects."

Jesse turned away from the window and walked over to his coat, placing both hands on the back of the chair it was slung over.

"Then delegate and have those people report to you."

"I would if I could trust the words they spoke with complete efficacy."

"Sir, let me put this another way then: if you try to do everything you will only do as well as one person split a hundred ways can: one-hundredth the quality. Surely this is not what you meant earlier when referring to trying your best?"

Jesse was about to say something when he realized Butler had a point. A flash of his father appeared before his eyes.

"Forgive the impudence," Butler continued, "but maybe what you need is someone to occupy your small time, allowing you to focus on the large picture; others can work the minutiae. A nice, worthy lady to hold on your arm, perhaps?"

Whispers of words spoken long ago came racing back to Jesse's memory.

…Do not follow the same path your old man did, waiting too long to love…

"I..." he began, mentally replaying the words of this father over and over. "I agree that I could try to find someone."

"Splendid!" Butler replied, emptying the singed contents of his pipe into the ashtray. He opened one of his desk drawers and rummaged around for a moment before removing a small, wooden octagon. Pressing a tiny button, the decorated lid unfolded in segments like a flower and there was more dried weed inside. He pinched himself another bowl full of it.

That was Jesse's signal to leave; he couldn't face another assault on his senses.

"But," Jesse said as he pulled his coat over his suit; Butler gave him a guarded stare as he lit his pipe again. "I need someone to challenge me... complete me, if you will."

"Easily done! There are plenty of young ladies in the city that would be more than pleased to be chosen to fulfill that need *and more*."

"No," Jesse blurted out. "I mean actual *love*, not some arrangement made out for expedited convenience. I do not think it's possible to find that with anyone from here."

"Why would you think that?"

"There are so many yes-men and women that one could be forgiven for thinking seizures are contagious in Diablo with all nodding," Jesse said, making sure to stare at Butler directly. "There are also far too many judgmental high and low-lives that can kiss ass quite well."

Butler did not reply to Jesse's vulgarity, drawing from his fresh pipe instead.

Jesse knew the conversation was over.

"Have a wonderful day, Foreman," he said, moseying to the exit, "and please be sure to inform me of any *real* issues that surface, beyond the harmless wants of a girl."

With that said, Jesse left, closing the door gently behind him.

Butler then turned away, blowing smoke as he dropped his greasy demeanor and resumed his keen watch over the factory floor.

"Oh, you will not have to worry about that, Mr. Winthrope. Such reports are already on their way…"

THIRTEEN

THE SKY WAS UTTER DARKNESS; a sheer wall of empty black. Then, a pale light began to flicker out on the western horizon. Beating like a heart, it swiftly sprang to life, growing until it was so bright that it rivaled the sun.

In the center of it, the silhouette of a man appeared, standing tall on the cracked wasteland soil. Beneath his bare feet, mud squelched and plants that were withered became green again. Smoke as white as snow rose from the ground and encircled him, swirling like great gears as they rose high into the sky. The air churned, becoming hot and sticky, kicking up flecks of dirt. Snapping on a pair of goggles, they glinted in the light as the man looked away from a woman who had been standing in front of him.

It was Jenny, also on the forsaken plains. She was wearing a tan leather corset, gripping its oversized clasp as she also looked away, forlorn.

The wind sent plumes of dust into her hair, frolicking with her frilly white dress and scratching at her lenses. It was becoming hard to see anything in the thickening cloud, yet not a word was spoken or exchanged.

The cloud surrounded them, darkening the sky and it became cold; a vast feeling of loneliness spreading out across the obscured vista. Despite the impending dark and thunderous noise, Jenny's heart remained steadfast. Driven, she plucked up the courage to look in the man's direction and as soon as she did, a line of gleaming blue tore across the sky, sending the dust to the ground with a tremendous crash.

In front of her, the shadowed man had done the same and was looking straight ahead. Feelings of hope and joy washed over them both, and again with no words they started walking toward each other, arms outstretched to embrace just as…

… a low roar echoed from across the plains.

Jenny opened her eyes quickly, waking up in a pale world shrouded in gray and blue. She was lying on a coarse blanket atop a grassy patch of ground. The air looked as if it would be chilly, but the breeze blowing across her skin was humid and warm.

What a strange dream, she thought, trying to interpret some kind of powerful message contained in it, but she ultimately decided it would be easiest to blame dinner.

The roars continued, mixed with low grumbles, and shifting, Jenny positioned herself to look out across the plains from their high vantage point. She gasped at the sight she saw: a herd of five camelo was wandering northward. Mind-bogglingly tall and graceful, the sight of those lumbering giants was captivating.

"They bond for life, you know," Aftershock said quietly, squatting at Jenny's feet to observe the herd. "The tall ones there on the outside are males, the females are beside them in the middle."

"And the little one in front?"

"Offspring from one of the pairs," he told her. "The other two will aid in watching and protecting it from predators. Then, when their time comes, the original pair will assist. It's actually pretty sad, isn't it?"

"What's sad about it?" Jenny asked, finding it beautiful.

"Sad that those beasts get the whole 'caring for each other' idea better than people do."

Jenny simply nodded, mesmerized.

"Never in my life would I have known such things existed," she said, "and so close to where I lived, too!"

"Makes you feel small and dumb as shit, doesn't it?" Aftershock asked as the herd ambled far enough to vanish in the mists.

"I wouldn't say it as quite as bluntly as a raider, but in a manner of speaking, I guess so," she replied.

Aftershock wore a half smile.

"Another fact you learn when you're out here – pretty fast too – is that no matter what you think you know, there is always something out there to teach you a lesson you didn't know you needed."

"Sort of like you did with me," Jenny said, sitting up to stretch.

"In a manner of speaking…" Aftershock repeated, followed by the other half of his smile. "Come on, let's get something in our stomachs. We have a long march ahead of us."

Jenny frowned, not looking forward to more of Aftershock's version of fine cuisine.

THREE HOURS HAD passed since the two of them left camp on their way to the outskirts of Diablo. The sun had yet to make much of an appearance beyond bright spots in the overcast sky, affording them a quicker pace across the endless, unchanging scenery.

Jenny slowed down to adjust her rucksack. Made of hide, it itched fiercely and was much heavier than she was used to carrying. The tops of her shoulders were sore. Inside were their provisions, along with matches and kindling, some first-aid supplies, and the beat-up canteen – refilled when they passed a watering hole not thirty minutes ago.

Aftershock was a few paces ahead of her. Reaching into the front pocket of his scraggy denims, he removed a brass disc decorated with an embossed border that resembled piping. In the center was a mound of red glass surrounded by leafy patterns. Depressing it with a thumb, there was a brief *click* and the entire front flicked open, revealing itself as a lid. Beneath was a fancy compass, its finely crafted arrow settling.

Jenny spied the device in Aftershock's hand, wondering if he had obtained it during one of his past raids. She was about to ask, when he spoke first.

"It looks like that little detour to avoid those razorjaws didn't put us off track to badly," he said, turning a few degrees to the right before snapping the lid shut. "I'd guess we added about fifteen minutes to the overall trek."

"I'll take a fifteen-minute delay over fifteen rows of sharp teeth," Jenny answered, catching up to Aftershock.

"You and me both," he replied, removing a waterskin that had been hitched to his waist. He took a quick sip. "I've seen what those critters can do and let's just say their name is the most understated part."

Jenny began panting, relieved they came across the agile

THE *Steam* TYCOON   137

creatures in the light, shuddering at the thought of their burnished black bodies lurking around in the dead of night.

"Speaking of understated, I'm glad the sun has been such today. Hopefully this cloud cover stays put until well after noon," Aftershock wished, studying the sky as he began to walk northwest. "That should let us easily make up the lost time, unless we encounter more along the way."

Jenny fell in behind Aftershock again, trying not to think about deadly bites. To help, she took a liberal look at Aftershock's shirtless back and shoulders.

It's not like they are going to have much of that where you're going, she justified with herself. *So, you better make the most of it while you can and he doesn't notice.*

But Aftershock was fully aware her eyes were still finding themselves stuck on him. With a subtle groan, he adjusted the bag slung across his left shoulder. Then, reaching behind to a rifle scabbard nestled down the center of his back, he used it to scratch an itch, making sure a few extra seconds were used for gratuitous flexing.

Jenny liked what she saw but knew it wasn't possible. That didn't change the fact that it was a form of torture, like looking at the goods displayed in a baker's window, while starving, without the money to buy a thing inside.

Aftershock quickly spun his head to see if he could catch her, but she happened to be faster, already pretending to look away at something more interesting in the distance.

Silly girl is still holding out a little hope, he thought, turning his attention back to the way ahead. *Not that there's anything wrong with having hope. She seems like a good soul, if I believed in that sort of thing. I hope she finds what's best for her in the devil's city, before the worst there finds her.*

Another few hours went by, excessively bright and scorching, and the pair was relieved to see the sun disappearing behind a widespread bank of clouds again.

"At last," Jenny said with relief, though she felt far from it being covered in that much sweat.

Aftershock was shiny too, stopping to wring out a white headband he had donned.

"Yeah, next time remind me not to curse us by mentioning our good fortune with the weather," he said, taking a sip of water. "By the way, you best get a drink yourself. From here to the city is where things get a little more interesting."

Jenny didn't think that sounded too bad. The last six, or maybe was it seven, hours were nothing but tedious.

"What kind of interesting?" she asked, interest piqued as she pulled the canteen from her bag.

"There's *two*," Aftershock replied, holding up as many fingers. "The first kind would want to kill us because I'm with you and the second, they'd want to do the same because you're with me."

"I… um…" Jenny said, blinking rapidly as she tried to process what was said. "I think your definition of interesting is *much* different than mine." She put her hands squarely on her hips. "What happened to that get-straight-to-the-point raider mentality?"

Aftershock pointed at his bald head before replacing the headband, saying, "Must've burned away in the heat."

Jenny wasn't laughing.

"In all seriousness," Aftershock continued, "the territory ahead is controlled by a smaller clan known as the Devil's Shadow."

"Their name sounds ominous enough," Jenny said.

"Exactly. Don't be fooled like many people are; as raiders go they're just as deadly, even with their few numbers."

"Why the Devil's Shadow?" Jenny asked as she took a drink and per the canteen away.

"Because they live in 'the shadow' of city Diablo, cast when the sun sets around the rocky outcrops at the Pitchfork. Oftentimes it's there that trade caravans or other travelers are ambushed, especially when they make the journey at night."

"Thankfully we don't have that problem."

"Still, it's in our best interest to keep our guard up," he said, voice getting even more grim. "There's still seven hours left until we get to the borders of Diablo, around the time we reach the Pitchfork. If that weren't enough, there's also Rangers and sentry bots roaming that area.

"Defending folks from the bandits?"

"Exactly, so you can imagine they'd be hard-pressed to take you in if you're spotted with me."

"We'll just have to make sure that doesn't happen."

"My plan exactly," Aftershock said confidently. "I know the area well enough, so we should be fine."

FOURTEEN

THE AIR WAS FULL OF CHAOTIC noise and Aftershock fell to the ground face first, eating a mouthful of sand as his pistol was flung out of reach. With the wind knocked out of him and grit between his teeth, he stayed still, but to get out of there alive, he knew that he had to move.

"Jenny!" he shouted, finding the strength to crawl on his belly toward the gun. He reached out and using his fingertips, inched the grip close enough to take hold. Twisting his body around he readied his finger with little chance to aim, screaming, "GET DOWN!"

Jenny leaped forward, crashing into the ground in a dusty haze.

BANG!

Bullets zipped over her flattened body in both directions, Aftershock rolling out of the way and behind cover just as three struck the sand where he was.

"You said we'd be fine!" Jenny shouted; her coarse throat made it sound more like a groan

"You can kill me later!" Aftershock yelled, firing more rounds toward a formation of rocks that gave the area its name. There were shrouded figures tucked amongst the stones. "Though let's get out of here first! I could really use your help right now to take down these goons."

Jenny didn't argue, grabbing the junk pistol from her holster while Aftershock swapped his for the rifle. The two aimed, then fired, sending a jacketed volley toward the attackers that blocked the way to the outskirts of the city. Jenny lost balance from the recoil but two of the bandits were struck, falling to the ground where Aftershock finished them off with headshots.

"Told you that gun had a kick," Aftershock said.

Jenny stared harshly at the kit-bashed weapon, then right at him.

"I'm used to my old one," she said, popping off a few more loud rounds.

Aftershock covered her as she reloaded, but more raiders came rushing in from the side.

"Shit!" he spat, firing the rest of his ammo into the mob. Hitting the mark each time, those attackers toppled but the rest kept coming. "Jenny, take care of the ones that are still under cover up ahead! I'll be right back."

"Okay..." she said calmly. "Wait, what? Where are you going?"

Pulling out a sharp blade that was strapped to his leg, Aftershock gripped it tightly in one hand while his pistol was primed in the other. Breathing deeply, he abandoned cover, bounding into the plains.

The ravagers drew closer, bringing with them axes, clubs with impaled blades, and gloves fitted with nails and razorjaw teeth. They shouted with bloodthirsty hatred, ready to kill.

Aftershock was no less enraged. He roared back at them, his battle cry fierce and when they met at last, metal clashed against metal, and skin, and bone. The attack was swift and brutal, the lone raider hacking and slashing his way through the Devil's Shadow until only a few of their more skilled units were left. Some turned to strike, struck down by Aftershock's bullets.

"Is that all you got?" he challenged, body coated in still warm blood. The raiders that remained began to scatter. "Thought so…"

Suddenly, a deep, pitiless laugh replaced the fear filled cries and a behemoth of a man strode through the chaos. The fleeing men froze in fear at the sight of him. He was beastly, adorned with an iron helm of horns from which a scruffy, square jaw jutted. His armor matched and powerful arms held an oversized sledgehammer. One end of it was flat, the other balled and spiked, both caked with stuff that reeked with the stench of death.

Aftershock recognized him right away as the leader of the Devil's Shadow.

"Dante," he whispered, the name too bitter on his lips to say any louder. "Long time no see."

"Well, well, well. If it isn't ol' Seth Colton of Skinner fame," Dante responded in kind, his voice fathomless. "Well, *former* Skinner fame. What the hell brings you this far out west, boy? It's not the urge to fuck my men, is it?"

"Fuck you," Aftershock snapped back, face red with anger. "You should know by seeing their bodies all around that it isn't."

Dante shrugged his large shoulders, which were at least twice as wide as Aftershock's.

"Funny that I've been hearing different about you," he replied.

"Yeah well, sorry to disappoint you, big man. Now, if you'll just let us by…"

"Who? You and the whore over there? I don't think so, Colton. It's not that easy to waltz your way through Shadow lands."

Aftershock sighed, licking his dry and gritty lips. He readied his finger on the pistol's trigger, glancing to Jenny who was still occupied with the shooters holed up in the rocks.

"Okay, have it your way. If it's trouble you want…"

"Nah, Seth, it's not what I want, but it's certainly what you're going to get."

"In that case, at least get my name right. It's Aftershock these days."

Dante chuckled, knocking over one of his own gang that had been standing too close. Struggling to get back up, Dante put his boot square on the man's chest. He then pressed down with all his weight.

CRACK!

The man cringed, tearful as his helmet was flicked off by one of the hammer's barbs.

"Chief!" the raider begged. "No, please!"

"Aftershock you say?" Dante questioned with disdain as he raised his weapon high. "Interesting choice for a name. Perhaps you'll reconsider it after you know what real ground-shattering power feels like!"

"Nooooo!" the pinned raider screamed as the flat end of the hammer came down on his face, smashing it like a melon.

The ground trembled; Aftershock recoiled.

He knew violence, having seen all kinds in his years, but that was one of the most ruthless.

"Vile!" he condemned, mainly due to the lack of honor he showed his own men. But Dante was unfazed, falling into a cold, bloodshot stare.

"Do you not have the stomach for such things anymore? Now I can see for myself why the Skinners got rid of you. Their time will come, but enough talk for now! It's your turn to quake!"

Aftershock's eyes widened as Dante moved with unexpected

quickness. Swiftly, he was upon him and Aftershock was forced to leap out of the way.

Firing his pistol, a single bullet soared from the barrel only to ricochet off Dante's chest plate. He was out of ammo with no chance to reload.

"Shit!"

Dante reached out, receiving a knife blade to the elbow where his protection was weakest. Blood pooled then splashed on the stained ground to join that of his men. He tried for Aftershock again and was sliced again, his target deftly weaving and carving between each of the massive man's attempts to grab him.

Furious, Dante struck the ground several times with his hammer. The land shuddered with each concussive blow and Aftershock toppled, having to roll away from strikes and dart between fallen bodies to avoid being flattened.

The skirmish continued, Aftershock growing more tired as it raged on while Dante, now moving more slowly, expended far less energy.

"You're a persistent pest," Dante snarled, launching another oncoming swing.

"You're welcome," Aftershock smirked, dodging again. He leaped backwards, air rushing by like a tornado as the hammer missed. "I could do this all night."

However, as he landed, Aftershock's feet struck a nearby body, causing him overbalance. Falling hard onto his back, several spikes on the dead raider's armor pierced his hamstring.

"You still haven't learned the art of modesty, have you?" Dante said as he approached.

Aftershock was stupefied, the glower spread across his face a reaction to the sting in his leg, which was sharp but bearable. With little choice, he gripped his blade tightly, not about to take what Dante was going to give without a fight.

He didn't have to wait very long; the beast of a man looming overhead with the sledgehammer resting across his broad shoulders.

Dante glared at Aftershock, laying beneath him while his imposing shadow stretched over the downed raider's body.

"Here, let me show you how easy it is to be quiet," Dante said, hoisting the hammer above him.

"I'll pass," Aftershock said as he threw his knife, and the last of his hope with it.

Dante jerked his forearm down and the blade sunk in with a clatter. Grumbling, he grabbed the fluttering end and yanked the blade free, chucking it into the dead body's side.

Aftershock's eyes grew, knowing he was completely out of options. Dante's did too, savoring the thought he would be the one to end the infamous Seth Colton.

Breathing proudly, Dante raised the sledgehammer high and was about to bring it down…

BOOM!

The metal of Dante's helmet *clanged*, a sudden pain surging in his right temple. He staggered back amid loud ringing, righting himself before he fell and…

BOOM!

There was a flash of intense white light, more ringing, and tight pressure at his temples. Dante's vision became blurry, but he could make out a slender figure approaching as he turned his head toward the right…

BOOM!

Warmth flooded the space between skin and metal, running down the bridge of his nose. Dante fumbled as if he'd had too much Cactus Wine…

BOOM!

Pain came, Dante's brain afire. A torrent of high-pitched

whines and bright colors came then went, ending in eternal, silent black. Watched by his surviving men, Dante stumbled around aimlessly, chunks of his head and helmet scattered on the blood-soaked ground. They all had expressions of horror, awe, and even relief when his bulk finally hit the damp soil.

Jenny advanced uneasily, still aiming down the sights of her smoking gun. The air was still and quiet, the haze that had been stirred now settling.

"Aftershock?" she called, unsure if he was still alive but unable to check since her focus remained on the remaining raiders that were congregating ahead. They were distracted, but she didn't know for how long.

"Jenny..." Aftershock answered, much to her relief. "I'm over here, skewered on this dead fellow."

She didn't feel comfortable looking away, not even for a second; these bandits had been so determined to kill them just seconds ago.

"There happen to be a lot of dead men laying around, AS," she said, prodding Aftershock to speak more.

"AS?" he replied crankily. "So we have little pet names now?"

"I'm only being concise like you're used to. Maybe I should add one more S to the end, just so it's clear we are talking about you."

Getting her wish, the stream of words that followed her snippy comment let Jenny know exactly how well, and grouchy, Aftershock was. It also let her know *where* he was without the need to take her eyes off the Devil's Shadow. Zeroing in, she picked up her pace. As she moved, the gang didn't seem to notice or care, transfixed on their leader's dead body.

When she arrived at Aftershock, she took on a similar impediment, all her concerns about the raiders fleeing from her thoughts.

He was on the ground, flat on his back with both legs up as if lounging on the dead body like a reclining chair. Yet judging by the expression he bore it wasn't as comfortable as it appeared to be.

"Are you all right?" she asked, dropping to her knees.

"Been a lot better," he answered, pointing to his leg. "But all things considered, it's better than the alternative."

Quickly, she maneuvered herself to get a better look. Blood was flowing from underneath his right leg, the area dark and wet. Jenny noticed the spikes studding the armor and realized that's what Aftershock meant by his predicament.

"Does it –"

"Hurt?" he finished for her, heavy breathing stifled by coughs answering the question.

There was a rustle and some indistinct shouting. Jenny looked over her shoulder toward the bandits; they had started to remove parts of Dante's armor, clamoring for possession of each piece.

"Time's short; seems our friends are getting themselves worked up. Let's get you off there so we can get the wound cleaned and us out of here."

Aftershock winced as Jenny moved her hands into position, slipping her fingers under his leg into a gross and sticky wetness. After counting to three, she pulled as he did his best to lift, and his leg jerked free with a disturbing noise.

Aftershock let out a gasp, curling his teeth over his lower lip.

"When you get to Diablo, please avoid becoming a nurse."

Jenny ignored him, tearing the denims away to get a look at the damage. Rough and bloodied holes lined the back of his leg. They weren't too deep but were large enough to make her stomach flutter.

"Going by that look, are things bad?" he asked.

"I think it looks a lot worse than it is."

Conclusion

Thanks again for taking the time to read this book!

You should now have a good understanding of fibromyalgia, and have some strategies for treating and improving it.

I wish you the best of luck in your battle against fibromyalgia. Remember to stay positive, and that you're not alone. Many others are fighting the same battle that you are, and many have managed to overcome it! Keep on fighting, have the right mental attitude, and you too will be able to achieve relief from fibromyalgia!

If you enjoyed this book, please take the time to leave me a review on Amazon. I appreciate your honest feedback, and it really helps me to continue producing high quality books.

Be Active Whenever You Can

When you need to get out and do a bit of strenuous activity, be sure that you only do so if you're feeling up to it. That is why keeping a journal is crucial as you will know the best hours that your body is fit for any activity. Exercise when you are well, and you can follow a schedule around your peak hours. Doing this will help you to do more things as well as help you feel better about yourself.

"Famous last words," Aftershock grumbled.

Seizing her rucksack, Jenny started tending to him. She pulled out the canteen along with a small bottle of whiskey. Using the water to rinse her hands, she followed up with a couple splashes of alcohol. Then, taking a clean cloth from the bag, she applied gentle pressure to the holes.

"So, the man I killed…"

"He was known as Dante. Honestly, I don't even know if he had a last name or where he came from; not that it matters now that he's worm food. What I do know is that he was leader of the fine group of bandits that tried to kill us."

"I thought as much. The big armor gives it away."

"Yeah, maybe I should break my old Skinner gear back out. Less narcissistic than the crap he has on, though."

Jenny tried to imagine Aftershock in a set of overelaborate armor, but what she visualized was more silly than intimidating.

"Yeah, yeah laugh it up," he continued, seeing her expression, "but I wasn't too bad back then. Anyway, that ruthless son of a bitch came into power over the Devil's Shadow about, hmmm, four years ago now. The area was being shook up by some expansion efforts out of Diablo. At the time, the gang was a lot weaker and ripe for a takeover. However, from the stories I heard, confirmed with my own eyes today with him killing his own man, Dante's rise to power was fast but fueled wholly by fear."

"What's that mean exactly?"

"Means good luck for us, especially now that you killed him. The gang isn't likely to finish carrying out his orders now; we'd probably be dead if they were. You see, for a raider fear is essential but it only gets one so far, the rest needs to be sustained by respect, amongst other things. I can tell you that there's no respect for him here, because he had absolutely none for them."

Once the bleeding stopped, Jenny took a quick look at the

squabbling raiders, seeing what Aftershock meant by the way they defiled their leader's body. Brushing away the grime collected in his wounds, she rinsed the area with more water afterward.

"There should be some lutrine salve in the sack," Aftershock said tersely.

Jenny opened the bag, rummaging through it. She didn't see it immediately.

"It'll be in a small jar," he clarified. "Probably fit inside your palm."

Jenny found the little container soon after, removing it then unscrewing the cap. She scooped out a Cog-sized portion of the creamy substance – it smelled a bit citrusy – and slathered it over the injury. She repeated the process three more times to get good coverage before dressing his entire thigh.

"You're going to have to get more salve, but nonetheless you're taken care of," she said spritely.

"Thanks."

"Can you try and stand? We need to get a move on."

Aftershock slowly sat himself up, refusing Jenny's attempts at help. Scooting around, he slumped his back on the dead body while avoiding the spikes and took a deep breath.

"Gosh, he already stinks," Aftershock said, reaching over to pull out his knife. He caught another whiff of something foul and cautiously raised his own arms. "Well, shit, it's me."

Jenny wasn't fooled by his attitude, able to see Aftershock's face riddled with stress plain as day.

"You are all right to walk, aren't you?" she asked.

Aftershock was picking little pieces of debris out of his beard, but before he could say anything, Jenny was already answering for him.

"You aren't able to, are you?" she asked, her voice breaking.

Aftershock finally shook his head. Jenny looked upset.

"Oh come on, it'll take more than some gaudy armor to knock me out of commission," he said, "but, for the time being, I need to get some rest. That's down time *you* unfortunately don't have."

The other outlaws had stripped Dante bare, his scarred and naked body catching the light of the falling sun. Most of them were departing with their new spoils, heading deep within the rocks and caves littering the Pitchfork, but a few lingered for unknown reasons.

"Don't be silly. I haven't got a deadline."

"No, but the sun's going down and a pretty thing like you isn't going to be very safe in this territory once it gets dark."

"Yet, you're going to be fine by yourself? Injured as you are?

"Yes! Look, I can handle those stragglers if they try anything. Done it many times over the years."

"I'm sure you have," said Jenny, though she had a hard time believing him. Aftershock's words always seemed to turn on him like a curse. Not only that, his tan skin was looking pale.

"Aftershock…"

"Jenny," he replied somberly, seeing that her eyes were already sparkling with tears. "You've known me for, what, less than *two days*? Trust me when I say I'll be fine. As for *you*, you shouldn't be this attached. I'm pretty much still a stranger and trusting someone so blindly could get you hurt in this life. You don't know the baggage I carry. It's hard enough as it is without –"

"Family?" she asked. "Or friends for that matter? I know that I'm naïve about a lot of things, but I'm not stupid."

"I didn't mean…"

"My life has been full of nasty people that prove your point ten times over," she stressed. "I know not to trust everyone, but I am trusting *you*. Considering I just lost the last of my family – my entire life until yesterday – it's a blessing to already have someone I can call a friend. Especially in this harsh world, no matter how short a time it's been. You're a friend and I think even you could agree with that."

Aftershock reflected on her words.

"Guess you're right," he muttered. "I can't argue since I rescued you for the very same reason. But… and yes there *is* a but… that still doesn't change the fact that my goal is to get you to safety. That means out of here."

Jenny felt more words forming on the tip of her tongue. They were ready to lash out, but knowing how stubborn both of them were, she stopped.

"Okay," she said briskly, watching the sun creep its way toward the horizon "Where do I need to go from here?"

Aftershock was surprised she conceded so quickly, having mixed feelings about it. As much as he didn't want to admit it, it was nice to have someone around for a change. It had been so long.

"The fringe of the city is past the rocks over where we had the gunfight," he told her. "Oh, and speaking of guns, we should reload while I'm talking, unless the Shadows took them."

Aftershock didn't need to worry about his rifle; Jenny had it and the scabbard slung over her shoulder. She handed them over, then began looking around for his pistol. It was gone, so she focused on reloading hers.

"Damn Shadows took it, didn't they" he barked toward the few that remained. "Shit. Well, never mind, it just happened to be my favorite."

"The directions?" Jenny pressed.

"Yeah, sorry. So, from the rocks you're going to head west. You'll go that way for about ten, maybe fifteen minutes before you come to a collection of metal buildings. They're nothing to gawk at, but they do mark the outer reaches of the city. They should be unoccupied, so you shouldn't have any trouble out that way. The structures are used by Rangers when out in the field for storage, shelter, that sort of thing, so don't go breaking in unless you're looking for trouble from them. Once you're past those buildings though, your technically in Diablo and safe."

He paused, taking a long, hard look at his bandaged leg.

"You know, this injury may be a blessing in disguise. I had planned on taking you there but if we were together and someone else happened to be there when we arrived, things could have been messy. We would've had to deal with anyone we came across so you could get into the city with an unspoiled story. Even if nobody was there we'd have parted ways to avoid being seen by the watchers along the wall."

He continued to tell her more about the city's wall and the process of getting inside the gate, at least for non-outlaws.

"So be sure to tell the guards about the attack on the Gulch and you're a survivor. I'm sure word has reached the sheriffs across the Barrens of what happened there."

Jenny seemed okay with the plan, but one point did nag at her.

"That's all well and good," she said, "but what if I'm asked details about *how* I made it out this far by myself?"

Aftershock mulled over it, noticing the few remaining Devil's Shadow members approaching.

"Good point; you're probably going to be asked that very thing. It's best that you tell them you were captured. Even though there are Eliminators, the guards know that raiders like to get their hands on female prisoners. You could have escaped during the night, coming the rest of the way to the wall. That sort of thing happens all the time. Keep your scrap pistol on you but leave the rest with me. That should be enough to convince the guards. Also, as much as I might like how mouthy you are, remember

Diablo's a different animal, like the Gulch times a thousand. Be sure you don't end up raising more questions than you need to, trying to start a new life. As tough as it is going to be, just go along with what you see and hear."

Jenny nodded, observing the raiders approaching herself. She stood up quickly, knowing that she had to go but was struggling to say goodbye.

"Come with me," she said impulsively. "I'm sure there are opportunities, and at least medical help, for you there."

She knew it was an impossibility, given the state of things there, but the words certainly felt good to say. They felt good for Aftershock to hear, too.

"If only you were in charge, Jenny, but we must part ways," he reiterated. "It's the only way you are going to get inside. I may be different from your average outlaw, but those within that wall aren't going to take the time to find out about it. Anyway, like I told you before, the city isn't meant for me by any means."

"Where will you be?" Jenny asked unwillingly.

"Out there, amongst the grit and tumbleweed. I'm going to see if I can find out why the Vipers were so coordinated; something is definitely wrong with that. Hell, maybe I'll earn some new contacts along the way. Sort of like these fine fellows here."

Jenny didn't know what Aftershock was talking about, but when she turned, members of Devil's Shadow were already standing close. They had been fast and quiet, reaching out to grab her.

"I don't think so," Aftershock said, chambering one of his newly reloaded rounds. "Leave her be."

Jenny had already brought up the junk pistol when the raiders stopped. They just stood there, staring, making her feel even more uneasy.

"Get going," Aftershock said.

"But…"

"Go!" he insisted. "Now."

She gulped, wishing she had the level of confidence he had about getting out of the situation alive. It was an awkward situation. Why weren't the other raiders attacking? Why weren't they even talking? What did they want?

With little choice and no answers to the questions filling her mind, she wished Aftershock well and began to step away. The wall of raiders didn't budge.

"I'll be just fine, Jenny, just like these men will be if they just let you continue on your way."

Two of the ruffians grunted, stepping to the side. Jenny slid through the gap between them.

"And Jenny," Aftershock said to her as she walked away, "thanks for reminding me there is still good in the world. If ever you need some wasteland help in the future, you know where to find me."

With tears in her eyes she carried on walking, deciding it best if she did not turn around. She marched to the rocks, threading between them until the area opened back up into a wide desert. Ahead on the horizon was the broiling skyline of Diablo, dark against a vivid orange sunset.

Trudging toward it, she was worried about Aftershock, thoughts reeling about what was happening behind with each step forward.

I should have looked.

I should have helped him.

I haven't heard any gunshots.

That must be a good sign.

Unless they used a knife!

Oh, I hope not…

I should have looked.

She wanted to scream, indebted to him, a raider of all things. Without his help, she never would have made it this far. She didn't care who he was, vowing then and there on her grandfather's memory that if she didn't get swallowed by the deep recesses of the city, or otherwise happened to lose her way, she would make sure to find him and repay him, assuming he was still alive.

Nervously checking her pocket watch, she really didn't care what time it was. The rusted metal buildings were coming into view and immediately, her mind switched, packed with more questions. How was she going to find food? Earn money? Look for a place to stay?

Jenny knew that she didn't have to figure it all out before she got to the wall. With the losses of her home and her family, those questions would still need answers no matter the location. However, as she walked with her heart as guide and long shadow as company, she was grateful to have some time to consider things alone.

Yet a faint prickling at the back of her neck made Jenny feel on edge and unbeknownst to her, high atop one of the rocky outcroppings bordering the western edge of the city, a Frost Enterprises guard was watching her exit the Pitchfork, radioing its findings back to headquarters.

FIFTEEN

ANOTHER DAY HAD DAWNED AND Jesse was up early to walk the bright streets of Comprass, an edge borough on the eastern side of Diablo. Wearing some of his less showy finery, he still managed to stick out amongst his surroundings.

The area was rough and its proximity to not only an exterior gate but also the rail station added to it, akin to a catch basin filled with residents, immigrants from the four corners of the world, hunters, trappers, and the dregs of society. As such, the feel was much different than Chester Avenue or the segregated Grayson Market. There, things were orderly and clean, whereas Comprass – like all the edge boroughs – was more free-flowing and jumbled. When viewed, it was difficult to believe it was all part of the same city.

Jesse passed by squalid shops topped with houses on both sides of the slender thoroughfare, their arches chipped and windows so filthy he couldn't make out anything inside.

Overhead, children dressed in nothing more than rags tottered along the roofs, nonetheless with innocent smiles on their faces. Behind them, rising fifteen solid meters, was the city's defensive wall.

Even as Jesse stared at the pauperism around him, he couldn't help but be impressed by what he saw. That particular day marked four hundred years since civilization fell and instead of disappearing into history, humanity rose from the brink, at least from an architectural and technological standpoint. The hearts of men, though, could still use improvement.

Jesse's eyes came upon a person from the Mudlands – evident by his mannerisms, clean-shaven face, and strangely colorful attire – arriving at a jeweler's storefront. While browsing the inexpensive wares through the dusty shop window, the man received judgmental glares from several passersby, their offhand statements carried over the soft beat of their footsteps. He seemed unbothered by the commentary, but Jesse shook his head at the notion that clothes alone could be the cause of such contempt, especially when not knowing the character of the person wearing them. It was in his experience that the best dressed oftentimes had the most to hide.

Speaking of such people, the store owner – who was a substantial man with no due to the size of his beard – was also watching raptly from the other side of the glass. One of his eyes was wide open while the other squinted hard, both eyebrows crooked with ill-placed concern.

The man at the window continued perusing, liking the appearance of a garish silver chain that was set amongst a few equally kitschy rings in the display. Wanting to purchase it, he moved toward the shop's entrance.

The owner was visibly troubled by this development, having kept his eyes locked on the man the entire time. He bolted toward the door faster than a dueler's hand to a pistol, barring the Mudlands resident from entering, not for being a brigand, but based solely on who he was. Words were flung between them, voices rising in volume, and before long fists were flying.

Every time Jesse saw things like that happen, which was nearly every day in Diablo, he wished the vision he had for the people could come to fruition before they tore each other apart. It wouldn't come close to eliminating the deep-seated hate residing in people's hearts – other things would need to change for that – but hopefully he could lift everyone out of the pits of destitution into the light.

As security forces arrived to break up the scuffle, Jesse sunk his hands in his suit pockets and continued with his business. His destination was a saloon near the rail station, about a five-minute walk through the crowded streets. A meeting had been scheduled for half past seven with a man named Drake Nelson, the new head of Barro's ostensible Master Mechanics. The group was the authority on all technological and engineering deals the City of Soil struck with outsiders, similar to what Duncan's Magisterium does for Lagos.

Jesse had no shortage of excitement to meet the old man, displaying a little pep in his step. It was his goal to convince Drake that Winthrope products would benefit their city more than the less efficient compression engines currently in use.

Today's the day, Jesse thought happily, riding the high from his success with the water trade deal. *Something great is about to happen, I can feel it in the air!*

Jesse was conveniently forgetting that Barro was highly untrusting of Diablo, resistant to deal with the city and any of its officials since the current mayor came into power. However, at that moment the past dealings of politicians didn't matter to Jesse. Instead, he was focused on the future, motivated by the fact Drake accepted the meeting in the first place.

Weaving through the increasing throng of people, the road widened into an irregular quadrangle where Jesse came upon a selection of booths that filled the open space with frayed white canopies. Banners flapped above while below, metalsmiths, chefs, and traders from settlements out in the Barrens mingled with borough natives. There were many things for sale; from foods like bread, salted fish, beef, pies, and cakes, to decorated tools, armor, and weaponry, to hand me down clothes and clockwork accessories, second-hand pocket watches and books, candles, and cutlery. Most in the edge boroughs depended on these vendors, everyone trying to scrape a living off the top of the anniversary's festivities. With good fortune, the earnings made that day could stretch to nearly a week, maybe more, though hefty percentages were often consumed on overdue accounts or failure to follow the law.

"Permits!" a Crier called, loudly clanging his bell to draw attention to his words, some ducking behind their stalls in poor attempts to hide. "Be sure your permits are displayed or there will be fines to pay! You there! Yes, you! Where is your permit for today?"

People churned between the stalls; those that could afford to buy tawdry charms or food did so as they went. Most were content with consuming juicy gossip and spicy scandals, regularly paired with critical glares toward their fair-weather friends and stRangers alike.

Only the youngest amongst the seething crowd, those that had not yet learned the art of being negative in all aspects of their lives, could just stand and enjoy the simplicity of a toymaker collecting his clockwork birds as they returned, landing gently on his top hat. He would then take each one in his palm and wait, looking at them through a pair of eccentric, latticed goggles while the brass buttons on sleeves gleamed in the morning light. Their little fluttering wings would slow, then stop, and he would grasp them by the tail to wind them back up. Tossing them away, they caught the wind and soared over the children's precious, smiling faces.

It was a little magic, in an all-too-real world.

Jesse was clapping across the street from the toymaker's stall, a smile tugging on the corner of his lips. One of the clockwork birds flew directly overhead, landing on a rectangular sign that had been tied to a jutting pole. The painted letters read The Junction.

"Ah! Here we are," he said excitedly, having arrived at the saloon.

Taking one last look at the mechanical bird before it took off again, Jesse climbed the few crackling stairs in front. He landed on a short railed porch, ahead of him a pair of swinging double doors that were hung in the middle of the frame. Placing a hand on each side, Jesse pushed as noise and smoke wafted from the top to welcome him.

While coughing, Jesse's eyes adjusted to the dimly lit interior. Even though the boroughs were supplied with power, many people couldn't afford the cheapest rates due to overwhelming administration fees or if they could, had the lights off most of the day to save money.

The room itself was very thin and long. On Jesse's left, a bar stretched from the front of the place nearly to the back. Its top was polished while foot rails of made of brass ran along the bottom, dirtied from excessive use. At the bar's far end, a surly fellow stood in front of a large box organ, cranking its wheel while long scrolls of perforated paper slid through the machine, filling the place with cantankerous music.

Through the stinging haze of smoke Jesse could see all kinds of patrons in all sorts of moods. He began to walk through the place to get better looks at them, bumping into shoulders, elbowing backs, and hearing disapproving grunts along the way.

In one of the corners was an elderly gent in a dark pinstriped suit and maroon cravat. His tall top hat was resting on the table next to an empty glass. At first glance, Jesse thought that he was Drake, but upon looking closer he found the man crusty – his attire too – and the droopy expression he wore indicated that he was probably a drop of liquor away from collapsing to the floor.

Scanning the crowd, a streak of crimson caught Jesse's eye. It was a colored wisp in an attractive young man's otherwise light brown hair. His boyish face was brushed with stubble and his smile was bright as he carried on a cheery conversation with some of the hardest looking folks in the place. His outfit was no less eye-opening and probably the topic of the lively current discussion. He wore pair of hole-strewn black denims with leather armor strapped across his chest and upper arm. There was no shirt underneath while on top, a front mounted scabbard held a rare flint lock pistol.

"I should have asked Drake for a lumograph," Jesse moaned, regretting his excited forgetfulness to even ask for a description.

 Continuing his search with a shrug, Jesse wound up at the edge of the bar. Everyone he considered ended up being too smarmy or young for such a high ranking official position.

Perhaps I could convince Barro to adopt holotubes[5] while I'm at it? he thought, resting his elbows on the top of the mahogany bar. Knowing their affinity for living underground, that proposition would likely be a dead end, the broadcast towers being unsightly and tall.

"What can I get for you, Mr. Winthrope?" asked the barkeep

___
5   Holotubes are like television sets, receiving monochrome still & moving images and sound over radio waves. Used primarily for communication by government officials, the units are also prevalent in large corporations and public spaces, where they are used for announcements and entertainment. They require huge, powerful antennas for transmissions.

as he wiped away some loose debris. His mustache twitched from side to side with each sweep of the cloth.

"Oh," Jesse said with a hint of surprise. "You... you recognize me?"

"Even in that getup, sir, who wouldn't recognize the famous Steam Tycoon?" he replied and then with a wink said, "or infamous, depending on which stories one's heard."

Jesse glanced over his outfit. He didn't know whether to be proud of that last statement or bothered by it, but ultimately his chest swelled.

"I... why... thank you."

"Of course, Mr. Winthrope. Name's Marcus Branston and welcome to the Junction; my humble establishment."

Jesse took another look around as Marcus gestured around, feeling more welcomed than he had been with the elites for a long time.

"It's my pleasure. So, as far as drinks go is it too early for a brandy, or do you have another recommendation?"

Marcus was already reaching for a glass, pouring a generous helping of amber liquid.

"It's not too early in Angelus, is it?" he smirked, handing over the drink. "On the house."

Jesse dug into his pocket and tossed a couple of Cogs on the bar.

"Don't be silly," he said as they clattered noisily. "One good turn deserves another."

Marcus wasted no time using one of his beefy hands to scoop up the money.

"No arguments here. So, if it's not too forward: what brings you out here to the edges?" Marcus enquired, putting the change in his pocket. "Not often do we see your class out of folk out here; most of your fellows stay tucked in on the inside, or fly overhead out of our leprous reach."

"Well, most of them don't know what they're missing, either," Jesse replied, taking a little sip. The brandy was surprisingly good.

"Or care..." Marcus added.

"Touché," Jesse continued, "and regarding your question, I'm actually here for a meeting, though my associate seems to have wandered off." Jesse hoped he was hiding his white lie well enough. "Perhaps you've seen him? He's a man from Barro, named–"

Before Jesse could finish, a hand came crashing against his shoulder, clamping tight.

"Winthrope?" asked an excited voice.

Jesse craned his neck, coming face to face with the oddly dressed man he saw earlier. Up close, his skin was mottled with dirt, especially noticeable around his bright grin.

"Yes?" Jesse replied hesitantly. "Can I help you?"

"I certainly hope so!" the man said, smoothing his red-streaked hair before holding a hand out to shake. "You and I have a meeting that should have started, oh, five minutes ago."

Jesse's mouth fell open as their hands shook and it felt like someone had poured cold water over him.

"You feeling ok?" the man asked, grabbing Jesse's glass and giving it a great big sniff. He turned to Marcus. "I'll have what he's having."

"I still swear you don't look old enough boy..." Marcus grumbled.

"What can I say? We keep ourselves well in Barro." He grabbed hold of his flint lock tightly. "Plus, this thing tends to remove any lingering doubt."

Marcus chuckled, muttering something about men compensating for their shortcomings while grabbing some brandy. He refilled both of their glasses and spotting a few new patrons, he bid the two farewell and drifted down the bar.

Perhaps he's Drake's assistant? Jesse reasoned with himself. *Yes. He must be. Surely he isn't…*

"Drake Nelson," the man introduced while taking a sip of his drink. "Though if you don't mind, I prefer to go by Pyrofly. Long story, but explosives are kind of my thing."

Jesse looked at his expressive face, eyes slowly rising up to his red tuft of hair.

"Fitting…" Jesse said. "My apologies for being late Drake, I… I mean Pyrofly. Admittedly, I didn't know who I was looking for, expecting someone much older."

"Nothing new for me," he replied. "I get that a lot since taking this job. It must be because the alternative meaning of 'master' in the title is 'one with gray hairs and wrinkles.'"

"Right, because the other Master Mechanics are twice your age."

Pyrofly shook his head, holding up three fingers as he casually took another drink. It was hitting a much-needed spot, warming him slightly.

"THREE times your age?" Jesse blurted out. "Exactly how old are you? Wait! Actually, never mind. I don't want to know."

Pyrofly laughed.

"Truth be known Jesse… may I call you Jesse? I was expecting you to be quite stuck up."

"Sure and who's to say I'm not?"

"Yourself," Pyrofly said, "by even agreeing to meet me in person in this less than savory part of town. I imagine there aren't many opportunities to impress when you're away from your peers."

"I hope that you find me a lot different than my peers," Jesse said. "Places like this make me feel more at ease; like I can be myself. Therefore, I feel the conversations can be more honest."

"I agree with that," Pyrofly replied. "I like the fact this part of the city looks a bit lived in, too. It feels a lot like home. Rich parts of town feel like museums to me and I'm often afraid to touch anything."

A sly look on Pyrofly's face hinted that he probably touched *everything* as the two relocated to a vacant table set between a pair of narrow windows near the back of the saloon. There they conversed for a while about their business, Jesse discovering Pyrofly was a lot like Duncan, yet with a technological slant that let them both flex their mental muscles.

"They're quite ingenious if you think about it."

"What was that?" Jesse asked, momentarily distracted by what he thought was the pretty face of a woman rushing by the entrance. She had a frantic expression; Jesse wondered why.

"The saloon doors," Pyrofly continued. "Clever design, really., though not nearly as much as those steam capsules of yours."

"How's that?" Jesse asked, never giving it much thought beyond the aesthetic. He took a big swig in anticipation, nearly emptying his glass.

Pyrofly inhaled deeply before diving into his explanation.

"Those surprisingly simple shutters keep out a lot of dust, yet allow for ventilation along the bottom and smoke to vent from the top. Drunks have an easy way in or out without worrying about pushing or pulling – so they more time to think about staying upright – and if well-positioned, they can shield any shenanigans from the outside."

Jesse smiled as he sipped on the last of his brandy.

"Well, there's my fact learned for the day. Do you often think long and hard about things like that?"

"Not really," Pyrofly replied indifferently, "just while waiting for business associates to show up."

Pyrofly might have had a fresh attitude but also possessed experience beyond his years. Jesse was unsure whether he should be doing business with him or ordering rounds of whiskey shots to party. In the end, the entire session went well.

Jesse glanced at a worn clock on the wall; a little over an hour had gone by and he needed to head back for Winthrope Limited.

"So it sounds like you have an interest?" he asked hopefully.

"Everything you've described and offered sounds intriguing," said Pyrofly. "I certainly am interested, not only in the WHESE, but also those steam capsules you mentioned – fascinating concept. Pride's gotten in the way of a lot of the Mechanic's decision making, especially from the prior head of the group. We need to move on."

Jesse agreed, especially with the last part.

"Our machinery may be robust," Pyrofly continued somberly, "probably some of, if not the, best in the world. But it's old and unreliable. Your devices alone will let us leap ahead, at least to where we should be. It'll be good to make some much-needed improvements."

"That's my intent for everyone," Jesse said. "I'd love to talk more about this in the coming weeks."

"Or sooner, perhaps. Prefect DuBois must approve all of this but I don't think it'd be a problem with a high recommendation from me and a meeting, face to face, with you."

It sounded promising, even though Jesse hadn't heard that name in a while, years in fact having dealt only with the Master Mechanics. He hadn't met Prefect DuBois in all these years, having been swept away into the corporate tower once his father's funeral ceremonies had ended.

"That'd be wonderful," he said, and Pyrofly perked up at the prospect.

With all the dealing out of the way, both men sunk into the backs of their hard chairs with well-deserved relief. It would have been nice to relax for longer, but the time to go their separate ways was approaching. Jesse was the first to stand, his chair squawking in protest.

"So, as far the rest of this fine day goes, do you have plans?"

"I think I'm going to take in the sights around the market – there was a particular set of merchants on the far end that had some interesting weapons attachments for sale. It's not often that four hundred years of anything comes around, so I want to take in what I can and see if there are any deals to be had."

"I wish I could join you," Jesse said with a grin, wondering if Pyrofly would face the same ridicule as the man at the jewelry store. Part of him thought he would face even more trouble due to his appearance, yet now that Jesse knew him a bit better perhaps not. Pyrofly's carefree attitude was rather infectious and an effective barrier against that sort of thing.

"Pyro…" Jesse began, pausing to see if he'd be corrected for shortening the name. He wasn't. "If you aren't doing anything for dinner, I'd be happy to have you out at Winthrope Limited later, before all the evening festivities. I think someone like you would enjoy the fireworks"

Pyrofly was excited, but only for a split second. His face turned into a deep-set frown.

"I haven't seen a good firework display in, well, never. Would have stayed until tomorrow, but I'm catching the Sunset Express to Bala so I can make it to Barro by the morning. No rest for the wicked it seems; you can blame another *boooring* meeting with the Prefect Council for that."

Pyrofly rolled his eyes so far they were mere slivers of white and Jesse laughed, knowing the feeling. They both navigated the crowded saloon on their way toward the exit. Pyrofly waved frantically at the barkeep while Jesse remained more collected.

"Well, you might be able to see some of them from the train," Jesse said. "I think the Express leaves around the same time they start. I suggest the last west-facing seat on the upper deck. There are some good views from there."

"I hope so," Pyrofly replied, sounding sad. He snatched his glass off the table and polished off the thin line of honey at the bottom. "As great a time as I've had, I don't want to take up any more of *your* valuable time, Mr. Winthrope."

"Firstly, call me Jesse," he insisted. "It only feels right after addressing you as Pyrofly this entire time instead of Mr. Nelson."

"I'm glad for that, too."

"Secondly," Jesse continued, "please take up as much of my time as you want to. I'm due to meet with Mayor Randolph and some of our mutual banking cronies in about an hour. The only thing more fun than that and their fees would be to impale myself with a hot poker from a fireplace."

"I would *hate* to keep you from that," Pyrofly said jokingly.

Things hadn't changed outside except that it had gotten far more crowded and noisy. After a prolonged handshake on the Junction's porch, the two said their final goodbyes and parted ways.

Jesse watched as the energetic young man disappeared, that fringe of red hair the last of him to vanish amongst the drab crowd. Something told him it wouldn't be long before their paths crossed again, likely the desire to close a deal with Barro as soon as possible. But before any of that could happen, Jesse would have to get his next impending meeting out of the way, no matter how much he didn't want to.

After he turned, starting back through the marketplace, something striking caught his roving eyes. It was the same woman that had passed by the saloon doors earlier except he was able to take notice of the stress and unease stretched firmly across her face.

Jesse deduced, or perhaps wished as he watched her pace back and forth, that she was not from Diablo. The style of her clothes in general was different, like that found in a wasteland settlement, while her head and eyewear he specifically recognized as 'Gulch Gear.'

I wonder if she's a survivor of that horrendous attack? he pondered, having read some of the preliminary reports about the Gulch massacre on his desk earlier. He could visualize Frost's face with each brutal word, ecstatic with the news.

Jesse's curiosity got the better of him and he started to move in her direction. As luck would have it, no more than three steps in a shrill voice cut across his path as a shriveled man wrapped in dirty clothes struck him on the side. Both men were nearly knocked to the ground, Jesse more by the man's body odor than the impact.

"I told ya to get away!" the owner of a food stall shouted.

About Jesse's age, the vendor was already balding, a thin strip of greasy, hair combed over in a poor attempt to hide the fact. Rubbing his pimpled nose proudly, he settled back behind his stall after pushing the elderly man. Many people in the crowd had noticed the commotion and peered out from the corner of their eyes while speaking to each other in hushed tones. The illusion of normality was maintained as everyone pretended to carry on with what they were doing, secretly craving more.

"What's all this fuss about?" Jesse asked with irritation, brushing himself off before helping the other man stand on his wobbling legs.

At first the vendor acted as if he didn't hear, but Jesse knew by the size of his protruding ears he should have no trouble.

"I asked you a question, SIR," Jesse said, slow and bold.

"I told the gaffer: mudsills or hard cases, especially ones ya can smell before ya see, ain't welcome. Besides, he ain't got no coin to fork out, which means no grub in my book."

Jesse reached out to the old man beside him, pulled up one of his dirty sleeves, and grabbed his hand.

Instinctively, the nomad recoiled, but started to relax when he felt then heard several Cogs clinking into his palm.

"There we are," Jesse said to both men. "It's all been settled." He directed his gaze at the vendor, adding, "Now, if you would please, let the man eat."

"Ya might have fixed one problem but I'm not sufferin' for the other," the stall owner persisted, crossing his arms defiantly while flaring his piggish nostrils.

"Very well then, have it your way," Jesse said hotly. Walking over to the next stall, he purchased two full loaves of bread from that merchant without a second thought before tipping him an entire Gear for it being the anniversary.

The original vendor's arms stayed crossed but his mouth drooped slightly before snapping shut in a snarl.

Food in arms, Jesse returned to the old man, asking his name as he handed everything over. Leaning in, the man whispered Wallace into Jesse's ear while trying to give the few Cogs back. Jesse politely refused, closing the man's wizened hand over the money.

"No sir, Mr. Wallace," Jesse refused warmly, "this is yours to do with as you please. Yes… yes… the food as well."

Mr. Wallace's eyes glimmered as though Jesse had given him some great fortune, and as soon as he smiled the tears spilled over, leaving clean streaks along his cheeks and chin.

Jesse couldn't help but smile through his own shimmery eyes. Taking a deep bow before he started blubbering, Jesse took his leave promptly and carried on through the market for his meeting. As he weaved away, many were shaking their heads disapprovingly, but he couldn't have cared less at that moment.

Jesse might have been interested, but remained unaware,

that there was another amongst the sea of faces that also wore a smile. The woman he had spied earlier and wished to speak to, was now standing near the Junction saloon and had watched the entire thing transpire.

It was Jenny, stopped in her frantic search for work by the act of kindness she saw. Not expecting to see anything like it within the city walls, never mind so soon.

"Who was that man?" she asked ardently, the bartender joining her there on the porch to see what all the fuss was about.

"You don't know?" asked Marcus with surprise as he leaned up on the rail, shooing away one of the toymaker's little birds. "That, my lady, was Jesse Winthrope and despite what some might say – from the deadbeats who know no better all the way up the ladder to the elite – he's a good man with a great heart. One of the best in this woeful place."

Jenny could feel the incident, though small, burning away her dwindling hopes. Confidence boosted, she turned toward Marcus and asked him if he had any work available at the saloon.

SIXTEEN

'M SO SORRY, BUT I DON'T HAVE ANYTHING that I can offer right now... Marcus' words repeated over and over in Jenny's mind, lining up perfectly with everything she'd been told since she arrived and attempted to find work.

With every rejection came more misery and a feeling of immense worthlessness. Staring at a large building in the distance (Frost Enterprises), dread crept into her gut as she realized she was just a tiny part in a *very* big machine. An unemployed woman in a sprawling city that only saw women in limited roles was a daunting prospect, one that made her crave the feel of a shovel or working the unforgiving soil with her bare hands. At least there was some independence.

The barkeep had been much kinder than the others though, forgoing any added insults or outbursts, unlike the man Jenny had asked at the fraternal building a few doors down from the saloon. He just screamed, so loudly that his face became puce, and he used a stiff broom to jab at her like some rodent.

Honestly how did you expect things to be, Jenny? her inner voice gnawed. *Different from the Gulch? Where everyone would suddenly be lining up and begging for* you *to work for* them?

Moping through the marketplace, dispirited by her own roaming thoughts, Jenny spotted another structure peeking over the rooftops toward the southwest. Enrobed in a shroud of steam, it was tall and made of latticed metal. She thought it might be the city's broadcast tower, since it resembled a much smaller version back home, but she didn't get much time to think on it before a wave of shoulders jostled her. One deliberately hard shove managed to snap her out of the slump and evoke the words of her grandfather, Mr. Johnston, and even Aftershock all at the same time.

They told her simply not to give up and that the current situation was a test of her resolve. Taking the timely arrival of those words to heart, she lifted her head with a modicum of pride. She watched and listened to those around her, hearing dark murmurs about the raiders attacking the Gulch and a lot of choice words about how stupid and deserving the settlers were to live out there in the first place.

Jenny became heated, wanting to tell those women how ignorant they were, but then a cascade of thoughts refocused her and she realized she was at a disadvantage; every opportunity for work and lodging in the borough was exhausted.

Thankfully, she had picked up some leads by overhearing conversations during her search. Unfortunately, they were mostly disreputable and located deeper within the city, leaving her with little choice but to try, no matter how much she wanted to avoid it. Imagining Diablo like some great tree, the outer, inner, and center areas were like concentric rings in its trunk. The outermost edge regions, like Comprass and its sister boroughs, were akin to bark, most rugged and varied, whereas the inner portion was far more uniform and regimented. Much of the support that bore the brunt of society's weight was there, while the very center, most insulated and hardest to reach, was where the most money and elites dwelled.

Most the work Jenny got wind of were for show and slop shops, producing cheap, bespoke and ready-made articles of clothing craved by the masses to satiate their thirst for outrageous fashion. Uniforms for the clergy, Rangers, and prisons were also coveted, and all detested by legitimate tailors that catered in fine-crafted attire for the wealthy. Not that the idea wasn't loathed by Jenny as well, with little desire to sweat and sew her fingers to the bone by hand in modest light. However, it was money no matter how pitiable the pay, anything greater than zero being a blessing.

From Comprass she reluctantly headed to the northwest and was soon entering a neighboring borough, passing beneath a large stone arch with a placard attached to it. It said Ganado, or at least did at one time; the letter N was worn away and the O was caked with a layer of grime so thick it was illegible. The sight didn't do a thing to prevent Jenny having second thoughts about proceeding. Nevertheless, she continued down thin paths no wider than alleyways and with each step the light seemed to drain away while the walls closed in. The color of the masonry also faded as the very warmth was stripped out of the air.

Somewhere, unseen in the distance, livestock brayed between the sounds of jeering men and cracking whips, the noise echoing off the unsympathetic walls before getting lost in the noise of the busy market. Catching a whiff of dung and the blood, its metallic taste hanging in the back of her throat, Jenny shuddered, visualizing a scene of carnage on a scale that was difficult to purge, even though she was used to slaughtering animals from life on the farm.

Similarly, Jenny thought she knew what it was to be destitute, until Diablo challenged her on that front, too, like some sick talent. Gloomy people with obscured faces were crouched and laid in front of similar properties, all alive with insects. The sight made her skin scrawl as she passed by many poor souls lining both sides of the street.

The classes weren't neatly demarcated in Diablo, or elsewhere in the world for that matter. Workhands, craftsmen, artisans, and even educated working folk were all cowering against the despair of the world, having no hope of earning an assured wage due to illness, disability, or other maladies. One thing was certain among the uncertainty: there wasn't a single trace of anyone elite gracing those dark roads[6].

Jenny scurried through the area as fast as she could, feeling as though wandering eyes were on her even though they were all either dipped or hooded. She passed from the frying pan into the fire, entering subsequently seedier areas of town.

The next one was rife with organized fighting; dark-skinned wanderers being pitted against a few raider hostages that day. Emotions and bets were high, as were raised boos, cheers, and fists. Jenny could tell two of the bandits were from the Devil's Shadow, being familiar with their style of outfits, but the others must have been from different clans.

She moved on and into another commercial zone where clunky, angular robots were being used for manual labor. Having heard stories of marvelous machines that looked, walked, and even talked like people, she was disappointed by what she saw. Those tales were obviously exaggerated, since these things were

---

6   When work was plentiful, workhands and other laborers could make up to five Spurs (half a Gear) per day while craftsman and fine artisans up to triple that amount. Educated workers could earn up to five Gears per day while trappers and hunters made the most of the 'low classes' since they also had some of the most dangerous duties. Depending on the beast, earnings could be up to ten Gears per day. The pay scale for elites and government officials far exceeded that of the other classes, ranking at hundreds to even thousands of Gears per day independent of workload.

just glorified tools, beeping and whirring instead of conversing with anyone around.

Reaching a crossroads, two longstanding timber signs indicated she was, ironically, on Opportunity Walk; the other road was called Fisher Lane. She had no idea where these places were, nor where to go for that matter. Looking up and down the intersection trying not to worry, she saw a few recessed alcoves and tight backstreets that were shaded from the bright sun.

Seeing nothing of concern, she chose to go right, gasping when a couple of oily men unexpectedly emerged at the end of the closest alleyway. They loitered in high leather boots and tight trousers, staring at her with eyes full of wicked intent.

"Hey lady!" said a husky man on the left in a pleasant, but obviously rehearsed, tone.

The man beside him was taller and less appealing; that is if the first could even be considered such.

"Are you lost?" he probed. "If so, we'll be glad to help get you where you need to be…"

"I'm fine," Jenny cut sternly, starting to walk past them.

No way am I going anywhere with you two, she continued in thought, instantly reminded of Jebidiah. *There's always someone like this in every settlement and in this city, there's probably so many that it rivals the population of small town.*

"Aw, come on," the tall one persisted, shifting agitatedly on his feet. "I know that you want to."

"We have a *lot* of things to offer," said the husky one, advancing. "You traveling all by yourself? This place can be a maze if you aren't sure where you're going."

He reached down and grazed the front of his trousers before extending his arm.

"Get off!" Jenny demanded, recoiling as he tried to latch onto her.

She flicked her arm hard and it struck his. He stumbled backward into the lanky man.

"Wow! Did you just say no? To *me?*"

"Pretty bitch did more than that, Garrett," the lanky one answered, sliding one of his busted-up hands into a pocket. He pulled out a knife, which caught a beam of sunlight and shined. "I think she needs to be taught a lesson."

"*I* think that I've learned plenty about this place for today," Jenny told them, "and recommend that you not even try what you're thinking."

Both men hooted, Garrett producing a similar blade which he tossed skillfully in the air.

"You hear that Tony?" he said, snatching the embellished handle as it spun. "She thinks she can tell *me* what to do."

"Maybe she's confused by her place," Tony replied, "thinking she's got something dangling between those legs? Come here sweet thing, you don't look like a man to me. I've got the proper tools so let me check things out. I'll promise to be gentle, at first."

"You heard me," she warned. "Don't even try it."

Tony grunted, moving toward her anyway, a swell now straining against his front. Garrett followed, both so close that their foul breath caught in her nostrils and moved her hair. Tony smiled, flecks of meat crammed in the spaces between his teeth.

He was first to put a hand on her shoulder…

… and Jenny whipped around fast. There was a soft *thud* followed by a pained groan, her boot having met him right between the legs. He hit the ground seemingly in slow motion, wincing and clutching at his crotch.

Garrett launched himself at Jenny, wasting no time swiping at her.

Jenny spun out of the way of each pass before making contact, smacking his knife arm. The blade few off, clanking down the alley and before Garrett even realized, her fist smashed into the side of his ratty face.

"You stupid whore!" he roared, using a thumb to wipe away the stream of blood that started pouring from his lower lip.

He didn't remove much, smearing it more than anything. Glancing down, he grabbed hold of a revolver mounted to his belt.

"Now you're going to get…"

Click.

The all-too-familiar sound of a hammer cocking reached his ears. Lifting his eyes slowly, they met the end of a junk pistol's barrel.

"I happen to have the proper tools, too," Jenny said confidently. "So how do you want this to end? By letting me go about my business, or your brains adding a bit of color to this dingy place?"

Tony was still groaning on the ground, his excitement gone, replaced with rage.

"What are you waiting for you idiot! Shoot her!"

Garrett used a forearm to wipe his deepened brow, slinking over to Tony. Hovering over him for a second, he leaned over and eased the man onto his knees, then his feet.

Jenny's heart was beating fast though you wouldn't know by her expression, forged well by her encounters with Jebidiah. She traced their path the entire time with her gun, patiently waiting for an answer.

"Garrett, you lose your manhood somewhere?" Tony muttered, turning attention to Jenny as his deep breaths filled the alley. "That piece of shit you're holding probably doesn't even work."

He snatched Garrett's gun and pointed it right at her.

"This one, on the other hand, just killed a loser far worse than you this morning."

"Mine works just fine," she replied calmly, the back of her neck sweating. "I would show you, but that'd just be a waste of a bullet on my part."

"Better a wasted bullet than you drawing anymore wasted air! I'm done talking!"

Before Tony could act, another voice spoke from behind.

"Are you sure about that?" it asked smoothly. "You shoot and I'm positive you'll be doing far more talking, but to the authorities. I am sure such fine gentlemen like yourselves wouldn't want to deal with Frost sentries now, would you?"

Garrett and Tony didn't turn but Jenny leaned to her left, trying to get a view of who was there. Down in the shadows stood another woman, wearing a lacy black dress and matching corset. Her collared top was tan with short sleeves and its plunging neckline was crisscrossed with thin black straps. She had a rather ornate pistol drawn herself, pointed right at the thugs.

"Evelyn," Tony sneered. "Don't you have anything better to do than pester us?"

"Well, that all depends on the answer you have for this lady; she's waiting."

Garrett stayed quiet while Tony was visibly annoyed. His teeth were grinding against each other as an eyebrow twitched.

"I really don't think this should be that hard of a choice," Evelyn said, smirking. "Or maybe it is, since she addled your lower brain with that kick."

"Fine!" Tony yelled. "Have it *your* way Evelyn, just know we're not going to let this little incursion go unpaid."

"You keep my tab open, precious. Now, be on your way."

Evelyn watched keenly as the two men crept by Jenny and raced down Fisher Street. Tony, despite his best efforts, seemed to struggle doing something akin to a gallop.

"Thank you," Jenny said, sighing with relief. She holstered her pistol.

THE Steam TYCOON   181

"You're most welcome," Evelyn replied, doing the same. "Sad thing about deadbeats like that is they'll be back, like some persistent sickness you can't get rid of. But we've wasted enough time talking about them, let's talk about *you* for a second. It's not often I come across someone that skilled in handling the trash, especially one wearing a dress."

Jenny blushed, finding a little comfort in the complement.

"Not from around here, are you?"

"Is it that obvious?"

"Yes, it is and to be honest I couldn't be happier," Evelyn said, looking thrilled. "As you've probably seen, it's terribly regimented around the city as far as what roles people play; what they can and cannot do."

"I've seen that pretty much everywhere I've been," Jenny replied, tinted with woe.

"Doesn't make it right," Evelyn said, looking at their surroundings. "Come on, though, there are better places to talk than this grimy place."

Jenny nodded as Evelyn motioned her hand back toward the street and the two women began walking down Fisher, making another left turn a short way down.

"Thankfully I hear it's not the case *everywhere* on Eaugen, but areas like Lagos and Barro are few and far between," Evelyn continued. "What irritates me the most is that the only person who seems to be doing anything to help is Winthrope, though he is still mired in playing elite games and his scope seems broader. As far as the rest goes, inaction when you know for a fact something is amiss is just as bad as the action itself, at least in my humble opinion."

That was the second time someone had mentioned how good of a person Winthrope was, making Jenny regret her decision to lump him amongst the worst of society. Now, she found herself intrigued, especially having seen him at the market earlier. Though the notion was downright silly, she held onto a small hope that she would be able to meet him one day.

"So where are you from?" Evelyn asked softly, not wishing to jolt Jenny from her thoughts.

Jenny answered with her name, then proceeded to tell Evelyn about her life on the farm outside of the Gulch, and about the horrific raider attack that came on them not two nights ago. Using the captive tale that Aftershock crafted, she omitted his part in her rescue entirely for reasons of trust.

"I had heard of that attack just this morning and can see how someone like you managed to escape their clutches," Evelyn observed. "Poor souls, the rest of them. We're living in frightful times if our own borders and the officials can't keep chaos at bay. So, you've come to this city looking for work?"

"Yes," Jenny answered hopefully, "and lodging."

"I'll be honest with you: times have been tough, more than I've seen in a long time. I'm not sure if that and the raider attacks getting worse are related in any way, but we're still affected nonetheless."

"Are you saying there isn't any work here?"

"Oh, there is work in Diablo, further in. Good work. There's nothing left like that in Comprass, the borough you came from, or here in Ganado," Evelyn stated. "I'm sure you saw the wonders along Opportunity Way. Most of those people have given up with life and are but a whisper away from death. Others that can't handle the work at the factory houses have turned to other, less honorable means of making money."

The two entered a wide-open space with what looked like abandoned livestock pens. Deep in their filthy recesses pairs of legs were raised and swaying in tune to the sounds of grunts and low thumping.

THE *Steam* TYCOON   183

"It's not pretty is it?" Evelyn said. "But, it's something to put food on the table, especially when the alternatives are so limited and grim."

Jenny caught a glimpse of several bots, more advanced than the ones she'd seen performing manual labor, tending to some garish men at the back of one of the stalls. There were real women there too, all intermingled in disgusting and smelly glory.

It was off-putting and something Jenny could never see herself doing, but something about it managed to cause her soul to ache.

"Many of the girls here see themselves doing this for a few years, since it's an easy way to build up finances for bigger and better things."

"The conditions though," Jenny said in disbelief. "They're hardly clean. Surely diseases…"

"Manage to cut those plans short?" Evelyn finished for her. "A lot are. Quite a vicious little circle of hell Diablo is, especially since foul wards aren't the best place for a young woman to be spotted if she wants any chance at normality after her few years in the game."

Evelyn noted Jenny's manner. The reality was hard to swallow and she knew that Jenny wouldn't go down such a path just by the look on her face now.

"But that's where people like me come in," Evelyn continued. "You gave me your name but I've yet to give you my full one. Evelyn Richards, owner of Eeevee's Brothel and Safe House. It's not the best profession, but is one that gets girls out of places like this."

Jenny was hesitant to shake her hand based on the discussion they just had, but sucked it up and did so out of goodwill. She imagined Evelyn's place to match her attire: graceful, comforting, and clean despite the nature of her guests and their clients.

"Every little bit helps," said Evelyn, escorting Jenny from the pens into another street and even though the passage was tighter, it didn't feel as confining.

"I think so, too," said Jenny. "I hope that I can see the day things change for the better, like back home before the fall. It would have been great to not worry about the land being seized just because no men survived."

"Exactly," Evelyn said. "We are still human, despite efforts to make us feel less. Hell, none of them would be around if we weren't! It's one of my deepest beliefs that all of us share common privileges granted by nature and yes, even other people. If I can convince any one of these forgotten souls of that, then I feel like my work is meaningful, even if not viewed as moral. Our society, the current one at least, values classes, and money, and power over all else, when at the end of the day we never purchased a thing – especially our freedom – when coming into the world, nor will we take anything with us when we leave it. We are all equal in that regard and that fact will always be. Who is then to say that one person is more deserving of a right than another, and if so, on what basis have they been granted such authority?"

Jenny didn't have those answers, nor thought she ever would. She did have a question of her own, though, developing as they walked for some time with nothing new to see.

"You mentioned something earlier about factories?" Jenny asked at last, having had her fill of stale brick walls.

"Yes, the factories are in a borough called Sucio. It's three away from here, to the south. Ah! Here we are."

Evelyn lead Jenny down another alleyway and after much winding, it opened into a brighter and more populous area. Filled mainly with women, they were all dressed well in similar fashion and topped with lively faces. Straight ahead, a handsome building of dark brick and wood rose above the dull cobblestones. Pretty drapes hung in the windows and between them more young girls stared out into the square. The front door was also open, teasing at a warm and inviting interior as the youngest of them swept the foyer.

"It's getting on a little," Evelyn said, pointing up to the sky. Some of the women had gathered around, more interested in Jenny's new face than anything else. "You are more than welcome to stay here with us for the night. Sucio is not far as the birds fly, but by the time you navigate the all the streets to get there, it will close to dark. There are no inns around the factories, either. Only shantytowns, though Winthrope does keep his workers well, unlike Frost, or any of the other proprietors."

Jenny looked once more at the building then all the congregated faces with respect. They were gemstones amongst the miserable surroundings and she felt genuinely welcome. That alone made her want to stay.

"Jenny, I know you can handle yourself, but please join us," Evelyn urged. "I can then accompany you in the early morning if you like."

"Did you say Winthrope?" she asked.

"Yes, he is probably the best person to work for in all of Diablo, not only from the lodging and wages standpoint, since he's also not that bad to look at."

Laughter filled the square and Jenny recalled Jesse's face from the market… there was something about it that sent her heart fluttering…

"Frost is one to avoid," she continued. "He's just a self-interested bastard out for himself. It would be a win on both counts if there were an opening at Winthrope Limited, but realize that factory work is not easy work at all. There are long hours without many breaks, and the foreman is one piece of work."

"What about him?"

Evelyn lifted her shoe, which had collected a thin layer of wet grime on the sole, and pointed at it.

"That's a pretty good description of the man."

Jenny didn't know whether to laugh or cringe, but either way the pros did outweigh the cons in the situation.

"Lovely," she said, requiring no more to persuading to stay, much to the excitement of the girls. "Evelyn, words don't seem enough thank or repay you for this hospitality."

"It's my pleasure," she replied casually. "Just remember everything we talked about today as you grow, as I know you will. That's all that I can ask for. Well, that and if you could please assist Martha with tonight's dinner. Poor thing; it's her turn and she can't cook worth a damn. It might be the anniversary of the Burning, but I don't think that it's meant to apply to the food."

SEVENTEEN

FROST WAS HUNCHED OVER A cherry wood desk, elbows firmly planted on the surface. His eyes were struggling to stay open in the dark and windowless room while his arms strained against the tight fabric of his black dress shirt, unbuttoned nearly halfway until he needed to put on a tie for the evening's celebrations at Grand Hall.

A lamp comprised of a single bulb of orange glass was screwed into a series of interconnected bronze armatures, bent at angles like pipes to illuminate an array of parchment splayed across the work surface. Some of the errant light caught in the hairs that peeked through the top of his chest. Upon the paper were schematics for several devices, the largest yet simplest of which was a cylinder one half meter in length and half that again in circumference. Per the plans, the other devices on the page were to be placed within it, along with a material referenced only as Soil.

Frost mumbled incoherently as a peaceful sleep took over, until a loud buzzer woke him with a start, snatching away a dream where he had been victorious in his plight against Winthrope. Jumping at the noise, he struck a knee on a sharply decorated panel.

"Damnit!" Frost yelled, pain shooting up his leg while his fist came down, rattling a half glass of liquor and sending a pair of magnifying lenses dancing across the parchment. "What is it *now*?"

Kicking back from the desk, Frost tugged at the bottom of his shirt before marching toward a faint glow on the other side of the room.

Aero happened to be there, unconscious as he laid in two halves on a metal table. A dim, blue light emanated from beneath him (the table itself was glowing) and tubes had been attached to open compartments across his forehead. His legs were separated and unmoving, while both of his chest plates had been cracked open like a parcel, exposing a radiant canister in the middle. Made of silver, it pulsed erratically, red light mixing with the blue hues to cast a purple glow on the monitors that beeped and gauges that joggled above.

"Aaron, why are you being so difficult," Lucas whispered gently, rubbing Aero's soft hair while his eyes darted between the displays and incessant flashes of red. It wasn't long before he found the cause of the alarm.

"The new alloys failed to keep the temperatures moderated," he spat, noting several indicators were pointed at zero while others were pegged on the maximums.

With an annoyed grunt, Frost grabbed hold of the cylinder and yanked it out. The slick lubricant covering it was flung everywhere, even more of it splashing when he slammed the whole array on the table beside Aero.

"Fuck you!" he shouted. "FUCK!"

Pressing a small button just below the steel table, a long drawer slid out without a sound. Inside, there was an identical silver cylinder resting on a bed of silken fabric. Frost took it, then jammed the unit into the slot left in Aero's chest. Once far enough, there was a subtle *click* followed by a low, building whine. A faint blue glow appeared a moment later, pulsing with a steady rhythm like a heartbeat.

"That's how the *other* one should be!" he shouted, his mechanical eye whirring madly in its socket. "I need these damn modifications to work!"

Pushing back from the table with such force that Aero's body shook violently, Frost marched over to a large device about three meters to the left. There, a heavy glass screen was suspended above an array of buttons, knobs, and levers. An inviting leather chair was placed front and center.

Opting to stay standing, Frost rested both hands on the soft, padded edge and squeezed hard. It wasn't doing much to calm him, though pretending it was Jesse's neck helped tremendously.

You are leaving me with very little choice, Frost thought, placing blame for his failures on the enterprising Winthrope instead of his own inept staff. *I WILL get my hands on your secrets and my plans WILL succeed, even if it means getting you out of my way.*

Frost was working to improve his bot designs and accessories, like those illustrated in the collection of plans on his desk, for mass production with better alloys that were independent of Winthrope and his affiliated mining operations. So far, attempts to do so had gotten close but ultimately met with failure, his teams unable to replicate or even steal the formulations Jesse was using to perfect his proprietary steam capsules.

"I'll have to find out what he's paying those damnable technicians and triple it. And more if necessary," Frost murmured darkly, scratching himself a note with a fountain pen on a scrap of paper. It simply said 'field bonuses'. "I'm sure that Mr. Butler would not mind a receiving one of those to help me discover that information."

As if to add insult to injury, another chime shrieked, slicing through Frost's focus like a whetted dagger. Ahead of him, an amber light flickered to life on the console, drawing his threadbare attention as it grew in brightness.

"Your timing is impeccable as always," Frost groused, a hand perched just over the light, ready to press down. "Once I am done with Winthrope I guarantee my full attention will be on taking care of you."

Dipping a finger, the button clicked and another light above it came on and was green. Frost cleared his throat and spoke clearly toward the screen, "President Archer, to what do I owe this great honor?"

The glass display burst to life, a jittery field of mossy static filling the holotube from edge to curved edge. After a few seconds, it dwindled, replaced by a deep-toned warble that remained until the distorted, almost three-dimensional image of a man appeared. He was obviously tall and quite broad chested, the tinted display making his black suit look a shade of forest green. A subtle damask pattern was noticeable in the fabric, along with a neat line of four buttons on his each of the lapels. Lengthy, peppered hair dangled gracefully in front of his eyes while his beard was comparable to Frost's own.

"Let's not start adding formalities while pretending to be enthusiastic about my calls," President Alistair Michael Archer said bitterly. "I know you despise them half as much as I do."

Frost couldn't disagree, choosing to remain silent instead; his sour expression answered on his behalf.

"So tell me, how are things advancing with the new power

source?" Archer asked forcefully, chin raised high in anticipation though his low-slung eyes predicted disappointment.

"Well enough," Frost said quietly but clearly, "but we have encountered a slight… hindrance to mass producing the unit."

"A slight hindrance?" Archer barked, followed by a tremendous sigh. "*A major problem* is what you mean to say."

"Not at all…"

"Then explain to me these delays!" Archer bellowed, his hair shaking wildly as his head quaked with wrath. "Frost, I am growing weary. No, correction: I AM weary! You have already spent far too much time working this matter with no further, measurable progress. How is it you can build a single unit in a comparable fraction of the time *and* have enough gall to place it in that disgusting plaything of yours, yet you cannot seem to find the aptitude to develop another one after a few more years?"

"A3R0 has nothing to do with this!" Frost retorted hotly; obviously, a nerve had been struck. "I built that prototype cell at great *personal* cost! Do you have any idea the finances required to produce such a complex thing AND keep the entirety of its production hidden from the officials?"

On the other side of the room, Aero stirred at the mention of his call-sign, opening his blue eyes. Readying to piece himself back together so he could join them, Archer's words booming through room at the top of his voice kept Aero quiet and motionless. Shutting his eyes again, he listened covertly.

"I *do* know the cost of such things!" Archer snarled, his face flushed with red although the screen remained a steady shade of green. "I am sure you would not want to find out yourself how deep *my* pockets actually go."

"No," Frost submitted, plunging his head in a reverent bow.

In the span of a blink, Frost envisioned Archer burning in flames so intense that his screams echoed all the way from

Angelus, across three-thousand kilometers of wasteland until they could be heard resoundingly in Diablo. Frost struggled to make sure a smile did not appear, gazing back at Archer with an expressionless face.

"Then we both agree that mass production of these self-contained arrays must be completed as soon as possible?" queried Archer.

"Yes, but the President does understand that perfection takes time…"

It was as if Archer heard him, yet didn't care.

"I understand that *progress* takes time, but don't be silly Frost. Verily, perfection only exists in Angelus. We will, of course, be sure to make do with whatever solution you come up with, provided it is, actually, a successful one."

Lucas averted his eyes in haste, looking back toward Aero who was still deactivated on the table. His mind wandered into his own plans, where those perfected energy cells would power the next generation of soldier bots, capable of operating out in the dry environment of the wastes without the need for frequent refueling like the current steam units, nor ineffectual winding like older clockwork models. With such a force at his command, Frost could sweep across not only Diablo but the world – including the lofty Angelus – until all was under his authority. He would not stop until his name was not only known, but chanted from all corners of the world.

Frost!

Frost!

Frost!

"FROST!" Archer was screaming, at last regaining the man's attention after nearly thirty seconds of calling. "A word of warning as you devise your course of action: do not overstep your bounds, or what you may *think* your bounds are. Make no mistake, the devices you are developing are for Angelus and Angelus alone." He leaned forward with a very contemptuous look on his face, filling the screen to the point that it looked as if he would bump his head on the glass. "If at any point something to the contrary becomes evident, you had best be prepared for a great hand to come reaching out of the sky to smite you and all you have ever known."

Frost's nostrils flared at the not-so-veiled threat and his mouth curled at once as if ready to hurl an insult.

The President withdrew from the screen, preparing to receive a verbal volley but no words came, causing Archer to simply smile at Frost's pitiful response.

Before the heated exchange could resume, a muffled voice unexpectedly came out of a voice tube in Archer's luxuriant office.

"Sir, pardon the interruption, but I have the update you requested."

"Go on," Archer replied, bending an ear toward the device.

"Two and a half kilograms of Soil has arrived from Muelle Esta by rail. It is currently being screened in customs, secured on platform nine, pending your inspection and approval before being flown to the facility."

Archer's face grew wide as he beamed, a definite contrast to his look when speaking to, or even glancing at, Frost.

"Thank you. Alert the dock agents to prepare for my arrival. I will be there within the hour."

"Yes, My President," the voice replied in such a way that Frost pictured the person on the other end gesticulating obediently. "All hail Angelus."

"All hail Angelus, indeed," said Archer, now speaking directly to Frost. His sullen face had returned. "So you see Lucas, we have been more than ready for you to deliver on your end of this bargain."

Frost scrutinized Archer as he cleared away strands of long hair that had fallen in front of his eyes. Both his left hand and arm were constructed from the same synthetic material as Aero, bordered and hinged at all the joints. On his wrist was a present from Lucas' father: an elaborate gold chronometer affixed by a thick brown leather band. Exquisitely, it ticked away each passing second since being gifted in far better days.

"How long do I have?" Frost asked hesitantly.

"Thirty days at most," Archer offered, "though I would preferably like to see action in half that time."

"I can work with that timeframe, assuming Winthrope cooperates with his technology."

"Cooperation is the very last thing on that man's mind, brilliant as it may be. Especially you factor in it." Archer's reply was ominous. "You know as well as I do that we need his assets in hand and the man himself gone."

Silence fell between the two men as they stood, poised on a point of no return.

"Get rid of him," Archer stressed, shattering both the quiet and any remaining reservations Frost might have had. "I don't care how it's done, just do it."

Aero's eyes sprung open with worry and as much as he disliked the treatment from master at times (there were times it seemed two versions of Lucas existed in the same body), he hoped that he wasn't going to go down that path. Without time to ponder the outcome, Aero snapped his eyes shut again for fear of being noticed and consequently deactivated.

"And what of the others?" Frost asked, his expression becoming sinister. "Mayors, prefects, sheriffs…"

"All in due time," Archer responded, his words initially grating against Frost's ears due to the President's insistence that he hurry, while others need not. "Their palms can be greased for now and, ultimately, they will be compelled to comply."

Frost liked the sound of that. With the joint drive from both of their extensive bank accounts working on the development of the energy cells, and with Winthrope out of the way for good, they – no, HE – would become unstoppable.

"Then we are done here," Archer said hollowly from his side of the screen. "Don't disappoint me."

"Of course not," Frost replied, the soft green light bending the shadows across his features into dreadful shapes. His brow and cheek-tops were especially rutted, as was his Cheshire smile.

"That remains to be seen," Archer replied with doubt dripping off his words and not a second later his image disappeared from the screen with a dull hum and no goodbye.

The moment Frost was sure the signal was disconnected and all the green light had faded, he dropped his counterfeit smile.

"What remains to be seen, *President*, is how long I shall tolerate your belittling once these units are produced."

Still talking to himself about malicious things, Frost swept past Aero, rapping his knuckles on the steel table as he continued to a distant door tucked off in the shadows. Opening it, light cascaded into the room from a line of lamps along the wall of a long passageway. The fixtures resembled oil lanterns, held by brass hands with orange bulbs instead of flames. Frost stepped into the hallway, still muttering, and closed the door behind him.

Aero waited for a few minutes after hearing the door latch before he made any moves, just in case Lucas returned. When all remained clear, he opened his eyes and pushing himself up and around, dangled himself over the edge of the tabletop. Reaching for his legs, he attached each one to his frame, bending his knees and wiggling his toes. He didn't get down immediately, instead setting his elbows atop his thighs and his face into his padded palms. A prolonged sigh escaped and if he were human it would have been followed by tears.

I am torn, Aero thought to himself, *between the duty I have for my creator and the lives he is about to affect.*

He struggled with which option would take precedence, considering both would violate one, if not more, of the fundamental principles hardwired into his brain.

Aero remained, head in hands as he mulled over his options, deciding that he would pay close attention to Lucas and his dealings going forward. Pressed to act, it would not be long before his master made moves and Aero would be there, watching.

EIGHTEEN

IT WAS NEARING SIX O'CLOCK IN THE morning as indicated by a large ironware clock that hung over the entrance to the factory floor. Jenny entered through the heavy doors, having trudged across the murky yard. The entire area was soaked by tenacious drizzle, as was her cloak and bits of uniform beneath it. Removing the outerwear, she folded it up and set it on a small shelf beneath her station along the central tables. Brushing out what wrinkles she could, she looked around at the same time, thankful that Evelyn had brought her to Sucio just over a week ago and was able to pull some favors so Jenny got in at one of Winthrope Limited's locations.

While many of the neighboring mills and factories had already been at work for an hour or more, steam had yet to collect overhead in any of Winthrope's facilities, the hefty machinery that normally hiccupped and belched the vapor to the rafters still dormant like some great, sleeping beast. In the shadows of pipes and pistons, Jenny stared at those unnerving work bots as they moved around, preparing to wake it.

I wonder why Mr. Winthrope doesn't just upgrade those things to look more...

Suddenly, the doors burst open and Jenny's attention fell on a stream of ladies flowing into the room, their light outfits reminiscent of a river cascading into channels formed by the tables. It was an impressive sight, all the women ready to get their long days started, though due to Winthrope's generosity they would end an hour before everyone else, too.

"Today's the day!" sang a somewhat round woman as she took a seat beside Jenny and cracked her stubby knuckles. Her gentle face was full of excitement, even though it was somewhat dirty.

"For what, Penny?" Jenny asked with a smile, clueless about what she was talking about. Nonetheless, her good mood was infectious and a great counter for the horrible weather.

"A visit," whispered Amelia Ward giddily from Jenny's left, her face red and nearly bursting. She looked like a matchstick.

"A visit from who?"

"Mr. Winthrope!" Penny and Amelia said together and the building literally shook with the sheer amount of swooning breath that was drawn in at that moment, then sighed melodiously out.

"T-that's today?" Jenny said, now recalling a mention of something about it a day or so ago. She was trying her best to be indifferent, but inside she was happy for the chance to meet and hopefully thank him for being so upstanding.

"Really now," said a downright depressing voice.

It was uttered by a harsh-looking woman with graying hair drawn up into such a tight bun that years of wrinkles were removed from her face. As she continued to speak, her long and un-tight neck wobbled.

"Decorum, ladies," she underscored sourly through pursed lips. "This is a place of business, not one for girlish fancies or frivolity. Need I remind you Miss Ward that the last thing you need is for the foreman to catch you again. He'll have you out on the street before your last swoon is out! The same goes for you Miss Langsdale."

"Oh, come now," Jenny said as the first set of pistons cranked. "If we must put in the work, why not get some enjoyment out of it?"

"Because it is pointless," the woman hissed, stressing the S so much Jenny waited for steam to vent from her ears and a metal part to be spat out of her mouth for assemblage.

"It is pointless... to be happy?" Jenny asked in disbelief, the real parts forthcoming.

"Quite..."

Without another word to the miserable woman (she didn't even know her name nor cared), Jenny snatched up the first of her components and set to put together a thing the other ladies called a controller assembly. The monotonous task continued for hours and Jenny fell into a mindless rhythm, allowing the time to tick by quickly until it was broken by two things that fast became just as repetitive. The first was not pleasurable in the slightest, having nothing to do with work but everything to do with the foreman and his salacious advances. One would be hard pressed to find anything that could induce vomiting faster than a detestable beard surrounding an equally loathsome mouth that insisted upon getting too close to one's skin. The second had the potential to be much more satisfying, if it came to be. Periodically, the entrance doors would fling open and Jenny's eyes would nimbly shoot over each time, anticipating Mr. Winthrope standing in the doorway illuminated by the rising sun.

Unfortunately, that had yet to happen, her gaze – along with that of Penny and Amelia – were instead met by the bun-lady's cricked neck and dissecting stare. Jenny would make sure to frown at her, mulling over the sheer amount of spitefulness she saw in the workforce.

I can see why they would be bitter relative to the foreman and those always groping hands, she thought, *but to see it amongst ourselves, rampant where it should be minimal, is disheartening.*

In the week Jenny was there, she'd seen many overly catty reactions or heard judgmental remarks made by women about other women, but none were more the topic of discussion than she was. Perhaps it was because Jenny was the new girl from the other side of the wall, with a different look and differing point of view. To her, that was something that should be celebrated, putting on a united front against their issues instead of being constantly against each other in some competition without a prize. But apparently, such things should be suppressed, as done by people who needed a negative regimen as much as air to survive.

"Don't mind her," whispered Penny as she tightened some bolts with a wrench, slamming the tool down before handing the unit off down the line. "Until you arrived I was the target of her berating. To be honest, I always thought it was a means of deflecting the fact she's smuggling some of these parts out of here."

"Oh my! Really?" Jenny muttered, flabbergasted while casting a sideways glance. "How in the world?"

Amelia leaned over and Jenny dipped her head, expecting a juicy reveal.

"We think she has one shoved up front and another tightly in the rear," Amelia said in a voice so mousy she could barely be heard over the general noise.

Jenny gasped, conjuring a visual before the trio tittered.

"That explains *quite* a lot," she replied, catching a hawkish glare from across the table. They didn't care, continuing unashamedly until their laughs were spent.

A couple more hours wound their way around the clock and lunch had at last arrived with the strike of noon. The machines and bots still toiled away as the women filed out of the work area for their break. Penny and Amelia stood, followed by Jenny who rose stiffly between them.

"Your back doing all right, dear?" asked Penny, placing her arms at the low of her own as she stretched. "After all these years, mine is murder by this time."

"More like by the first hour," said Amelia as her joints popped loudly.

"That's because you need to eat more!" Penny said with concern, her narrowed eyes hunting for any sign of meat on the girl's frame. "There's no cushioning for your bones! You look like a rail."

"I would if I could afford to," Amelia scowled, now glancing at her thin arms in comparison to Penny's plump ones.

Penny shook her head saying, "You earn the same wage I do and though it pains me – as nosy as I am – I'm not going to ask what you end up doing with yours. Nope; it's none of my business!" Though she just denied it, she really did look as if she wanted to know. "Come on! Time's wasting and you *do* need to eat!"

The pair of them set off but Jenny delayed.

"Are you coming?" Amelia asked, halfway to the door already. "We've only a half hour…"

"I'll join you two shortly," she said, wanting to spend a moment alone.

"all righty, just be sure you don't lose track of time and go and miss break; we still have six more hours to go!"

"I won't," Jenny said as her two friends disappeared through the door and down the passage leading to the dining hall. She turned back around and sat for a moment, looking at the floor.

"I miss you..." she whispered, pulling from around her neck a filigreed silver locket attached to thin chain.

Placing it between her thumb and forefinger, she flicked the locket open and looked at the tiniest lumograph of her mother. The short banter between Penny and Amelia reminded Jenny of her mother's often failed attempts to get her to eat vegetables growing up and, for some reason, the memory came in and hit her like a locomotive.

The minutes passed and while she reminisced, several footsteps approached behind her.

"Oh sorry, you two," Jenny said, closing the locket and putting it away. "I did exactly what I said I wouldn't and lost track of ..."

"Your place?" said a voice that didn't belong to Penny or Amelia. It was far more shrill, predatory.

Jenny rose slowly and turned right into a pair of beady eyes peering from beneath a familiarly taunt bun.

"I beg your pardon?" Jenny snapped.

"Oh look at her now, acting all innocent-like," said a shrew-like girl with kinky hair that looked like it had been grabbed in too many random fits. "We know all about you now, don't we Miss Persimmons?"

"Undoubtedly," the uptight woman replied, her eyes never wavering. Behind her, the group of women grew to number a half dozen.

Jenny could feel her skin prickling, knowing where this was headed. Looking around for the foreman, he must've been at lunch himself; the space where he was normally perched in his window empty.

"If you would please hurry, Miss Persimmon, is it? I would like to spend what little time remains of lunch alone."

"Persimmons," she corrected, still hissing like a snake. "Funny that you mention you'd like to be alone *now* my dear Miss Boone; perhaps the company you keep at night keeps you quite... occupied."

There was a round of heckling sniggers, punctuated by Miss Persimmons' pretentious throat clearing.

"What?" snapped Jenny.

"Stop pretending!" the ratty girl charged. "We heard you arrived with Evelyn Richards! Some of us seen you! That louse is only good for one thing!"

"I hear she's good for a great many things," Miss Persimmons corrected snobbishly. "Especially when basking in the glow of a red light..."

Knowing how kind-hearted Evelyn was and that she was trying her hardest to champion equal rights for all, even the bitch in front of her, Jenny became enraged.

"I would strongly suggest that you watch what you say," Jenny told her, leaning compellingly over the table.

"Or you'll what?" Miss Persimmons asked, unfazed. "Show me how a wasteland jezebel handles a situation?"

"You seem to be doing just fine with *that* all by yourself..."

The mouthy girl's jaw hit the floor, her bucked teeth chewing on the air.

"How dare you!" she squeaked, and a split second later she was shoving a palm right into Jenny's forehead.

There was a flash of light followed by a flurry of intense spots, Jenny stumbling backward in a stupor right into something hard. As her vision returned, fuzzy at first, she leaned against the wall and saw the faces of Persimmons and her motley crew, aghast.

"Oh. My. Goodness! My *sincere* apologies!" Miss Persimmons insisted, dropping her shaking hands away from her mouth.

Jenny groaned before replying, "I'm not sure how sincere you can be considering..."

"This must have been an accident," said a man's voice from very close behind.

Jenny bounded away from the wall, spinning to discover it was no wall at all. There, standing in front of her was none other than Jesse Winthrope, debonair as ever in his tan suit and brown trench coat, even with a stack of crumpled documents piled in a heap over his leather shoes.

For a split second, it became so quiet one could hear a pin drop. The other ladies were still recoiled, arrested by fear and embarrassment while Jenny could only manage an awkwardly flattering stare right at Jesse's face.

What are you doing?! she screamed at herself, becoming mortified.

Yet, before she mustered the energy to flee, something soothed her, something so astronomically impossible that she wanted to pinch herself to see if she was dreaming. Staring back at her from those beautiful brown eyes was the exact, same look.

"I… I am so sorry," Jenny said at once, dropping to her knees where she started collecting the fallen documents.

He followed, planting a knee to the floor (and the ladies watching nearly fainted at the sight), smiling at the one time the sound of rustling paper could fill his heart with joy.

This is her, he thought excitedly. *The woman from the market. What are the odds! I must speak with her about the attack, find out…*

He stopped thinking as soon as his hand brushed up against hers.

What was this strange thing he felt? It was like the enjoyment he got out of his work but so much deeper. Something had passed between the two of them at that perfect moment, unseen but certainly felt.

Her skin is so supple and smooth…

Jenny felt the same way, obnoxiously thoughtless while her head swam in a cloud of delight.

His skin is so soft and warm....

They both looked at each other, wearing smiles inside and out, bursting with a feeling that should be long brewed, yet given in a moment of breathless surprise.

Their hands began to reach for each other to embrace.

"My goodness, what is the meaning of this!" came the voice of the foreman. Even his tone managed to foam like his lips, quickly snapping the duo back to reality.

Butler reached down and snatched Jenny's arm away from Jesse's, forcefully using his grip to jerk her to her feet.

"Mr. Winthrope! This incident is all my fault!" he proclaimed apologetically. "I assure you that I only stepped away for a mere few moments." He looked at Jenny with revulsion. "I will see to it that Miss Boone is severely…"

"Excused," Jesse replied tenderly, and Butler's disgust turned to aggravation. "We cannot go around reprimanding workers that have done nothing wrong, other helping a clumsy fellow pick up his mess."

We cannot go around consorting with employees nor those in classes that are beneath us either! Butler imagined himself shouting back to Jesse, but of course he stayed silent.

Jenny grinned but Butler looked more annoyed than usual. Releasing his vice like grip on Jenny's forearm, she rubbed on it, a sharp pain shooting between her wrist and elbow.

"What are you all gawking at?" Butler exclaimed, looking around at the room, now full of ladies returning from lunch. "Back to work, all of you!"

The workers listened right away and there was a rush of breaths and a mass scraping of chairs as they all assumed their positions at the tables.

Jesse could not take his eyes off Jenny; there was something about her that had him held captive. She possessed not only beauty but an unbridled innocence that wanted to be tamed yet, at the same time, could itself tame the most savage beasts.

"What is your name?" he asked.

Lured not only by the question, but the soothing tone of his voice, Jenny looked right into his eyes again.

"It's Jenny," she said bashfully, amazed that he even asked.

"Jenny," he repeated softly. "I like the sound of that. Boone is your surname then, if I take Mr. Butler to be correct?"

She nodded.

The way the conversation flowed, it was like they already knew each other, even though they had never met until a few minutes ago.

"Jenny," whispered Penny as she tugged on the base of her uniform. "I like the sound of your name too but Mr. Butler doesn't seem to right now. He's looking quite heated! I think it's time for us to get back to work…"

Indeed, the foreman was cross, his bushy beard and brows standing on end. Jesse glanced at him, thinking he looked a mess.

"It's fine," said Jesse to Jenny, his words riding an audible sea of gossip that had started to rise. "Duty calls to us both."

"Yes, it does," Jenny said meekly, forcing herself to tear away.

As she did, Jesse leaned in swiftly as if he were going give her a kiss. Jenny nearly collapsed with surprise. He wasn't actually going to do it, whispering a message into her ear instead.

"Before you head for the shantytown this evening, please see me," he requested. "I have some questions for you about the attack. I'll return then and will be waiting outside the gates at quarter past six."

"I will…" she said, not knowing anything better to say.

Jesse pulled back, making way for Butler who was waiting impatiently with arms crossed and foot tapping violently on the floor.

"And Mr. Winthrope," she said, and he turned to look at her. "Thank you for being such a shining example for us all to follow."

Jesse smiled, reaching the foreman. The two disappeared up the stairs and into the upper foreman's office, Butler drawing the curtains once Jesse had closed the door.

The main clock's hands struck the half-noon position and a bell tolled. Immediately, the assembly lines began working and Jenny finally sat down in her seat.

Her head might have been pounding from getting punched by a ratty girl's fist…

Her stomach might have been grumbling from missing lunch with six hours left until the end of the day…

Her heart might have been beating so fast it could easily burst out of her chest…

Yet with all of that piling on top of each other, Jenny was more than content and for the time being, feeling good about her future.

NINETEEN

THE LIGHT RAIN THAT HAD started a few days earlier grew into a thunderous downpour that battered the city, only just starting to subside around an hour ago. Dark clouds still spat on the city from the broken sky while above the shadowy swirls, white tendrils gleamed in the blazing evening sun.

Jesse walked briskly down one of the glistening streets, puddled water like silver splashing around his boots and wetting the tails of his flapping overcoat. Checking for pursuers, he stopped and slipped on a pair of bizarre goggles. Flicking through various lenses that were attached to the front by little brass fasteners, he moved his from side to side. Normally, those kinds of accessories were used for magnification but the combination of special coatings on these allowed him to see things in better the dark, though this set were still experimental and needed refinement.

Jesse didn't notice anything suspicious through his clarified but slightly muddled view and once sure the coast was clear, he took off the eyewear and snapped them to the top of his bowler hat. Moving down the street, he stopped in the shadows just out from the light of an overhead street sconce, turned sideways, and disappeared down a narrow gap in the wall. Far too thin to be an alleyway, Jesse followed it as it turned left then right then left again, emerging into an area of roughly square shape with no other way in or out.

Jesse was amazed, for the area was like a garden bursting with life, supplied with water from a couple of redirected downspouts. Looking around at all the plants, wild and unkempt, he had never seen anything like it within the walls of Diablo before. Green flowed across the ground like a spongy carpet, climbed the walls like soft wallpaper, and sat on ledges like cushioned chairs. It was a tiny piece of serenity within a city sorely lacking it.

Yet, as spectacular as the verdant space was, in the center of it all was the most beautiful thing he had ever laid eyes on.

Jenny approached, clad in a gleaming white bustle skirt and corset, both with golden accents like swirling leaves. Her brown hair was swept around her face like the long petals of a flower and Jesse's heart had no choice but to bloom with delight.

"It's great to see you," Jesse whispered as she got close. "I appreciate you still wanting to meet, this time away from all those prying eyes. Most would be scared or embarrassed, wanting to avoid experiencing ridicule like that again…"

"Why on Eaugen would I pass up the opportunity to see *you* of all people again?" Jenny said with a smile. "Especially when I'd probably face ridicule from the others regardless."

"Touché," Jesse said, giving his shoulders a quick shrug. "I *am* that great after all."

"Don't flatter yourself, Mr. Winthrope," Jenny replied, doing a quick twirl in her dress.

"Point taken," he said with eyes wide. "I'd rather flatter you! That dress looks amazing; where did you…"

"Evelyn," Jenny said softly. "She agreed to let me borrow it after telling me about this place. Those other 'ladies' can say whatever they want about her, but they can't fault the woman on her style or willingness to help."

"I certainly can't," Jesse replied with a long exhale and a slow, methodical stare. "Nor can I fault the woman wearing it, at all."

Standing together in the peaceful garden, it seemed like an eternity since Jenny met Jesse that night outside the gates of the factory yard, yet only two excruciating nights had past, this being the third.

During their brief discussion, urged to haste by scornful looks and remarks from workers to Jenny as they left the property for the night, Jenny told Jesse about her family and prior life in the Gulch, right up to the point the terrible attack sent it all to ruin. With each word, she confirmed his prediction that all the posturing the raiders had done was a prelude to an assault.

Concerned about which settlement would be next to fall, Jesse struggled to figure out the how and why behind it. Also, as much as he would never tell the bastard, Frost might have been right in his desire to bolster security forces, and his work along the railways certainly helped to stem the tide.

Though his mind was locked on figuring all that out, along with how his resources and technology could be used to help combat those evil forces, Jesse also found himself distracted by the woman standing in front of him. Wanting to get to know her better, he asked if she knew of a place they could talk in private, not that he cared if people saw them together, but in those budding moments he felt it necessary that she have his full attention.

"This place… it's unreal," Jesse muttered as he looked around again, knowing the same could also be said of his situation.

Stifled, he removed his coat, letting the weighty thing slide off his shoulders to the flora below. Beneath it, he wore a lighter gray vest over a crisp white shirt. There was no tie to burden his neck and the top two buttons of his shirt were undone, chest hairs peeking out invitingly.

Jenny was speechless, the outfit and frankly everything about Jesse tailored to absolute perfection.

What is happening to me? she wondered, Aftershock's words of warning ringing in her mind. *Is this just my willful fancies taking advantage of me? But he said that I would find what I was after when I got here; that it would happen when I least expected it. Yet, this… it's so fast. So soon. It can't last…"*

"Are you all right?" Jesse asked, seeing the look of concern forming on her face.

"I… yes, I'm fine," she said. "You know what's truly unreal? No, remarkable? Seeing you that day in the market there by the train station. While the world seemed against that poor old man, you approached him with nothing but kindness and light, willingly aiding him without so much as a second thought."

"Why wouldn't I?" he asked her earnestly. "Just because he is different than I am? It may be an unpopular view, but I care about everyone. I guess that is why I pour myself into all this work and these projects."

His voice trailed off and he sat himself down on one of the spongy, moss covered ledges. Jenny walked up beside him but remained standing.

"There's nothing wrong with that, Mr. Winthrope…"

"Please, call me Jesse," he requested. "It makes me feel far less old."

"There's nothing wrong with that Jesse," she said with a nervous laugh. "You're helping people in your own, commendable way. You should be happy about the progress you've made."

Jesse nodded, shifting so he could get a better view of her face. Reaching out, he passed the outer edge of his hand along her silken cheek until he touched the outer edge of her lips.

"That may be the case," he continued, "but sometimes the happiness you see in someone's face – their smiling lips and eyes – are just a dam, holding back a flood of tears that have accumulated over a long time. I have sacrificed a lot in my pursuit of work, nothing more than love. As I told you, I have no other family other than Logan but I have always wanted someone to fill that space... someone out of the ordinary."

Jenny's heart fluttered and she brought her own hand up to meet his before guiding it along her neck to rest on her chest where he could also feel it beating.

Can it really be? he pondered. *Is this the one I have wanted yet did not have the time to look for?*

"I know you are thinking the same thing I am about this situation..." Jesse said, though the words were difficult to get out. "Is this really love or just –"

"Lust," she answered, confirming her similar worries. Her eyes plummeted to the ground, but at once he moved their joined hands to her chin and push up. Their eyes locked.

"I cannot explain this, but this is the absolute best I have felt in a very long time. Just please never mention that to my best friend Duncan. Is there any way something that appears so quickly can even be considered real?"

"I don't know," she admitted, "but my world has changed and that is certainly real enough for me."

"Mine, too," he replied, leaning forward.

"And what I'm about to say sounds incredibly naïve..."

"As most silly yet significant things do..."

"But I feel like a spark has set something aflame in my heart and though society may try to douse it with all their might, everything that should feel wrong at this moment..."

"...feels *incredibly* right," Jesse said, pulling her closer until their lips met.

Jenny trembled, kept upright by Jesse's sturdy grip. The kiss lasted for an age of the world, until the time their souls were satisfied. When they separated, Jesse collapsed back on the ledge and panting, inched over so Jenny could sit down beside him. She nestled her head at the base of his neck while he pressed his against the cool brick and vines.

"I hope that was the right thing to do," Jenny whispered, her hand finding its way back to his but twitching anxiously. "For the right reasons."

"You know what?" Jesse asked after a time. "I don't care..."

Jenny was quick to lift her head, eyes like saucers. Did he suddenly come to his senses and realize this was a mistake? Why hadn't she?

"Calm down! Don't worry, I'm not going anywhere," Jesse continued with a lighthearted smirk. He pulled her back against him. "What I mean is that life is full of so many important questions that go unanswered, and so many trivial ones that everyone seems to have an answer for.

"I don't know about you, Jenny, but I don't want to ask any more questions about this... about us... and just see if it is trivial and ends, or great and meant to be. Either way, know that I don't see you as just another woman; there are plenty of forgetful ones here in the city. What I see before me is a beautiful soul that longs to be cared for and I want to be the one to do it..."

Jenny thoughts began to swirl again; so much about this was unclear...

"Okay," she said at last, "no more questions. Let's see where this road takes us, the journey being the best part."

TWENTY

IT HAD BEEN NEARLY TWO WEEKS since Archer proclaimed his deadline for dealing with Winthrope, two weeks since Archer ordered production be restarted on the energy cells for Angelus, and two weeks since Frost had made no progress with any of it.

Whether caused by sheer arrogance or just the inability to overcome his nemesis, Lucas found himself in a terrible position. He was weary and stressed, his focus frayed just like the shirt beneath his toffee-colored coat. Grabbing the leather lapel, Frost yanked the coat's swooping line of polished buttons completely open before dropping into an unyielding wood chair.

Beside him on an otherwise empty table was a lowball of whiskey, calling out to be held. Frost reached out and did just that, placing the chilled glass right in the middle of his pounding forehead. The condensation ran in broad strokes down both sides of his nose.

If you don't get rid of Winthrope by tomorrow Archer is not going to be happy, Frost thought. *You have to do this; there is no other way.*

If Frost could have shed tears he would have, yet the stinging in his eyes was merciless and he was sure crying would be just as comforting as salt in an open wound. Besides, why shed tears for something that he had done numerous times in the past? If anything, he would do so for joy, his apparent success mere moments from his grasp.

Lowering the glass to his lips, he breathed in some of the whiskey's sharpness as a shrouded figure appeared in a distant doorway.

"Sir, he is here," said a man's voice, each word precise and clear.

Frost stood from the chair, striking the seat with his thigh. It made a dreadful screeching noise as it skidded across the floor. Once he managed to regain his balance, he gave his coat a quick flick, stowing any last-minute regrets. Then, sputtering, he downed a large gulp of whiskey before walking toward the next room, carrying the glass by his talon-like fingertips.

Crossing the threshold, Frost was in a dim, wooden hall lined with lumographs of some far-off coastline. The large man that had collected him was marching a short distance ahead. Frost followed, his footsteps light until they met the bare floor of the larger space. It was a saloon, dark and musty, filled with smoke that hung above tables of patrons, each wearing ten-gallon hats or hooded robes.

There were flashes of lighting and rolling thunder, suppressed by the sound of rain hitting the outer doors and a silvery, slow song that was playing on an elegant radio resting on top of one of the crowded tables.

The barman nodded as the two men entered, spitting some dip into a spittoon while he finished polishing some glassware. Once done, he collected a tray and placed on it a pot of simmering tea, along with cubes of sugar, some milk, butter, and several slices of bread.

"Ah! I'm so glad you were able to join me, Your Honor!" said Frost, happily taking another swig of his drink.

He was speaking to Mayor Randolph, who was settling in at the only open table near the center of the place. Dressed in a plain but very tight evening coat and top hat, a sopping cloak was thrown over the back of his chair. On either side of him, an elite sentry bot was positioned. Both were wearing rigid bowler hats, maroon shirts, and waist-length suit jackets; the rest of them uncovered, their coppery cladding shone with each flash of lighting.

"Why wouldn't I?" Randolph spewed like a deflating balloon as the barman set down the tray of jostling things. "You did say that there was an urgent matter, did you not?"

"Yes, of the utmost importance," Frost replied, watching Randolph lunge for the butter. He scraped a huge glob of it over some bread and took a large bite.

"Then you should have come to Grand Hall!" Randolph said while chewing, waving around his half-eaten slice of limp bread. "Or even my manor! Instead, you've decided to have *me* come to *this*…hovel."

The barman cast a menacing stare Randolph's way, but the mayor didn't catch it.

"A certain amount of secrecy is required at times," Frost replied.

"Times such as this, I gather?"

Frost nodded while sipping.

"Well then!" Randolph said flatly. "Out with it."

Frost set his glass down on the tray – there was no room elsewhere on the small table – and placed his hands at the back of his neck, rubbing.

"Wherever do I start?" he said troublingly.

"At the *point*," Randolph scorned, tempted to grab at his pocket watch to see how much longer this meeting would be, but a cup of tea worked just as well.

"Have you noticed that Mr. Winthrope has been distracted?" Frost began. "Ever since taking this new woman in his life?"

Far too many sugar cubes plunked into Randolph's cup, causing it to splash then overflow.

"Really, Lucas!" Randolph snapped. "Had I known you wished to discuss Jesse's private love life this badly I would have added it to the agenda of our meeting earlier this week! Instead you've dragged me from the safety of the core boroughs into dangerous –"

"Excuse me?" interrupted the barman, his gruff voice loud. "I thought you were the mayor for all the people? We ain't good enough here in the *dangerous* parts of town? I'd have thought these parts would be needing the most attention!"

"Yes, I am in this for *all* the precious voters," Randolph replied, "no matter the rat hole they reside in…"

The barkeep slammed his fist on the top of the bar, several glasses breaking, and Frost immediately shot his hand up.

"Case in point," the mayor said smugly, peering over his cup at the barkeep. "We didn't have to wait long for that."

"Gentlemen! Enough!" called Frost. "Your Honor, it is not about what Winthrope is doing I have issue with, it's who he is doing it with."

Randolph left his cup in place and waited for more.

"Can you not see that his judgement has been compromised somehow by that girl?" Frost insisted. "I am concerned about the supply of metals in the future. Winthrope Limited could do with, or rather needs, better control at the top."

"And that better control would, in fact, be you?"

"No, but he is in this room," Frost said, pointing straight ahead.

Randolph let out a blubbery laugh and lowered his cup.

"You know that officials do not control corporations? Other than laws and taxes of course. You suspect that sliver of a girl Winthrope has on his arm is nefarious?" he said with doubt. "She makes a fine arm band, Lucas, but is hardly some kind of spy."

"I did not say she was a spy!" Frost downed two huge gulps of whiskey, banging the near empty glass on the tray. "Do you not see? Winthrope has lost his mind and the cause is that unsophisticated girl! He has forgotten who and what he is! Not to mention she was spotted coming out of raider territory – Pitchfork – before entering the city!"

Randolph looked bothered, pushing himself away from the table as his chair let out a pained scraping noise. Frost belched and shook his head drunkenly.

"We have plenty of traffic that passes through that area, Lucas. It is apparent to me that you are the one without full control right now. Please, get yourself sober. The matter is closed."

Frost's eyes narrowed; there was a menacing gleam in his mechanical one. He shot upright, his chair falling backwards with a loud crash against the floor.

Randolph jumped at the noise. Flustered, he stood up and reached for his cloak as his bot guards prepared to leave.

At the same time, Frost reached for his firearm.

"The matter is NOT closed!" he shouted over the roaring rain.

Sweat poured from Randolph's forehead and collected in his armpits.

"Lucas…"

BANG! BANG!

Randolph's arms had risen in terror. Realizing he was still alive, he frantically checked his body for bullet holes. There were none. However, there was a loud *boom* to his left; the guard had collapsed, sparking from its head and chest.

"What is the meaning of this?" Randolph shouted, his fists now clenched and trembling. His face was so red he looked like a plump tomato about to burst.

"Doing what I should have done earlier."

Randolph shuffled his way behind the other guard, pointing his fingers at Frost.

"Why are you just standing there? Shoot him!"

The sentry remained motionless.

Grabbing what was left of his drink, Frost swallowed it all then flung the empty glass over his shoulder. It shattered on the floor.

Unexpectedly, the barman didn't say a word about the damage or the mess. He slipped off down his side of the bar to an alcove at the end, pushed a hidden door open, and was gone. One of the hooded patrons sitting at the bar got up and eerily took his place.

Randolph looked around nervously, breathing hard through his nose.

"You know, Mr. Mayor," Frost said, pacing, his pistol waving flagrantly, "obedience is a wonderful thing, is it not? At least for those of us in authority who are being obeyed. People like Jesse, they don't believe that they need to, doing whatever they want, even if it means undermining the very principles that makes this civilization so grand. I think of them as cracks, you see, weakening our foundation to the point of collapse."

"And your perversions with sex bots, attraction to the same sex, and even that ink you try so hard to hide are not such corrupting cracks?"

Frost scowled before continuing, "That may be your opinion, but opinions only matter when the people who have them matter, too."

Randolph scoffed.

"Which brings me to control, which makes you matter. Simply put: I have it, you do not."

"How dare you speak to me like this! I am the mayor of this city! Elected…"

"Three times yes, but are you the one in control or the people who put you there? I don't recall the number of petitioners who helped with your funding right off the top of my head but I *can* recall that none of them have faced much scrutiny from the officials because of it. So, I repeat: who is really in charge?"

Randolph stammered.

"Did you notice how smoky it is in here?" Frost asked, stepping over to a neighboring table. He positioned himself behind one of the customers. "Yet, somehow there is no smell of tobacco. I wonder why that is?"

Frost yanked back the man's hood and instead of flesh and hair, there was cold, unfeeling metal. The rest of the saloon followed, revealing them all to be bots. All but one, who kept his hood up over by the bar.

"Something is very wrong here…" Randolph muttered.

"There you go again with your opinions! You see, the good thing about those who have control, Mr. Mayor…"

Frost removed a cylindrical device from his jacket pocket, looking it over lovingly. It was short and had ridged grip on it, along with a blue button at the tip. The hooded man by bar leaned forward, his eyes flickering with worry as if he knew what it was he saw.

"…is that you always know where the pieces are and thus, the outcome."

Frost mashed the button with his thumb and grinned.

At once, all the robots in the room started to buzz and shake as if having seizures. Randolph watched, tucked in safely behind his guard who, strangely, appeared unaffected by the mechanical massacre. Steam violently hissed out the others and filled the rafters with more haze. Clockwork parts fell to the floor, jangling in a multicolored gear-strewn mess. Arcs of blue and white electricity erupted from their heads, some of the more powerful bolts jetting around the room. It was chaos.

Then, as quickly as it began, the calamity stopped and all the bots collapsed where they sat or stood. The silence that followed seemed to amplify the sound of driving rain and another slow song on the radio ten-fold.

Randolph was drenched in sweat and his eyes shook as he looked to Frost with dread.

"That's one way to make sure their memory banks are cleared. Don't you worry, Mr. Mayor, I was never going to do anything to you," Frost said reassuringly, looking at Randolph. "Your guard is going to do it for me."

Randolph jerked his arms away from the bot he was clinging to, looking worryingly at its emotionless features as it raised its arm.

"Stop! I order you to stop!"

The bot did not comply, a barrel unfolding from its forearm. It planted the end right between the mayor's throbbing and sobbing eyes.

"Lucas, make it stop! Lucas ple–"

BANG!

Mayor Oscar Randolph was dead in an instant, the bot then turning the pistol on itself.

Frost stood alone in the saloon, everything around him dead or inactive. He took a moment to let it sink in before turning. Walking over to the radio, he flicked a small, recessed switch on the side. The music was replaced by static, then silence as he unclipped a microphone from the back of the unit. Pulling up a chair, Frost sat down in it and kicked his boots up on the tabletop.

Frost depressed a button on the side of the microphone.

"Come in."

"Passcode?" a static-ridden voice replied a short time later.

"Winter."

"Message received. Clean up gang is now on its way. You should leave now so you aren't around when they arrive, sir."

"Yes, yes I know. Be sure the body is placed in Sucio as discussed," Frost said.

"Understood."

Frost took a moment to consider all the bots around him.

"One last thing: let A3R0 know that he best be ready for me when I get back. I need relieved of the stresses from tonight."

"We have not seen him, sir, though he may be off wandering again."

Frost sighed, but his happiness prevented him from getting irate.

"Very well. I'll just punish him harder."

Turning off the radio, Frost stood and stretched casually.

It's all coming together quite nicely, he thought, *and victory is within my grasp.*

Frost buttoned up his coat and walked over to the hidden doorway the barman had used, looking at the hooded figure lying awkwardly with head teetering on the edge of the bar. He smirked at all the mechanical carnage, grabbed his umbrella, and exited through the passageway.

Once sure Frost was gone, the hooded man at the bar rose to his feet, his contorted joints fixing themselves on the spot.

"Oh, Master… what have you done?" said Aero as he looked took in the death and destruction that was around him.

He started to approach the mayor, who laid in a puddle of blood with a good chunk missing from his head, though his mouth was still wide open in a begging plea. Aero didn't have long to loiter; as the lighting flashed, he could make out the shapes of several rough-looking men approaching the saloon's front entrance. Retreating into the shadows, Aero made way for the back door, racing off into the rainy night with the memories of everything that happened still burning bright.

TWENTY-ONE

JESSE AND JENNY WERE EATING A light breakfast, perched high on the roof of Winthrope Limited.

"I'm so glad we got to do this; I thought the rain was never going to stop," Jenny said as she nibbled on a warm, buttery crumpet, a little of it drizzling down her chin.

"I know," Jesse replied, quick to catch the honey-colored streak with his thumb. Wiping the butter away, he gave it a teasing lick. "It's been murdering your hair."

Jenny's cheeks went a pale shade of red and she sent up a hand, inspecting. Sure enough, her hair had grown bushy since the rain had started earlier in the week and was frightfully a mess that morning.

"Why didn't you tell me earlier!" she retorted, giving him a nudge with an elbow. "Anyway, the same could be said about *your* beard!"

Jesse recoiled in feigned shock, saying, "Nobody talks bad about *this* beard!"

They both fell into carefree laughs, spirits higher than the birds that soared overhead.

Jesse lifted a thin glass off the breakfast tray and took a long sip of freshly squeezed juice (Logan's mechanical arm had talents beyond fierce punches). Looking out at the city, there was a vibrant sunrise to the east, bathing the normally drab buildings with a gorgeous sheen of liquid gold. Rising above that were two structures, nearly as tall as Winthrope's tower.

Jenny recognized one of them from her time in Comprass.

"What exactly is that?"

"Hmmm? The metal tower there?" Jesse asked. "That's a radio antenna. Owned by Gibson and Large, Inc. They broadcast most of the music you hear, but also handle the communications traffic for the officials – sheriffs mainly – and the larger companies like mine. Even holotube broadcasts are directed through there."

"Ah, I thought so," Jenny replied, quite pleased with herself. "We had something that looked similar back in the Gulch." Her eyes saddened for a moment, then recovered. "Not as tall obviously, but I thought it served the same purpose. Good to know I was right. What about the other one, over there?"

"That would be Frost Enterprises," Jesse said with loathing, speaking of the imposing pyramid and spiraling tower off to the north.

Jenny needn't ask more; she had learned over the past couple weeks all she needed to know about Frost and his ways. As she looked back to Jesse, the wind swept through the strands of ebony dancing on his face and the sunlight hit him in such a way that she was reminded about a dream – the one she had out in the wastes the night of the attack.

"Jesse," she said softly, "now that we've started to get to know each other…"

Jesse's brows crumpled together and his face became a blend of dread and confusion.

"What is it?" she asked.

"Just preparing myself. That phrase often prefaces something surprising, or negative, or surprisingly negative."

"What does that even mean? It's nothing bad, I swear. I just figured I could tell you about a dream…"

"Oh no, that's bad…" he said with a wince, bobbing his head rapidly.

"Stop it! A dream I had not too long ago. I hoped to tell you and you not think I'm insane."

"I know you're insane, Jenny, that's what attracted me to you."

She wanted to punch him in the nose so badly, but his brown eyes had an effect of vanishing anger with the slightest effort. At least it worked on her that way.

"We'll see if that's still the case when I'm done telling you," she giggled, then began to recount the details of her dream – from the desolate wastelands to the city in the distance to the man and woman swept up in a storm.

As her words filled Jesse's ears, his eyes seemed to grow with familiarity and Jenny carried on for a few more rambling seconds until she noted his expression.

"Oh gosh! You think I AM insane!" she cried.

"Jenny, no… no… far from that," Jesse replied. Visibly stricken, he set down his juice, reached for her hands, and clasped them. "You are not going to believe this, because I really don't even believe it myself, but after hearing what you just told me… I might have had the same dream not two weeks ago. Well, not as a woman, but you get the gist."

Jenny sat in silent disbelief as her eyes darted everywhere other than on Jesse. Then, suddenly they snapped back.

"You're insane!"

She was positive that he was teasing her again, searching for a hint of it desperately, but when she looked deep into his eyes she realized that there was no joke behind it.

"That's impossible!"

"I know!" Jesse replied briskly, as if that would make the fact it was true disappear. It didn't work of course, and they both sank into thoughts about it.

Jenny was the first to say something.

"Hmmm, the figures are obviously searching for something," she said, trying her hand at some dream interpretation.

"Look at you, being all witchy," Jesse said flirtatiously. "You know, they used to kill people for that?"

"I'm sure there are still people in this city that do. In fact, one of them works for you and always has her hair drawn up in a bun," she smirked. "Though she wouldn't be able to charge me with much. It is pretty apparent, isn't it, that the figures are us?"

"Yeah, I was thinking the same. You and I both seemed to be on a search for something or… someone to fill in a hole in here." He pointed at his chest. "Lucky I think we might have been successful at it."

"Yes!" she said excitedly. "Hence the turmoil in our lives, represented by the dust storm, was sent away and the skies cleared when our eyes locked!"

"You've confirmed it for me: you are quite insane," Jesse said as her enthusiasm flowed over him. "And I mean that in the best way possible. So, let's say that it is indeed us, that still doesn't explain how the dreams were *exactly* the same, and the timing of…"

"Who cares?" Jenny said bluntly. "Why are you looking at me like that? You said it yourself, back at the garden. Why must we know the answers to everything? Perhaps, this is nothing more than destiny."

Jesse smiled and said, "If it is destiny, then it is everything. Do you believe in that sort of thing?"

"Well, I…" she hesitated, looking away to the east where the

Gulch used to be. "I can't say that my life has been full of blessings to make me think so. Do you?"

Jesse took in a deep breath, exhaling as he watched the climbing sun.

"My life has been the opposite of yours, its journey full of wealth and blessings beyond the lives of many down there. Yet, it was empty until I found myself here on the roof of my building, eating breakfast and talking to you, thinking that I must dreaming while knowing that I am awake."

Jenny took her hand and rested it gently on her chest as a light breeze billowed in her hair.

"We have both walked different paths through our rather mechanical lives," Jesse continued, "doing our daily routines, forever locked on a track that we think is inescapable – for fear of breaking ourselves, for failing, or losing our way. But for me, destiny is arriving where we arrive regardless of the path we take. Those of us who have not only mind and body, but spirit enough to be unbound can do it. I'd like to think that no matter what happened to either of us along the way, we would still have ended up here."

"What are you saying, Jesse? That we are destined to be together?"

"I'm saying let's not lose sight of the gift that's been given to us; something no contraption or timepiece can ever hope to possess."

"Love?"

"Yes… love," Jesse said, about to kiss her. "I guess that was my way of saying yes, I believe in destiny…"

"Isn't that the most sickening thing I have heard in a very long time," came a deep voice from behind the two of them. "Although I must say thank you to you both for being in the same place and making these fine gentlemen's jobs easy. Rangers, please, do your duty and place both of these murderers under arrest."

TWO HARDENED RANGERS tipped their broad hats at the man between them, then approached Jesse and Jenny with their dusters kicking in the breeze and badges glinting in the sunlight. Seized by the arm, unfeeling cold steel clamped over the couple's wrists and they were jerked to their feet, unresisting.

"Lucas!" Jesse shouted. The ranger holding him tightened his grip in case Jesse planned on lunging. "What is the meaning of this outrage?"

"Murderers?" Jenny exclaimed. "What are you talking…"

Frost sent a single finger skyward from his otherwise gloved fist, then brought it to his lips.

"Shhh… men are talking."

"Don't talk to her that way!" Jesse snapped, a shot of anger rising from his chest into a dagger-like stare.

Jenny shrank, her shoulders dropping, and looked down as Frost edged forward, each footstep clunking on the roof until he stopped mere centimeters from Jesse's nose. His golden eye glimmered with enjoyment as he looked down the bridge of his nose at his longtime rival.

"The meaning of this 'outrage' is to see the two who conspired against the goodwill of this city and its citizens – the wonderful Winthrope and his wasteland whore – punished for their crimes. The mayor is dead, found in Sucio with a gunshot wound to the face. As if you did not already know…"

Frost's words were dripping with an awful coat of gratification.

Both Jenny and Jesse looked at each other, lost for words. Jenny's expression turned from one of confusion to panic, having heard stories about Frost but seeing him in person was a different matter, never mind her first meeting being one in which he was having her arrested for a crime she did not commit.

"Dead? Shot?" Jesse mumbled, his mind racing and revolted at the images it was conjuring. "I have no idea what you're talking about, Lucas, but we need to actually get to the bottom of this!"

His sincerity fell on six deaf ears.

"Ah but you would say that, wouldn't you? Throw us off to prevent others in your little, or perhaps large, web of conspiracy to be discovered? Mark my words, if they are there, they will be found. I have already started the process to have your friend from Lagos investigated in this matter. What was his name? Duncan?"

"He's innocent, and you are jeopardizing this water trade deal with them!"

"Then he should have no fear of an inquiry," said the ranger holding Jenny.

"You seem more concerned about that deal and your pocketbook, Jesse, than the fact our people are suffering, potentially at the mercy of raiders. Then again, it all makes perfect sense as a motive when coupled with the taxes the mayor was going to levy on your expanded mining operations, themselves leaving us more vulnerable to wasteland ruffians like this woman beside you."

"That deal was *not* for my pockets, it was for the people! The same ones you claim I do not hold respect for!" Jesse shouted, his words rightfully spilling over each other in a near ramble. "And Jenny's own town was destroyed by raiders; she would do nothing to help them!"

"Is that wholly true, Miss Boone?" asked Frost. callous and unyielding.

"I would never help them," Jenny shot back.

"But one did help you," Frost said innocuously, looking right at Jesse when he did it. "Am I wrong?"

Jenny didn't answer that question and by that, Jesse's mouth drooped half-open, clearly shocked at the revelation.

"I'll explain…" said Jenny regretfully, on the verge of tears.

Jesse glared at her, about to say something when Frost cut in.

"Tsk, Tsk, Jesse, you really should be more careful with who you choose as friends, especially those you end up bringing into your little inner circle."

TWENTY-TWO

JESSE AND JENNY WERE FORCED down a long hall with heavy metal doors lining both sides. It was dark and would have been entirely black if not for a single circular window at the end, positioned high as to let a shaft of light in to see, but afford no view of what lied outside.

The lead ranger stopped outside one of the doors about two-thirds of the way down, unlocking three massive padlocks then sliding three substantial deadbolts to the side. Each made a ringing *clang* as it opened.

"Get in," the trailing ranger ordered and when neither Jesse or Jenny moved, he shoved them both hard.

They stumbled into a room nearly as dank as the hall, with its own slender window that was too high to look out of. Before they could thank their escorts' hospitality, the solid door shut with an echoing *boom*.

"What is going on?" Jenny asked now that they were alone,

shading her eyes as the light from the window gleamed right into them.

Jesse turned around and leaned on the wall; it was wet and he didn't want to think long on why. Moving away, he dropped to the floor and sat there with both of his hands on his head, fingers drumming.

"You tell me," he muttered while his shackles rattled.

"What? You think I had something to do with this thing and Frost?" Jenny asked, heart cracking from stress and sadness, breaking her from the inside out.

"Not this, Jenny, what Luc... what Frost said. About a raider helping you. That's the last thing I expected, if what you said about your escape was true."

Jenny's lips bowed and she sighed, trying to smooth the ends of her hair with her fingertips.

"Is it true? About the raider?"

"Yes," Jenny replied and Jesse's face went flat and empty. "But it's not what you think!"

"What else could it be, Jenny?" he bellowed, writhing as if an itch had taken over every part of his body and he couldn't ease it. "Did you conspire with them? Plan all this to use against me?"

"I'm in here, too!" she cried. "In case you haven't noticed."

Although it hurt to be accused of such a thing after losing her life out there in the wastes, she dove into a detailed, if not jumpy, explanation of what happened that night after the attack. She described how Aftershock helped her escape, provided shelter, and even escorted her of his own accord to Pitchfork.

"So, you see Jesse, he isn't like other raiders," she emphasized, leaving out the personal details he'd told. "I thought he was at first – like you and everyone else does – but spending time with him made me realize I was wrong. Frost can say what he wants to try and use it against you, but if not for Aftershock, I wouldn't be alive. I owe it to him to stay true to that."

Jesse seemed swayed, but then insisted with a last-ditch effort that, "He had to have an ulterior motive. Wanting *things* from you."

"I can safely say the answer to that is an indisputable no," she answered, a bit coyly and in different circumstances would probably have giggled. "Besides, you should be the first one embracing someone that doesn't fit into society's mold, since you manage to avoid getting lumped into a shiny, elite box so well."

Unable to deny that, and sensing the passion in Jenny's words, the tingle in Jesse's nerves started to fade away. He could breathe a little easier, although the musty room presented its own challenges.

"Thank you for that," he said softly, rubbing his head one more time before looking up at her. "When you first told me the story in the garden you stopped right after the attack. Now I understand why you had your reasons for not mentioning Aftershock before. But, since you've confided that information to me, that trust goes a long way."

Jenny smiled, and that drove away Jesse's torment, at least for a little while.

"What happens now?" she asked, getting closer to him but remaining standing.

"Being in the core boroughs we're lucky; even you not being an elite."

"Thank goodness for being in the right place at the right time," Jenny said.

"With the right person," Jesse clarified as he looked ruefully up to her. "I know that sounds egotistical, but it's not meant to be; they literally *have* to go through the process since you've been accused alongside me. That clearly assumes whatever is happening here is legitimate. If it is, there will be a hearing first, to see if there is enough evidence for a trial before one of the city's magistrates. With Frost trying to involve Duncan in this, and limiting his travels, I know that it's a blatant move to keep his legal prowess at bay."

"That's not good for us…"

"No, not at all…" Jesse said, trailing off worriedly.

"Something more?"

"Yes," Jesse answered a moment later, troubled. His eyes had been shifting quickly, as if he was reading through a set of documents in his mind. "The more I think on it, the more I think there isn't going to be a hearing."

"Even with your resources and influence they'd be so quick to put the noose around our necks?"

"We'd see the gallows by the end of this day if they could. All it takes is someone willing to pay more Gears than the other party to tip the balance in their favor."

Jesse's eyes started moving again as thoughts consumed him, the silence lasting a few minutes.

"Anything else?" Jenny asked with baited breath.

"Frost. I don't have any proof, I have a feeling he has something, if not everything, to do with this."

"I've been thinking the same thing in the back of my mind."

Jesse let out a frustrated grunt and Jenny jumped, startled by the suddenness of it. Standing back up, Jesse grasped Jenny by the shoulders and hugged her. He could feel her stirring restlessly in his embrace, so he kissed her softly on the forehead to take some of the worry away.

"We need more time," he told her, "a delay, anything to help us get the evidence we need to –"

Jesse stopped mid-sentence; he could hear someone scuttling around outside the door.

Did they hear us? he thought, wondering if they had been overheard. Looking around for a holorecorder or microphones, none were immediately visible.

Regardless there was jostling…

Followed by three ringing *clangs*…

Whoever it was coming in and doing it fast.

"Jenny, get behind me!"

Before Jesse had finished getting into position, the door flew open and hit the wall of the cell with a deafening *bang*. The duo slammed their hands against their ears for all the ringing that continued.

In front of them was a man, draped in a hooded cloak that covered his head and a dark, loosely buttoned shirt.

"Mr. Winthrope, Miss Boone, you must come with me!"

Jesse didn't recognize the voice, frantic but also boyish in tone. He thought, for a silly moment, that he might have even seen flickers of blue light coming from beneath the hood.

"Why would we go anywhere with you?" he asked firmly, keeping an arm positioned to guard Jenny.

The man immediately pointed to the open door.

"Well… um… okay…. then who are you?" Jesse pressed.

"Mr. Winthrope, please, there isn't much time. My name is Aero and I promise to answer your questions, but along the way! We must leave before…"

The alarm klaxons started sounding and the area was filled with a shrill whine that came and went in a repeating pattern.

Aero flung his cloak aside and tossed each of them a pistol; they were bulkier than normal with large barrels and rectangular ends.

"These are non-lethal," he told them. "But do pack a punch."

"Are *theirs* non-lethal?" Jesse asked cynically, eyeing his gun as if it were a toy.

"No, of course not. They're Rangers," Aero replied, "which means they would not have additional and *legitimate* charges filed against them should they kill any of you. Now come!"

Without another word, Aero tore down the hall.

"Self-defense is always a good go to," Jesse added, giving a quick look to Jenny. "Right?"

"I don't think that applies when you are escaping from a jail."

Giving each other a swift kiss, the pair bounded out of the cell, nearly stumbling on a body just as they came around to the left. They ran past several more Rangers lying on the ground as they ran, unconscious if Aero had used either of the pistols he off-loaded.

"Seems like our savior has been busy," Jenny said with quickened breath.

"Yeah, he has, though I'm not sure he's one of us, if you know what I mean."

Jenny's expression told that she wasn't sure, and when she answered "No" with great puffs of air, Jesse chuckled.

"You'll see."

Aero had stopped up ahead at an intersecting row of cells, three more Rangers coming through the door in front of him. As they raced down the hall, they fired their deadly rounds and he managed to nimbly evade them, leaving pockmarks in sections of floor that had been occupied just seconds before.

Jesse snatched Jenny and heaved them both to the side, striking the wall just in time for stray bullets to whizz by.

Aero continued to dodge his attackers gracefully, almost acrobatic in his skill. At one point he saw an opportunity, leaping up and off a wall, flinging his cloak off in mid-air. The heavy garment draped itself over nearby ranger, which gave Aero just enough time to land, spin, and kick him into the opposite wall.

Jenny could now see what Jesse meant as Aero continued his ballet. His shirt sleeves were rolled up to his elbows and along his forearms was a peculiar material that looked very much like skin, but carved lines separating it into plates broke the illusion.

Step by bullet-dodging step the two of them managed to get closer, at last retuning fire on the remaining two Rangers. They hit their targets after a brief exchange, the big ammo knocking them unconscious. Reaching Aero, they saw that he was not tired nor sweating like they were.

"Where to now?" Jesse asked, resting with a hand on his hip, taking in the strangeness of a bot helping them.

"We will be outnumbered and out of ammo if we go through the main entrance," Aero stated. The sound of more footsteps was in the distance; a lot of them. "Yet, we will also be pursued if we are seen going down either of these side pathways."

"Where do they lead?" Jenny asked, quickly looking at her shoulder, which had a dull and burning pain. A bullet must have grazed her, Jesse flying over to tend to it.

"Pardon me," he said, ripping off a large portion of her sleeve before wrapping it firmly around the wound to stop the bleeding.

"Could you get that any tighter?"

"Nope," he said while admiring his handiwork and her lopsided outfit. "There you are, all mended and setting new end-of-century fashion trends."

A quick series of beeps emanated from Aero and then he said, "To the left is a cafeteria and the right the garage; both have access to the city. I recommend that we head to the left; there will likely be fewer encounters."

"But won't that keep us on foot? There are vehicles to the right, correct?" Jesse asked, hearing those footsteps get closer with every word.

"Yes. That is often what you place in a garage."

Jesse sputtered and tried not to look annoyed.

"Well, do you think we can *commandeer* one and get out of the building? Possibly out of the city?"

"Accessing..." Aero said amongst more beeps. "Yes, there

are a couple of motor carriages in there; one is an experimental convertible unit that may be our best chance."

"Well experimental is my middle name!" said Jesse excitedly.

"Your middle name is Elliot, Mr. Winthrope."

"It's a... never mind... Aero, right?"

Aero nodded as Jenny looked distraught, the thought of leaving so soon after she arrived was exhausting.

"There will be nowhere safe for us to hide within Diablo," Jesse said, noticing her appearance. "The tower has likely broadcast our names and likenesses across the entire area by now. Plus, it's not like I can go many places and not be noticed. We must do this. I can stay in touch with –"

A gunshot rang out, the bullet striking Aero in the shoulder. It sparked upon impact, but the damage was minimal. Aero looked in the direction the shot was fired and saw a ranger preparing to fire again. Launching a few non-lethal strikes his way, the ranger was taken out of commission.

"We have lingered too long," said Aero, "neither of you can stay, nor can I now. But, where do we go from here?"

"Let's go," Jesse suggested. "We can mull on that once we are out of here."

"Jesse, we can drive it east!" Jenny said excitably. "Aftershock's out there. I know where to go."

The Rangers were arriving, the first starting to trickle in though the entrances.

"We are out of time," Aero said, and a compartment unfolded in his forearm. He reached inside and removed a pair of goggles with some extremely dull lenses. Ripping them in half, he held them out. "Take these and use them to follow."

"Follow what?" Jenny asked.

"Me."

Suddenly, from within Aero, there was a tremendous burst

of smoke and steam. Jenny shrieked as it flew forward, filling the room with a haze that was so thick it was impossible to see anything more than a half-meter ahead.

Disoriented, Jesse raised the goggle half in his hand to his eye and surprisingly, he could see! Not like he normally would, nor very clearly, but the faint lines around Aero's body that had appeared black were now glowing with a faint blue light through the glass.

"Jenny!" called Jesse.

"I got it!" she replied.

"Excellent!" said Aero as he charged toward the garage, unseen by the Rangers now mired in the haze. "Follow me!"

<hr>

A LARGE FOUR-WHEELED motor carriage ripped around the corner, sending people screaming and diving in all directions to avoid getting run over while its wheels skidded harshly on the bumpy cobblestone. The eccentric thing flew down the streets like a bullet, its wide passenger cab and sleek, silver lines tapering to two large lamps at the front.

"I seem to have lost our pursuers," Aero said, maintaining the high speed.

"Is it broken?" Jenny asked over a horrendous noise.

Aero made another daring swerve, missing a monger but crashing through his market stall, sending a rain of cheese splattering around the area.

"I'll pay you back for those!" Jesse shouted over the unique chittering noise from under the hood. Turning attention back to Jenny he told her, "It's nothing to worry about… just the sound of this particular steam engine. The old dirigible-styled airships make a noise just like it."

"I'm not so sure that reassures me," she responded, tossed around as the carriage rushed across several potholes. "You'd think the core boroughs wouldn't have any missing pavers!"

"You're correct in that statement, Miss Boone; we aren't in the core anymore," Aero replied calmly, his chest bearing slight electrical burns from their garage escape (courtesy of a ranger trying to short circuit him with a bo prod). "The holding cells are actually in Carcel, close to the western edge of the city."

"So, when we get out of here," Jesse took over, "we're going to have to loop around the city – taking a wide berth – to head toward your contact out east."

"That is if we get there," Jenny said. "We have company!"

Two monocycles and their riders had rejoined the chase, their colossal tires churning up the debris left Winthrope's wake while plumes of chugging steam were left in their own.

One of the drivers leaned to the side, wasting no time now that they were back in his sights. Firing his gun, the bullets struck the back window, right in front of Jenny's face. She screamed, yet the glass held and did not shatter.

"Who's vehicle *is* this?" she asked, swiping a finger across the jagged but intact areas where the bullets impacted.

"I've no idea," Jesse answered, "but I certainly want to get my hands on one after all this is straightened out!"

Another hail bullets struck and Aero flung the car down a narrow side street to evade, then again onto a main thoroughfare. Trash was thrown everywhere and more people leapt for their lives as the riders followed relentlessly through the zigzag of streets.

"They're still coming!" Jenny said, watching them weave past a smattering of grape crates Aero had just plowed through.

She was half-listening to Jesse – shouting at Aero about driving through a saloon next to complete his bill for the most expensive wine, fruit and cheese plate ever – while also observing their pursuers.

The closest rider pressed a large green button on one of his levers and his cycle suddenly sprang forward, closing the gap quickly. Pulling a different lever, a couple of armatures popped out from the front of the unit and began to drop, folding out like the arms of a praying mantis. They latched onto a space between the bumper and chassis and the car shuddered greatly.

Applying his brakes, the rider forced Winthrope's vehicle to slow down, allowing the second monocycle catch up and do the same.

"We're slowing down too much," Jesse muttered, hoping Aero had a plan formulating in that bot brain of his.

"Brace yourselves," Aero replied.

"Wait… what?" Jesse wasn't expecting anything so soon.

A split second later, Aero turned the wheel hard left and the whole grouping of carriage and cycles spun.

The first cycle hit the corner of a clockwork parts store, splintering into a shower of gears, metal, and wood. The second was hanging on tightly, its rider firing nonstop at the reinforced glass.

Aero spun the wheel in the other direction, takin the carriage precariously close to the building walls. Luckily for them, as they turned the cycle struck hard against an iron barricade, sending parts scattering all up and down the street. The largest fragment – the steam engine – cartwheeled overhead and took out the doors of a saloon.

Jesse tried not to think about the damage inside, instead opting to stare intently at Aero.

"You didn't hear a word I said about that, did you?"

Jenny would have laughed, but a bracing thought overwhelmed her.

"Gentlemen, not to put a damper on our escape, but given all this commotion won't the officials have the gates blocked?"

Jesse's expression went from sour to pale in the blink of an eye and as if in answer, when they rounded Sunset Boulevard the large doors of the western gatehouse were barred and a line of Rangers were ready to stop their advance.

Aero made another harsh turn down a side street, the carriage jostling harshly as the road was not meant for vehicles. The good news was there were no Rangers down this way. The bad news was the city wall was coming right at them.

"Aero, didn't you say this thing was a convertible?" Jenny asked with frantic haste. "What does it convert to?"

"I didn't get a chance to look," Aero said calmly. "I used the technical manual to beat the ranger that shocked me. Then it caught fire and burned to a cinder."

"Which is what will happen to us if we don't do something!" Jesse bellowed as he looked around for anything that would help.

Aero found a button marked with an ornate C and pressed it, the vehicle starting to hum promisingly before…

The roof flew off and crashed behind them.

With the wall approaching fast, Jenny and Jesse reached for each other and embraced while Aero continued to look for a solution.

"Ah, here we are," he said, flipping a switch that was engraved with three small letters: FLT.

Then, from the back, a large propeller-like engine emerged and wings sprouted from beneath and the sides like some graceful mechanical butterfly. Moments later, the motor carriage took flight and rose, higher and higher, until they barely crested the walls.

Jesse looked behind as they soared away.

Winthrope Limited, his family's crowning achievement,

seemed to weep as sunlight danced across the windows of the building. He then looked to Diablo itself as Aero banked starboard for the long loop back east. From that height, the city looked like a segmented clock, the intricate swirls formed by streets entangled with patterns formed by the rooftops, all set within more complex shapes made by interior walls, decorative features like the sundial of Grayson Market, and more.

Now, it was his turn to weep, and wiping tears from his eyes he apologized for leaving the steam powered city in the clutches of a cold man named Frost.

TWENTY-THREE

DUSK WAS CREEPING ACROSS THE land, Aftershock's mountain camp beneath a sky full of wheeling stars wrapped in a purplish hue. The blue of moonlight mingled with the red of a campfire burning at the crest of the northernmost peak, while spread out on the plains below were no less than a dozen other pinpricks of flickering crimson. Two dark figures huddled around the sputtering flames, light dancing across Aftershock's tired features. As he sat quietly scratching his beard, the other figure sitting across from him was looking out intensely at the surrounding vista.

The handsome man was named Wyatt Jameson – widely known as Lobo – and he was younger than Aftershock, but not by much. Their beards on the other hand were vastly different; where Aftershock's was thick and bushy, his was far shorter, thinner, and neater. A pair of large silver goggles were resting on top of his head, flattening his short black hair, and across his chest and arms were colorful tattoos. There was a leather pauldron strapped over one of his shoulders, gauntlet over a forearm, and across his back, a pipe rifle etched with a handmade pattern.

"You look like you're about to bust something in your brain thinking so hard, Lobo. Cog for your thoughts?" said Aftershock lowly.

"Huh?" the man replied, shifting focus to Aftershock. From his torn denims, an artificial leg studded with spikes and painted skulls gleamed in the firelight. "Oh. It's nothing really. Just wondering if I'm good enough for this. Things are changing so damn fast."

"Good enough for what? Leading the Devil's Shadow or…"

"Yeah that," Lobo replied quickly, plucking off one of the glass vials he had strapped across his upper left arm. He took a sip, his lips curling back over his teeth. "I'm sitting here wondering if I rushed into this. Someone like *you* should be in this position; not me. Hell, me just talking to you about this kind of thing shows I'm not fit to lead."

"It tells me the exact opposite, Lobo," Aftershock said, looking down at the campfires below. "It's a challenge no doubt, but the fact you realize you have imperfections is something half the clan leaders out there would never admit, the other half too dumb to realize.

"That gives you strength for this, since you know that you have to work for what you want and even harder still to keep it." He paused, seeing Lobo ease up a bit. "That said, I wouldn't talk too openly about it…plenty out there are looking for things to exploit. I'm a testament to that mistake. Keep it inside, knowing it, and owning it."

"Yeah that's why I feel comfortable talking only to you about it brother, especially since getting to know you over the last month. That was a bad situation for you and your blood. Not sure I would've made it." Lobo took another sip, offering some to Aftershock.

"I got stronger waiting for me once the others return with grub," he replied, waving it off.

"Suit yourself," Lobo answered by taking another swig.

"Besides, I'll leave the drinking of that lutrine spittle to you."

"Hey, I told you that there's only a couple of drops in this liquor! Keeps me looking young, fit, and with hair."

Aftershock's eyes narrowed and suddenly he looked ready to punch him in the throat.

"If looks could kill, right?" Lobo smirked.

"If only! At least I know how to grow a proper beard," Aftershock laughed, slipping back to a serious look shortly after. His fingers were restless. "Lobo, I wouldn't be around to offer any of these opinions had you not stepped in back at Pitchfork…"

"Nothing to it. I saw a brother in need, one that took care of that menace we called a chief. Didn't have a second thought about vouching for you before the others cut your head off."

"Technically, it was Jenny that took care of Dante…"

"True, but either way, you have my respect. That's something that's long been missing in this clan."

"You got mine too, and my loyalty. I don't forget where I've been or who's helped my needy ass along the way."

"Ah, yes, loyalty. I value that a lot; it's a core principle for me. Don't have it and your words are nothing but sounds and letters falling out of your mouth – empty and better left unsaid so you can keep your lungs full of breath."

Aftershock was beaming.

"And here it was, you were doubting yourself not ten minutes ago. Sounds like everything is as it should be."

"Hope it is," said Wyatt, popping the now empty vial back into its slot on his arm band.

The sound of crunching soil and murmuring rose over the cracking wood, both raiders turning to see three shapes – two men and a woman – coming around the corner.

"Ah there you are!" Aftershock boomed. "Finally, and just in the nick of time. Was about to lop off ol' Lobo's other leg for a bite."

Jenny was in front of the others, carrying two plates loaded with fresh beef, potatoes, and some greens. There was even a slice of cornmeal bread.

"Hey now," she retorted, smiling heavily, "you could have just as easily drug yourself down there with us."

"Nah, was too comfortable up here on these hard rocks. Plus, my friend here makes for good conversation."

Jenny smiled, walking toward Aftershock to hand him a plate, but Jesse cut in front of her and handed him one of the two he was carrying.

"There you go," he said wearing a thin smile in the trembling light. One of the logs in the fireplace fell awkwardly, sending a plume of sparks and flames into the air. "I'm sure it tastes just as good so be sure to enjoy it."

Jesse was having some trouble adjusting to Aftershock, appreciative of his efforts in saving Jenny but something else was digging in his craw. Jenny liked to assume it was because they were both so similar in nature and it clashed at times, but her gut was far blunter, suggesting it was because Aftershock chose to walk around without a shirt all the time and was in no way a traditionally hideous raider as expected.

As Jesse continued toward Lobo to give him his food, Jenny slid her eyes over to Aftershock with a repentant shrug of her shoulders. He didn't seem to mind, shaking his head coolly before shoveling meat into his mouth, its savory drippings wetting his beard.

Aero brought up the rear, carrying two pails full of long-lasting dried goods to place in the cave's compartments. Lobo eyed the bot's synthetic arms as he worked, wondering if his legs were of the same design.

"Hey, Jesse," he said, in part out of curiosity but also to diffuse the tension, "are those things expensive?"

Jesse was taking a seat next to him, Jenny handing him the plate originally meant for Aftershock, and answered, "Bots? Older editions aren't too much, finding their way into alternative uses and piece parts. But one like Aero there is unique. I've never seen one like him."

Lobo popped a wedge of potato in his mouth and chewed loudly.

"How about one of those legs?"

"I think it was about two-hundred Gears," Jesse answered.

"Just for the leg, eh? Never mind that!" Lobo said, giving his own artificial leg a thumb with his utensil. "I could buy a whole lot of shit for that kind of money."

"Hopefully it's good quality shit," Aftershock added and laughter made its way around the camp fire, even from Jesse.

"Well ladies and gents, I hate to be the one to talk business while we eat," said Lobo unhappily, "but now's as good a time as any. The Pack down there is starting to show signs of getting restless. I'll make sure that the Shadows are here for the long haul, but if we don't act soon – whatever that may be – we are going to lose that entire clan's support."

Grumbling and murmurs filled the air.

"I wish we could just pay them," Jesse said as he let his fork drop on the plate. "That would make all of this so much easier."

"It would for sure," Lobo replied, "but that's kind of the reason we have them here in the first place."

Aftershock and Jesse nodded in reluctant agreement but

Jenny had apparently missed that part of the conversation over the last two weeks.

"Sorry, but why would that be the case? I'd think anyone out here would want the money. Send it my way if not."

Aftershock chuckled.

"Normally that's the case," he said, "but for raiders it's an honor thing. Yes, money is plundered and people end up killed, but in a weird sort of way, they end up earning the spoils. It's not just given, which any true-blooded raider would take as an insult."

"Seems the Vipers were playing dirty," Lobo continued, using his fork to move his veggies around, "and the Pack found out about it. You see, there were whispers about two, maybe three months ago that their clan confirmed. Some city-dweller had plans to build himself an army. For what end game we don't know, but an army is normally used for one thing."

"Taking territory and then holding it after," Jesse said spitefully. "Yet, he needed to convince certain people that there was a major threat in the first place. Then, he would be able to do his work and build those forces without suspicion. Three guesses as to who we're talking about. I bet you only need one."

"Frost," she said sourly.

"Yep!" confirmed Aftershock, finishing his meal and folding his arms over his chest. "Turns out he was the one that supplied weapons and parts to the Vipers, and paid them well enough to attack the pipelines leading out of Diablo…"

"And the Gulch?" Jenny said, her sparkling eyes both sad and angry. With the plate resting in her lap, her hands vigorously rubbed her forearms.

Everyone stayed still and quiet except Aero, who had finished packing away provisions in the cave and had come to join them.

"Yes," he replied. "Master was quite vocal about it once he

had heard the news. Thrilled would be the word I would use to describe him."

Jenny was fuming. She had been standing no more than a meter away from the bastard that caused the death of her old life and she had no idea. None of them did at the time.

"It all makes sense to you now, doesn't it?" Jesse asked, recalling the weekly meetings with the mayor at Grand Hall. "He wanted sway the population into his waiting arms, thinking that more powerful and frequent raider activity would lead to an increased demand for security in Diablo."

"Speaking of there, has there been any word on how things are?" Jenny was concerned for the few nice people she had met along the way. "It's been nearly a week since we sent word to our contacts. With the mayor gone and you too, Jesse, he pretty much has free reign of the place."

Jesse frowned, so deeply he appeared to sink down into the stone a few centimeters.

"Got word from someone named Marcus at the Junction today," said Lobo, causing Jesse and Jenny to perk up with great interest. "Would have said something sooner but we were dealing with the stubborn Pack and their issues."

"What'd he say?" asked Jesse.

Lobo proceeded to summarize the report he'd received (from those monitoring an old radio Aero had fixed up), starting with the fact that Frost didn't seem to bothered by their escape.

"He's not calling for searches or anything like it," Lobo said, though he is incredibly angry with the bot." All eyes fell on Aero. "He's made it quite known that you are at the top of his shit list…"

Aero's eyes looked away from the rest, and he placed his arms across his thighs.

"But yeah, he went straight for it and assumed control while things were in chaos," Lobo continued. "I guess it was all sparked by your departure and he did so in the interest of, how was it Marcus put it? Peace and stability."

"What kind of control?" Jenny asked as Jesse stood up and started walking around, still within earshot of Lobo.

Lobo watched Jesse carefully as he continued.

"Someone named Evelyn reported that Frost went for Winthrope Limited."

Jesse immediately kicked the ground, a dusty, stony cloud of debris launching from the spot. He wanted to scream but spared the others from seeing his anger spill over. Frost was walking around *his* home, looking through *his* things, and stealing *his* inventions.

"You all right Jesse?" asked Aftershock, removing a flask from his pocket and flinging it at him. "You need that more than I do right now."

"Do you want to know more?" Lobo asked out of courtesy.

Jesse opened the flask and swallowed two hefty gulps of liquor. It burned as it went down but he couldn't care less. Holding onto it for a little longer, sure he'd need it, he nodded.

"Lemme guess, he's been busy making steam capsules for all sorts of things?" Jesse said, taking another preemptive guzzle.

Lobo shook his head saying, "Marcus didn't mention anything about steam capsules, whatever those are. He did say that several of your factories are making parts for something called a battery, while his are using your alloy specifications to make new bots."

Jesse's groan could have been a herd wild creatures for how loud it was. He stormed off to the edge of the overlook and took another drink. Aftershock got up and swaggered over.

"How are the people doing, Wyatt? Okay?" Jenny asked.

"Marcus didn't say all too much, but I gathered from what he did tell me, and some reading between the lines, that there's a menacing air hanging over the city. Citizens are confused, wondering where the officials are, and being mistreated by Frost's emboldened security forces. Violence hasn't erupted, yet, but tensions are running high."

"That's dreadful!" Jenny said, horrified. "We have to do something!"

"What, just waltz up in there and ask Frost to stop being mean?" Jesse said on his way back with Aftershock, who was now holding the flask. "We've been thinking about this for two weeks now and not finding many options on the table, fewer still to make all the wrongs done right again."

"So, what are you saying?" Jenny snapped. "Now you just want to live in the wastes?"

"That isn't what I said at all!" Jesse yelled, his voice cracking at the height of strain. The two of them stared at each other, equally stressed, and suddenly Jesse felt as if the stars were watching, judging, laughing at his plight.

"all right everyone, just calm down," Aftershock urged. "I'm the first in line for a good fight but we don't need to be wasting energy ripping each other's throats out."

Lobo dropped his shoulders and looked down at his boots; there was a hole worn into the left one and his toe was sticking out of it. Wiggling it, he sighed.

"I hope a plan forms soon, because if it's something that we want to involve the Pack with, it needs to be soon."

The group fell quiet as they ate their meals, the long days and nights with little sleep starting to show signs. Nerves had already been frayed and every little nuance, glance, or loud chew was enough to shred them that little bit more.

Aero sat and watched them alertly, neither tired nor hungry.

"Might I say something?" he asked politely, breaking the strangling silence.

Aftershock and Lobo were the first to look his way; both didn't know what to say. Lobo felt a bit disturbed by the whole notion of bots, especially this one who looked more alive than any he'd seen before and acted like it, too. Aftershock on the other hand was intrigued, starting at the bot's ice blue eyes and thinking, for a second only, that there was more.

"I think you're entitled to that," Jesse said. "You did save us from the gallows, after all."

Jenny smiled, a little hope rekindled, saying, "What do you have for us, Aero?"

The bot exhaled intensely, a strange thing to see and hear which caused the others to breathe in sharply in expectation.

"Evidence that could be used to disgrace my Master and restore innocence to both you and Mr. Winthrope."

It grew deathly silent again.

"Wait... what?" asked Jesse, his senses resurrected. "Did I hear you correctly? You have evidence on you?"

"Not on me," said Aero, "in me."

Jesse was an emotional rollercoaster again, hardly gentlemanly. He flung his arms up in the air and they came crashing down to his sides again, unable to grasp a single question in the mental storm going on in his skull.

Jenny looked at him, upset, wondering if he was going to explode.

"Well go on!" Jesse exclaimed, latching on to the most burning question he had. "What is this evidence that you've withheld from us, for two weeks no less, while we've been out here in the wastelands?"

Aero closed his eyes in shame.

"I was there the night Master murdered the mayor..."

Jenny gasped and Lobo leaned forward to better focus as Aero told them in detail about that night. Jesse paced, still listening, while mulling over a litany of his own thoughts.

"Master believed that by short circuiting all the bots he had involved in the conspiracy that he would be able to wipe all traces of his crime away. However, he did not factor in nor want me being there, recording everything I saw while saving it to my memory banks."

"Why weren't your robot brains scrambled?" Lobo asked doubtfully. "And how do we know you aren't recording what we say and sending it back to the boss?"

Aero tipped his head and considered what Lobo was asking.

"To answer the first question," he replied, "Master built me to be unique, more human like if you will. So, while I still have a means to be deactivated, I am not tied into the same systems as the rest of the control systems. Therefore, when he sent the purge signal to their receivers, I did not receive it."

"And the second?" asked Aftershock, shifting his weight from one hip to the other while his arms were crossed tightly across his chest.

"You don't, other than by trust."

Lobo sputtered his lips as he stood, joining the rest in the seemingly more comfortable position of standing.

"Aero," said Jenny, the only one of the group still seated with Aero. She sensed something good in him, even though he should just be a collection of bolts and gears wrapped in fake skin. "Why... why did you wait to tell us this until now?

"Loyalty," he said without hesitation and both Aftershock and Lobo gave each other surprised glances. "Of course, I have it for Master... for Frost, as he is the one who created me. I would have no basis for all other judgement if that were easily dismissed."

The group looked at each other with surprise.

"You think that's all preprogrammed in there?" Lobo whispered to Aftershock. "Has to be, doesn't it?"

"I have no damn idea," he replied, looking over to Jesse and

Jenny to see if they were faring any better with the bot that had a conscience.

"Over the last two weeks," Aero continued, "between the all the stress you have endured, I have seen so many examples of laughter and joy and happiness, things that I have only ever witnessed at a distance, such as through a spyglass. Never have I seen the complexities of your interactions up close; you all show each other such a dynamic of friendship, of family, of love... that contrasts with my world view of abuse and pain."

Jesse felt an odd feeling in his gut, tearing him in two directions. Aero talking about such highly emotional topics was moving, yet the ease at which he was divulging it was uncanny, both aspects shaking the notion that this was just a machine saying it all, no different than the vehicle they crossed the wasteland in before it crashed. Yet, right there in front of them was something more.

"Aero, you mentioned the fact you were there at the murder scene. How did you find out that the meeting was happening in the first place?"

"I was undergoing diagnostics, minor repairs, and fluid refills," Aero said as Lobo cringed, "and overheard a discussion between Frost and –"

A series of jarring beeps sounded.

"Between Frost and –"

The beeps sounded again.

"It seems that I cannot say," Aero said with distress, closing his eyes for a quick second. Another series of tones trilled before he reopened them. "There is a block that I cannot bypass."

"Curious," said Jesse lowly. "The burrow goes even deeper than we thought. Aero, if you can, continue trying to breach that wall. It seems like there are pertinent details waiting on the other side."

"I shall."

"Thanks," Jesse replied, rubbing his eyes while trying to stifle a yawn. It escaped anyway. "Well, everyone, given this information it seems like we still need to develop a course of action and determine who to show it to, and soon. No pressure."

"If we can get to the broadcast tower," Aero said, "I may be able to hack in and interface with system to transmit the recording over the radio and holotubes."

"That's brilliant!" Jesse said. "Do you think it will work?"

"I honestly have no idea, but based on my capability and calculations, it's probably our best chance."

At that second, everyone saw a pinprick of light form at the end of the long tunnel, Jesse starting to say something else but not before he yawned again.

"I agree that's probably our most promising option, Aero," Aftershock said, "but looking at everyone made of flesh around this fire right now, it's like the dead have come to life. We need to get some rest and finalize this in the morning, taking everything into account. Lobo?"

"Yes?"

"Do you think the Pack could wait for two, maybe three days for us to make sure this will work? I'm not even sure we will need you guys yet but this has me motivated."

"I'll try my best, Aftershock. Three days is doable for the Shadows; the Pack may start to leave before then."

"Try your best, but if not, that's fine, so long as we have some aid," Aftershock replied. "If we are going to get Jesse back into Diablo, it's not going to be easy and we will need all the help we can get."

TWENTY-FOUR

EVEN THOUGH THE AIR WAS WARM, Jenny felt wonderful tucked into Jesse's deep embrace as they made way for the cave. Lobo had just said goodnight, walking with his slight limp back down to the base of the mountain to let the other raiders know what was decided.

Slipping beneath the rocky canopy, Jesse let go of Jenny and removed a tan canvas bedroll from the alcove, spreading it out fully on the ground. Jenny then added a thin blanket and even thinner pillow to the arrangement, Jesse looking down as he put his hands squarely on his hips.

"I don't think I could live in the wastes for my back alone," he said, stretching. There was a painful strain, then a relieving pop in his spine. "These two weeks have nearly done me in and just looking at that bed makes me uncomfortable."

"Maybe we can make it a little more comfortable," Jenny said while her hands were lowered, then slid around to massage his lower back.

"Ah! That's the spot, right there," he said jubilantly. "I would like to request that you never stop, please."

"I don't plan to," she said, resting her chin on his shoulder, "though you can be quite a handful at times."

"I think you like that about me, though you have yet to see the best part," he said, one of his eyebrows arched high though hidden from her view.

"Maybe I do like it, maybe I don't," she said playfully.

She increased the pressure she was applying and Jesse rolled his eyes until they were merely thin lines of fluttering white. The satisfaction he was getting from the massage, even through his clothes, was grand.

"You know, I have said it before, but I've never met a woman quite like you. Most are coy, obedient, and proper…"

He winced, that last rub she gave deep.

"While I'm just brash, rebellious, and improper, right?"

As much as he wanted to keep getting massaged, Jesse turned around. Looking Jenny right in her eyes, his weren't the only part of him straining.

"Exactly," he replied, "and that makes you the perfect woman for me."

"I see what you mean by handful," she said, her gaze having drifted down to the rise in his trousers.

"My eyes are up here," he said with a gentle laugh.

She ignored him, still staring.

"In all earnestness," Jesse muttered, taking a hand to her chin. As he lifted it, her smile rose too. "If you'll have me, Jenny, going forward I plan on being there and providing for you, no matter what life tries to throw our way."

She looked to the side ever so slightly, humming pensively before replying, "I think that I can live with that."

Those words sent a surge of powerful desire through Jesse like a great river, full of life and hope and…

"Love," he said. "What a strange and remarkable thing. This time a month ago, I was walking the streets of Diablo an empty man with nothing but my work as company. Yet here we both stand today and I feel fully alive with you beside me. In my greatest moments of invention and within my wildest dreams, I never thought something like love could be as grand as it seems."

Jenny moved in closer, placing her head on his chest where she found his powerful heart beating. Closing her eyes and lifting her hand to caress his bearded cheek, she said, "Me either. It's as if life before was dull and pallid, now bursting with color and life. I do not wish to go back to the way it was before, so full of sorrow and strife."

"Promise me that won't happen; just the thought of you being away turns my heart to ice."

"I promise!"

That was enough to send their lips crashing into each other, melting away any lingering thoughts of cold and the past.

Hands alive with exploration, Jenny pressed herself against Jesse, her fingers roving all over his back and shoulders while his worked feverishly to remove her clothes. They were no match for his determination and once the last slip of fabric fell to the ground, Jenny was standing before him, a smooth vision so glorious in the desert that it had to be a mirage.

He groaned as she pinched her fingers on the topmost button of his shirt. Though he might have been efficient, she was going to savor her turn. Twisting, she released the button from its hold and down the line she went, first exposing his furry, heaving chest and then his flat stomach, rippling with muscle and heavy breaths. Flinging the shirt apart, Jenny kissed Jesse's exposed neck and took in his scent, thrilling as his soft beard touched her skin like a thousand tickling feathers. She pulled the shirt taunt as her kissing strengthened, slowly dragging it over his shoulders until, at last, it rolled down his back and was off.

He leaned in to nuzzle her ear then breathed softly into it, "I want you." Her hands left his back, launching straight for his belt, immediately undone and gone. Then, just as she did with his shirt, her fingers found themselves poised on the button of his trousers.

Jesse was aching below her grasp, tight against the textile prison, begging to be released.

She could sense all the want, wrapped in his musk. Knowing that she had the control, it took an eternity to unclasp his pants before slowly plunging the zipper toward the base. With the cage door open, she reached inside and gasped, for he might have had ample in length, yet his girth was overwhelming.

"Go on," he whispered as Jenny pulled it out, a glistening strand dangling from the tip, mesmerizing. "I know you've been wanting to."

Without a word, Jenny slid onto her knees, making sure to bring his trousers all the way down with her. She bit her lip as she grabbed hold of him and squeezed tightly hands unable to close. He moaned as she started to move them back and forth along his now slick shaft, her tongue like a match to kindling, striking a fire that surged from his groin all the way down to his feet and up to his head, riding high in the sky.

Weaving his fingers through her hair, Jesse wrapped those gossamer strands of brown up and over as he drew them into a fist. He used it to guide her lips up and down, watching her strain with his dark eyes in both sinful pain and pleasure.

"Take it," he said forebodingly, stretching her lips as she went down, providing her with fleeting relief on the upstroke before forcing her down again. "More... yeah... all of it..."

The feeling was incredible; bursts of passion rolling in ever mounting waves of heat. The sensation grew with each tantalizing suck and lick, rising like steam from boiling water until it all neared the point of bubbling over.

Yanking her up while he could, still drooling from the end, they kissed again. Jesse turned so Jenny's back was pointed toward the bedroll, and he guided her down to the canvas in one graceful swoop, their bodies folding atop each other until she was laying safely on the ground.

Jesse grabbed each of her thighs and spread those silken legs wide as she leaned her head against the pillow, arching as he loomed over her in admiration. Smiling, he positioned himself with the tip of his shaft teasing her, right up to the point he pushed inside.

It was tight, wet, and warm. She winced as he went deeper, then moaned as she struggled for the snaps that lined the sides of the roll. She clutched them tightly as Jesse filled her, spread her apart, and made her feel like she was on the top of the world.

Jesse had bottomed out, pulling back before grinding forward again with a low growl riding each thrust. He was being gentle yet his size was not, Jenny breathing in tiny puffs of air as she whimpered.

"Damn," Jesse muttered as Jenny started to clamp around him, a wetness flowing that made his motion easier. Lifting her legs, dove in and ground himself rhythmically against her skin.

She cried in bliss; he felt so good all the way inside her. Forcing her eyes open she watched… and felt… as Jesse moved, now writhing in chaotic thrusts.

Jesse's balls were tightening, an orgasm building inside him as their bodies splashed together like the salty sea upon the shore.

"Oh God… that's it…" he bellowed as his body exploded, Jenny's buckling beneath his.

They both sighed, and smiled, Jesse coming to rest beside Jenny. He didn't want to move at first; perhaps he couldn't with how drained he felt. Eventually propping himself up on an elbow, he looked over at her, panting and covered with faint

266   GOLDEN CZERMAK

drops of sweat. They glistened against her curves in what light was coming in from outside and within him, something stirred again.

"Do you think he heard us?" Jenny asked with a giggle.

"Who? Aftershock?"

"Yes," she replied with a tinge of embarrassment, stretching calmly. "At least we're done."

"What are you talking about?" Jesse said, a stern look in his eyes as he slid beneath her and urged her on top. "That was just the start... now the real ride begins."

The two locked lips again, hands tangled in each other's hair as their passion continued in darkness of the cave, the stars and moon shining brightly outside.

THE CAMP WAS quiet, the fire dying down to its last few remaining embers. Aero had relocated off to the edge of the overlook, sitting on a rock while looking out across the wide-open spaces. Even though he had seen maps and globes adorning Frost Enterprises, he found that the world was far larger and more impressive in person than he imagined. All he had ever seen until the day they soared over the walls of the city were the dreary walls of Diablo, the lavish luxury that saturated Frost's home, or the stark cold of the laboratory. That was his entire world, and it was smaller than a single grain of sand in the vast desert below.

Speaking of sand, Aero's leg joints were beginning to stick again – a hazard of being out in the wastes – so, grabbing hold of his right leg at the knee, he pushed it in then twisted counterclockwise. There was a gentle hiss and a pop, then the unit disconnected. Holding it up in the moonlight, shaking, fine grit worked loose and the motes glinted as they fell back to the ground like falling stars.

"Fascinating," said Aftershock approaching from behind.

"Ah, hello there Mr. Aftershock. I thought that you would be sleeping, considering you were the one to suggest that to the rest."

"You can just call me Aftershock, Aero and trust me, I definitely want to be asleep right now, but let's just say Jesse and Jenny are making quiet a lot of noise."

It took Aero a moment to register what he was talking about.

"Ah! Well, that is too bad. For you. Not them."

Aftershock chuckled, a rare and full smile appearing in his beard.

"May I join you here for a little while?" he asked, noticing how Aero's eyes were like sparkling sapphires in the light. "At least until they're business is concluded."

"Of course," Aero replied with a grin as he continued to shake out his leg. "The pleasure would be mine."

Aftershock crouched then plopped himself down on the dirt, watching the odd sight up close. Reaching into his pocket, he removed a rolled smoke and a single match, lighting the latter with a firm strike off his thumb nail.

Aero replaced his right leg, moving on to the left one, which came off with the same oddly satisfying *pop*.

"How often do you have to do that?"

"The cleaning?" Aero asked continuing once Aftershock nodded. "I could get them once a week in the laboratory, but being out here it has been a daily, sometimes twice, part of my routine."

The raider took a substantial draw of his smoke, then held out a hand, beckoning with his fingers while asking, "May I?"

Aero pondered the request and didn't see a problem, so after shaking his leg a couple more times as a courtesy, he placed the thing into Aftershock's waiting palm.

Expecting it to be heavy, Aftershock lowered his hand marginally as it made contact, but the leg was surprisingly lightweight, around the same as one of his longer rifles.

"That is amazing," he said, flipping it over and admiring it from all angles. "You really have to get right up close to tell it's not real skin, though these dark channels give it away. What're they for?"

"They serve multiple purposes, the top three being flexibility, thermodynamics, and separating the limb into easily replaceable panels."

"As me how to make a rifle out of junk and I can have you one in half an hour… I have no idea how one even begins to make such a thing, but that doesn't diminish its wonder."

"Your words are very flattering, Aftershock," Aero replied, taking possession of his leg again and sliding it back into place. "I can't say I'm used to that."

"Flattering maybe," he said, "but no less true."

"So, tell me, are there any other complements your otherwise gruff exterior has locked up inside?"

Aftershock jerked his head away.

What the hell are you doing Seth? That THING isn't a person.

He ignored his thoughts, wanting to know more.

"You're not a run-of-the-mill bot, are you?" Aftershock asked, trying his best not to make that observation sound offensive. "Ones I've seen over the years and long miles are made of entirely metal; often nothing more than fancy tools that hardly look approachable. You on the other hand look…"

"Different," Aero replied. "Indeed, I am unique. While the other bots such as myself are made with generic faces, I was crafted in the image of a person that Frost once loved, designed for the sole purpose of delivering him pleasure." Aero seemed to shudder as he spoke, the words cold and uninviting. "I suspect that he wished to relive the feelings of his past, long dimmed. Who wouldn't? Yet, this path could never be more than a substitute; I am not the one he lost nor could I ever hope to be. It was a doomed the moment it was first conceived."

"Aero, if Frost wanted to relive those happy times, why would he abuse you?"

"Because for some, no matter how happy things are for them or those they are with, control reigns supreme, manifesting in all sorts of chilling, and painful, ways. Both physically and emotionally as well, a toll is paid."

"Hell, if I could afford something like you, I would take care of that thing like my life depended on it."

Seth! You're being no better than Jenny and her giddy infatuations with you! Do you remember what you told her?

"That it was an impossibility..." he answered himself in the faintest whisper.

"What was that, Aftershock?" Aero asked.

The same applies here, Aftershock's thoughts reeled. *It may look like a man, but it is nothing more than a machine! A MACHINE!*

"Is he though?" Aftershock said under his breath before raising his voice. "Can you tell me more? The other models I've seen are run by steam, or clockwork mechanics. I haven't seen you do a single refill or be wound since you arrived. Not... not that I have been watching you too intensely."

"Of course," he answered happily, pointing to his chest. "It's in here, the reason those things are not needed. It's an energy cell that powers me, another thing that does not exist anywhere but here."

"So, this battery thing mentioned in Lobo's report, the one Frost is trying to mass produce, is this same device?"

"Yes, though Jesse's metals are being used as a more efficient and lightweight version," Aero said. "Ultimately though, mass produced items are cheaper, aren't they? Still making me the better edition."

"Was that a joke?" Aftershock asked, agog.

"No, it was just the truth," Aero answered with the gentlest of smiles, Aftershock returning the gesture with a couple awkward coughs.

This is beyond simple preplanned replies! he thought. *There is one more thing I must know.*

Aero had long finished with cleaning out the joints in his legs and had moved on during their discussion to his arms.

"One last question, Aero, if you would entertain an uneducated raider."

"I would say inquisitive rather than uneducated," Aero replied, spinning his arm around rapidly. There came more dust like a cloud of falling starlight. "In other words: feel free."

"Do you have wants? Or even dreams?"

Aero admitted to having both, his wants focused on doing more with his life, beyond his allotted role as a sex-bot.

"I think I've taken a pretty good leap along that path, getting Mr. Winthrope and Miss Boone out of harm's way. As far as dreams, I dream of the day humanity can put aside its petty differences in mutual support of each other. Sad to say bots are better at it than their own creators."

Aftershock is taken aback.

"Forgive me, but that is the same thing I feel daily. For myself, I would give anything to be a better part of society, but it's impossible since I wasn't born into it and this life as a raider would follow me to the grave."

"Perhaps one day the world can change."

"I don't think I'll have as long to wait for it as you do, Aero, but hopefully it'll come sooner rather than later. From what I hear about Jesse, he's making a great effort to that end."

"Agreed, which is partly why I am so willing to help him."

"As am I," Aftershock replied before thinking, *Change begins at home, doesn't it?*

Then, he yawned, unable to hold it in any longer.

"It seems that fatigue is catching up to you," Aero observed. "You really should try to get some sleep, as we have much to discuss in the morning, then to do in the coming days. Good things are on the horizon and the night is warm. Sleep out here if need be, under the watchful eyes of the stars… and me."

TWENTY-FIVE

IT WAS A PEACEFUL MORNING, AS MOST mornings were up at the northern fringe of Diablo's city limits. The sun smoldered between tufts of rolling cloud while a stiff breeze from the west shuffled groups of tumbleweeds across the arid ground.

Two Rangers were amid the rusted carcasses of old storerooms and a downed alarm bell tower, both clad in chaps and off-white shirts as they sat on roughened building blocks. Cushioned with makeshift padding made from their folded-up duster coats, one of them – a slack shouldered young man with a squirrelly mustache – was shoveling baked beans straight out of the can into his mouth. The other, older and a bit more refined, dug around for a match in his vest pocket so he could light his pipe.

"Another borin' day watchin' the fringe," said the young ranger as he looked from building to rusted building with nothing but dirt and a few scrubby plants peppered in between.

"Quit your bellyaching Kevin," the older ranger barked as he finally lit his pipe. It was filled with cheap tobacco that made plumes of foul-smelling greenish smoke. "Otherwise you'll jinx us and that's the last goddamn thing I need to happen. I'd rather be out here than toiling those scummy streets along the edge."

Kevin kicked out a leg, using it to drag his boot through the soil in an arch.

"This here is about as excitin' as it gets. I dunno, you might like sittin' around all day smokin' that shit, Hank," Kevin sneered as he loosened the frayed bandana around his neck, "but I need more *excitement* in my life. Keeps the blood flowin'… vitalizin' me for the ladies. Otherwise, I'd just turn into somethin' like you."

Hank chuckled as he puffed more sickly smoke, shaking his head slowly within the vapor.

"I have a hard time seeing you with any lady other than maybe one on a lumograph, son. As far as work goes, use your brain for a second, idiot! Out here, you earn more Gear for less work. Sure, it's fucking boring as bo balls, but when I can pocket three times what those edge-scrapers do, without having to deal with anyone, who's the dumb one now?"

"Whatever, Hank," said Kevin spitefully, "guess you're just too old to understand, your only company bein' one of those first-generation Vixens."

"If you say so, boy. Even a bot's more action than a picture," Hank replied, catching a glimpse of a what looked like a sandstorm coming in on the horizon. His forehead crinkled and for a second he looked much older. He stood. "Strange, the wind isn't coming out of the north. Be useful and fetch me a spyglass!"

Kevin saw the same thing and shot off toward their sleipnir. They were hitched nearby on a couple of rough-and-ready posts. Digging through their saddlebags, he snatched a brass, leather sheathed spyglass and darted back to Hank, who snatched it off Kevin well before he come to a stumbling halt.

Lifting it, Hank looked through and his normally stoic expression was gone, pale with distress.

"What is it?" Kevin asked as the distant cloud grew larger and closer. There was a low rumble and the ground seemed to be vibrating.

"Look for yourself," Hank croaked as he tossed him the spyglass. "You're about to get your wish… you fucking idiot!"

Without another word, Hank hastened toward his mount, having to ride back to the city and raise the alarm there. The fringe tower had been damaged in the last genuine sandstorm, but with Frost in charge it was too chaotic to get anything officially repaired.

"Goddamn city's going to shit! Giddyap!" Hank yelled and his steed tore away to the south, leaving Kevin trembling for fear of what he might see.

Raising the spyglass as the rumbling started to become a roar, Kevin eased it into focus. He gasped immediately, mustache a quiver. Dropping the thing, it shattered on the ground, and took off running at full speed for his steed. Leaping on its back, Kevin landed with such force that the creature reared, screaming.

"Whoa!" Kevin shouted but it didn't work to calm the beast, the sleipnir bolting toward the city while Kevin plummeted to the hard dirt flat on his back.

Groaning as he tried to move, a pain in his lower back kept him in position. He dropped his head where he laid, and looked out (albeit upside down) and waited.

For charging toward him with great speed was an army of no less than two hundred raiders, riding a herd of sleipnir and enormous wolves that kicked up a dust storm worthy of legend in their wake. Making for the northern gate of Diablo, they were led by a man known to some as Wyatt Jameson, but known to more as Lobo. A fire in his eyes to ensure his part of the went off without a hitch.

"WHAT THE HELL is happening at the north end of the city?" Frost roared at his subordinates, all of whom were running around in a manner that contradicted their chic sensibilities.

Top hats were toppling, ascots fluttering, and sweat was staining flamboyant fabrics that were supposedly stain free; all while panicked wheezing and shrieks of worry filled the room. Frost and his associates had gathered in Grand Hall, where he had been visiting for 'discussions' with then Vice-Mayor Bernard Webber, a man whose services would no longer be required as a replacement for the deceased Randolph.

"Well?!" shouted Frost, fuming that he was being ignored. In the chaotic shuffle, his leather-bound fists creaked, ready to strike at the puffy, red faces around him. "I'm waiting for an answer!"

"Raiders, Milord!" came a reply at last. "Approaching Frontera's gates!"

It was from a nervous man who was stooped low over a radio, cupping a speaker over his ears. Its curly wire was wrapped around his short finger, moving apprehensively.

Frost waited for more information, but apparently, that was all the man could make out for the time being, his eyes squinting hard as he tried to focus over the ceaseless noise.

"SILENCE!" Frost demanded so loudly that it seemed to shake the building. Everyone froze in place and he pointed back toward the radio operator. "Continue…"

The man listened for a few moments, bobbing his head, shaking it, and making a few strange expressions. Frost did not like the story they were telling.

"A large force of raiders is attacking the northern gate!" he said at last, cringing at the intensity of Frost's metallic stare. "Their numbers are vast... a hundred, maybe more."

Frost said nothing, his expression ice.

"They've requested reinforcements or will soon be overrun; shall we send some" the man continued. "If left alone, the attack force will spill beyond the wall and there will be no telling the damage and death that –"

"They dare to betray me?" Frost whispered, amused by the notion.

"Milord?" asked the radio operator, confused. It was not the yes answer he was expecting.

I will show you the price of crossing me, Frost thought, before shouting at his associates, "Order more sentries to the gate, bring turrets closer if need be! By God you'll be out there next if they enter the city!"

"And the X5-1?" said another man, off near the door. He was strangely thin with a gaunt, goateed face and slender shoulders that tapered outward to his hips. Upright with hands in front of his torso, his spidery fingers were pressed tip to tip while a glossy black lens was strapped over his right eye.

"No," Frost replied coolly. "I am saving that one to clip Angelus' wings..."

The mysterious man said nothing more. After a bow, he opened the door, slipped through, and departed. As the door closed behind him, there came a commotion over at another radio.

"Milord! A guard has just reported activity just inside of Comprass!"

"More raiders on the east side?" Frost asked, marching over with wrath in his eyes.

"I... am not sure, Milord," the operator answered shakily. "I- if they are, there are not many of them."

"It's like an infestation of rats to be exterminated. Is there any more information?"

"Not much. Milord, the guard, he's stopped responding. The last thing mentioned this small group was headed south.

"There are only two major points of interest in that general direction..." Frost said aloud but only meant for himself. "Winthrope's tower and..." Then, an unexpected rage overtook him, and his face blazed with red while his good eye filled with tears of frustration. "AERO!"

A fist came slamming down on the operator's table, nearly knocking his radio to the floor.

"I need a contingent of sentries, guards, whatever can be spared from the north gate to meet me at Gibson and Large!"

The operator looked up, clutching his radio as if it were a child and said, "The broadcast tower?"

Frost looked down upon him ruthlessly, eyes ablaze.

"YES! NOW!"

"DAMMIT THAT'S NOT good!" shouted Aftershock as the Frost guard off in the distance slumped, then fell, his radio dancing in pieces across the cobblestones.

"Was he able to get a message out?" Jesse asked, arriving at Aftershock's side while reloading his gun.

"I think so," Aftershock nodded, holstering his rifle and removing a pair of golden revolvers with mahogany grips. "Hate to say it, but I think our advantage might be on its last legs."

"Dammit, I was hoping for more time," Jesse asked, looking around the desolate streets. There were empty stores and stalls in both directions. "What time is it?"

"Nine twenty-three," Aero said, joining the two of them along with Jenny. She had a hold of her junk pistol and a sleek rifle across her back; Aero for all appearances seemed unarmed but after witnessing him at the holding facility, Jesse knew better.

"This place should be bustling with activity this time of day," Jesse observed, the group walking along a walled street. They were heading west toward a soiled archway that lead into the borough of Bagat. Trash blew by their feet, littering the area far more than usual. It was as if people had left, or were too scared to come out. Wishing he had time to investigate in detail, Jesse lead the team on; they would need to head through the area as quickly as possible, entering the borough of Chismear which housed their destination.

The journey through Bagat was eerie; more abandoned streets and stores, several of them smoldering. It was too quiet, the smell more wretched as they walked past dead end alleys looking for a westerly road.

"I know that smell," Aftershock mumbled, looking around for any signs he was right. His fingers were reliably hovering beside the triggers of his guns.

"I think I do, too," Jesse said over his shoulder, "but I don't want to know for sure."

"Count me out, too," Jenny said, "and if you can get rid of this feeling that we're being watched, I would be most appreciative."

Suddenly, a voice surged from the shadows of a nearby alleyway.

"Jenny?" it hissed. "Is that you?"

Her heart leaped in her chest, and spinning on the spot she aimed as the rest of the team stopped their advance.

"Who's there?" Jenny demanded. "Show yourself!"

Two figures stepped out from the shade, the indistinct forms of more barely visible behind them.

Jenny lowered her weapon upon seeing them, familiar faces yet battered and bruised.

"Evelyn! Marcus!"

They met and embraced, Jesse shaking both their hands (with Evelyn demanding a firm hug as well).

"You've done well for yourself, girl," she told Jenny with a wink, still feeling his arm.

Smiling at Jesse's awkward countenance, Jenny introduced them to Aero and Aftershock. Both garnered wide and disbelieving stares from the residents before being welcomed.

"Now that we've all had a chance to meet, can one of you tell us what's going on here?" Jesse asked. "The place is a mess; more than usual."

"Frost," Evelyn said and that was enough to answer most of Jesse's other questions. "It's been sheer Hell on Eaugen since he took over."

"He did all this?" Jenny asked, Aero looking miserable.

"No, he's been so damn occupied with building sentries. It was his guards that did all this… and so much more." Evelyn's voice broke, sadness flowing through the cracks. "Those monsters; parading around as men loosed to do whatever they want without consequence. They've killed many poor and unarmed protestors in Comprass. The streets were literally soaked in blood. Ganado had an incident or two as well. Just this morning, the same happened here."

"We're in the process of clearing and burning the bodies," Marcus said softly and Jenny suddenly knew what the odor that had clung to the air had been. "The last thing we need is another plague to appear on top of this mess."

It might have been too late for Jenny, who was feeling nauseous, amazed at how rancid a person's soul could become when given just a taste of power. Looking at Jesse, who was deep in his own thoughts, she realized how special a character he had to resist and want to help.

"Have you stood up to them?" Jesse asked, the anger in his words apparent.

"We've started to," Evelyn said. "It's been so hectic. First few days nobody knew what was going on. Mayor was dead, you were charged, vice-mayor disappeared, Frost took over to save the peace.

"What a steaming crock of shit *that* was," Marcus added.

"Then," Evelyn continued, "when things started to show their true colors it was too late. Now at least it's finally slowing down enough to let us focus and plan. Frost's forces still have an advantage over us with firepower."

"Come on," Marcus said, aggressively looking around at their surroundings, "we need to get off the streets. We have a lot left to discuss and should back at…"

"No, we need to get to the antenna at the broadcast building now," Jesse countered, pointing to Aero. "He is in possession evidence that proves Frost is responsible for the mayor's death and we need to get to that tower so we can spread the word both here and outside the city. Hopefully it'll clear my name, but it may also be a rallying call."

Evelyn and Marcus swapped glances. Jesse couldn't tell if they were joyful or anxious ones.

"all right then," Marcus said with a grumbling sigh. "I don't like this, but we'll take you to the square."

The six of them moved through the alleys, scaling discolored walls and other obstacles to avoid detection on the main thoroughfares. Eventually, they reached the end of a narrow passage bordering Gibson Square. Normally full of entertainers and happy crowds, it too was bleak and forsaken.

"There it is," Marcus said, motioning to large, unmistakable building dead ahead. Its multiple floors of ashen stone were topped by an immense radio spire.

"You sure you want to go through with this?" Evelyn asked Jesse, knowing what his answer will be.

"Honor is everything, so if I can both clear my name with this *and* help instill something in the oppressed, I'm all for it."

"You sir, are one remarkable man," Evelyn said, giving him another embrace. "Take care of my girl, will you?"

"You know I will," Jesse smirked, nodding to Jenny.

"Bar's always open for you, Mr. Winthrope," said Marcus, stepping up to slap his shoulder and shake his hand. "Drinks are on the house."

"Don't be silly, Marcus, we've gone over that before…"

With that and a few last-minute chuckles, the group was once again four, headed swiftly across the open square.

On their way, Aftershock waltzed up to Jesse, nudging him on the shoulder.

"Are you crazy?" he whispered harshly.

Jesse looked around before answering, wondering if Aftershock was talking to either of the others.

"What are you talking about? Have I done something wrong?"

"You turned down free drinks!" Aftershock hissed. "At a bar! For life!"

Jesse shook his head.

"When we get out of this, you let that barkeep know that your buddy will take him up on that deal."

"You got it, After –"

A bullet whooshed by, cutting the conversation short.

Jesse looked over to his right, narrowly escaping another bullet.

A squad of Frost's sentries and guards were barreling toward them. They fired again, and Jesse was grazed on the forearm. The wound wasn't serious, but he nearly dropped his weapon due to the harshness of the sting.

"Run!" he shouted, sprinting as fast as he could. "We have to get Aero to the tower!"

Raising his pistols, Aftershock fired successive rounds into the oncoming swarm. A couple of guards fell at once, dead, but the mechanical sentries that his bullets struck kept advancing. Focusing on one, he slung more lead at it, the sentries' head exploding in a shower of sparks and steam.

Aero was also occupied, arms splitting down the center, grasping four pistols holstered to his denims. In rapid succession he pulled their triggers, shot after shot impacting guards and sentries alike, sending them to the ground in heaps.

There was a sudden roar, the sound of hundreds of footsteps drawing Jenny's attention. Readying her pistol for the worst, her eyes fell upon the best.

Pouring out of the streets and alleys alike were the people of Diablo, armed with whatever they could find and carry, rushing the square toward Frost's forces with a single purpose in mind: liberation.

Jenny's heart swelled at what she saw, moving to join the rest of her group in their final dash.

With the guards and sentries engaged with the citizenry, the four of them sprinted to the tower's doors, flung them open, and entered.

TWENTY-SIX

THE TEAM ENTERED THE BROADCAST building, plunging from the bright sun into an ominous gloom. The interior was unlike anything in the rest of Diablo, sleek metallic lines curving along the surfaces and furniture, all basking in the green glow of neon lights spiraling up support columns in the large entry hall. Along the walls, eight large holotubes were hung, four different channels on display, their ghostly images a putrid shade of green.

"Nice to see they're conserving power," Jesse said sarcastically, approaching a reception desk. A red leather chair sat empty on the other side. "I always thought their bills were high just because of the antenna."

"You've never been here before?" asked Aftershock, taking in the weird environment.

"First time for me too," he replied, looking around for any indication of where to go.

"Lifts seem to be out," Jenny said, casually looking over

the guest area. There were fancy flyers spread across the tables touting the marvels of holotube technology ("You'll think you're there!" and "New Portable Versions Coming Soon!")

"Aero," Jesse called. "Where do we go from here? The signs in this place are dreadful."

Aero walked up to the reception desk beside Jesse.

"We will need to get to one of the broadcast studios. I suggest the largest one; it's on the top floor with the others. It will likely have the most direct connections with the antenna."

"Point the way and we'll follow," Jesse said, motioning toward the silvery stairs immediately behind the receptionist area.

"Of course. Lifts out, target's on the upper floor," Aftershock grumbled. "You all and your obsession with these sky-scraping buildings."

"This coming from a man with his home on top of a mountain overlook with a single, craggy walkway," Jenny replied with the slightest eye roll. "Let's go."

The team climbed many flights of stairs, finding broad rooms stuffed with arrays of desks on each floor.

"Guess everyone skipped work today," Jesse said, following Aero to yet another flight of stairs. "How many stories are in this building? I couldn't tell from the outside."

"There are twelve," Aero replied. "We are nearly there. After two more flights, we will need to cross an office area such as those we've passed; the stairs up to the studios are on the opposing side."

Within a few minutes, the team was advancing through the final office space, photos of families and personal adornments decorating each desk they streamed by.

The sound of something scurrying reached them, and they paused to assess the situation.

"We've got company!" Aftershock shouted as a sentry came rushing out of a side door.

He flung his hand at the bot, pistol whipping it with enough force to send it reeling backward. Aftershock then fired each of his revolvers, blowing big chunks of metal off its head, the thinnest piece of metal left running down the center.

Jesse was firing as he ran behind Aero, making way for the stairs.

"Almost there!" he cried, turning to see Jenny under attack. "Aero, go on! We'll be right behind you!"

With that he flew toward Jenny's attackers and both of them worked together, back to back and side to side, to take the guards down.

"Thanks!" she said with a huge exhale, looking right into his eyes.

"No problem!" he replied. "I like you well enough I won't say you owe me."

Jesse watched as Jenny's eyes left his for a split second, the sound of a gunshot ringing in his ears, followed by a loud *thud*.

"No," she replied, "but I will say you owe me."

She pecked him on the nose and made way for the stairs, and as Jesse looked down at the freshly sparking body of a sentry, he smiled.

"She really does it for me!" he said, joining up with Aftershock as they all made way up to the studio.

AERO HAD MADE it to the row of studios, two per side framing the door to the largest at the end of the hall. Rushing toward it, he burst through into a massive space filled with terminals, bulky cameras, and a couple of sets (one more relaxed like a family room, the other a dais with podium).

Aero swept up to the closest terminal. Finding a thick black cable dangling at the side of the box of circuits, he reached for it, simultaneously flipping a panel off the side of his head. Beneath it were several different connection ports, one matching the cable in his hand.

"Aaron!" said an all too familiar and unwanted voice. "Stop!"

Aero didn't comply, inserting the cable into the port where it made a slight *click*.

"I said stop!"

"I do not have to take orders from you anymore," Aero said as he began to key in a sequence on the terminal's keyboard, turning his head at the same time to survey the room.

Frost emerged from the shadows between the sets, dressed in a shiny, insulated suit with a pair of menacing goggles over his eyes. In his arms was one of his large rifles, steam venting from the barrel while arcs of electricity leaped across grills on the body of the gun.

"If you don't do as I say RIGHT NOW I will force you to," Frost threatened. "I made you and can end you just as easily." His voice lessened, almost passing as caring. "I nurtured you, Aaron, and THIS is how you repay me? With betrayal?"

"You're the one who betrayed yourself, Master, believing in things that could never be" Aero replied. "My name is not Aaron! It's Aero!"

Beneath his goggles, Frost's eyes boiled red with rage and he aimed the rifle without a second thought.

Jesse and company raced to the studio, entering just a massive bolt of energy like lightning tore across from back of the room right into Aero.

"No!" the three of them shouted in unison, emotions surging in all directions as Aero's body floundered in a cage of energy that burned most of his outer plates away.

Collapsing to the terminal, Aero's metallic frame was smoldering and he was barely recognizable except for his face, which still clung on to familiarity. Despite his condition, he pressed on, his fingers and hands splitting into twenty tendrils that rapidly keyed in the rest of the broadcast sequence.

A female voice, mechanical and without emotion spoke.

"Uploading..."

"Goodbye Aaron!" Frost yelled as he raised his rifle again. Aftershock saw him and sent a hail of bullets his way, puncturing the rifle's body.

Out of ammo, Aftershock shed his revolvers and slipped the rifle off the back.

"Eye for an eye," he said, pulling the trigger. The round blasted from the end of his rifle and finished the job the revolver bullets had begun.

Frost could hear the pistol whining and feel the tingle of unstable energy building through holes now in his suit. Tossing the rifle away, it exploded in midair, sending a shower of shrapnel and hot steam around the room.

"Sequencing..."

The room settled, Frost emerging from the swirl of fog to find Jenny and Jesse both with their pistols pointed in his direction.

Aftershock had rushed to Aero's side, his expression one of dread and grief as he found him lying face first next to the keyboard.

"So here we are again," Frost said smugly. "Two of the most powerful men in the world at odds and gunpoint instead of combining our efforts to –"

"You're not going to schmooze your way out of this one, Lucas. Besides, seems to me you're the one at gunpoint."

"A shame," Lucas replied. "You're sounding just like your father and his putrid ideas on how harmonious the world could be if only given the chance."

"Don't you dare speak of him and taint his memory!"

"Taint it?" Frost laughed. "Jesse, I MADE him the memory!"

A sudden chill blew over Jesse, becoming a fever moments later.

"Oh? Was it something I said?" Frost said, watching Jesse sweat. "You see Jesse, both of us are still armed with hurtful things."

As if possessed, Jesse's face became inhuman he pulled the trigger. A bullet ripped through Frost's right leg and he cried out in pain, stifled by his own pride.

"One good turn deserves another, isn't that right?" Frost spat, sinking to one knee.

"Did you pay the raiders that shot him down?" Jesse asked mechanically.

Frost was silent.

"DID YOU?"

Frost's pained wince suddenly became a crooked smile, until Jesse sent another bullet into his left arm.

"There is more to this," Frost warned, laughing maniacally. "So much more that you do not understand."

Jesse fired a shot at the back wall, causing Jenny to flinch.

Frost was unfazed.

"That one was meant for your head. I won't miss again. I'm not interested in any of the others right now," Jesse said, the tip of his pistol smoking. "Only with you."

Aftershock pulled Aero back from the terminal, his body slumping into a cradle formed by Aftershock's elbow.

"You did it Aero," he said. "The information is about to be sent to the whole city."

"S-succc- -ce-ssss?" Aero replied, his voice stuttering and failing.

"Yeah, buddy," Aftershock said sadly, watching Aero's eyes struggling to stay lit.

"F-factooo-ry," Aero said, repeating the word three more times before his systems were finally overcome and his eyes faded.

Aftershock dipped his head, Aero still in his arms as the terminal said the words they had all been waiting for.

"Broadcasting…"

Jesse sighed upon hearing those word, knowing that people were seeing and hearing the truth about what happened to the former mayor.

"What are you going to do with him Jesse?" Jenny asked, unsure herself. "The authorities are probably on their way here now. They'll likely take him away to face those hearings and trials you talked to me about.

Jesse stood with his pistol aimed right at Frost's head; he was still smiling that wretched smile.

"I don't think so, Jenny," he replied as Aftershock slinked up between them. "Lucas has way too much money shoved in far too many cracks, keeping them just wide enough to slither away."

"You're going to kill him then?" she asked apprehensively.

"I don't see any other options," Jesse said sadly.

Jenny sighed, knowing what had to be done but wishing there was another way to go about it.

"He won't do it," Frost goaded. "He doesn't have the balls to do anything other than dream the dreams of little boys."

"You're right, Lucas," Jesse said, lowering his gun. "I'm

nothing like you. Though we may share a lot of common traits we each take on vastly different forms like steam versus ice… so similar yet so different."

Frost chuckled at his apparent success.

"I knew that he…"

"I might have some hiccups. But my friend here," Jesse said, handing his pistol off to Aftershock. "He's like a totally different element, so doesn't have those same issues…"

Wide-eyed, Frost began to shiver as Jesse walked away, Aftershock filling his view while considering the pistol in his grip.

Extending an arm, Jenny walked up to Jesse and gave him a kiss, holding each other as they walked over to Aero to pay their final respects.\

EPILOGUE

WITH THE SUN RISING OVER THE plains, a new day was beginning in Diablo.

Word had spread to the four corners of the world about the events that transpired, which were unlike anything that had happened in a long time. The whole city had been turned right on its edge by malevolent forces, then slammed back again when they were repelled. As wonderful as the victory seemed on the surface, a great shift like that made sure things could not return fully to normal, while causing others that were long forgotten to rise to the surface anew.

It had been a week and day since Frost's mundane demise and the clearing of Winthrope's name. Frost's deeds had been heard and seen across the entire city many times, the shock and outrage of it no less potent. Holotube rebroadcasts had even made it as far as Angelus, where President Archer followed statements made by Lylan Laguna of Lagos and Prefect DuBois of Barro denying any knowledge or involvement with Frost's misdeeds.

"It is my hope that we can put an end to this heinous breach of public trust and confidence," Archer said in a greasy fashion that nearly matched his slicked back hair, Jenny and Jesse watching the transmission on a holotube in Frost's office. "I hereby pledge any resources from our great city in support of the honorable Mayor Webber and his ongoing investigations in the gre… desert city of Diablo, to uncover who else was involved in this conspiracy. I –"

Jesse turned the unit off, combing fingers through his hair as if to make sure none of the oil from Archer's had transmitted through the screen.

"Did you hear him get 'great city' in there?" he asked Jenny, wiping his fingers together in front of him as a final check.

Jenny nodded reluctantly.

"And that was how many times?"

"Four," she said glumly, holding up as many fingers.

"I believe that means I won the bet!" Jesse said, his eyebrows bouncing up and down. "My four to your vastly miscalculated one. You, my dear, owe me a home cooked meal tonight."

"I'll be glad to do it," she said, "but I'm pretty sure that it's not much of a prize for you. Grandfather absolutely loathed my cooking and Evelyn, well, she thought I could help out with dinner at her place, but soon found out she was sorely wrong about my culinary skills."

"I already know all about that," Jesse said as he grabbed Jenny's hand and gave it a quick kiss. "Evelyn told me, but that doesn't mean I don't appreciate the thought behind it. Feel free to give your list of ingredients to Logan later. He can collect them from Grayson Market for you."

"How did I end up this lucky?" she asked with an appreciative smile, "and thank you for sending Logan to fetch the ingredients. I still get anxious from all the stares out there. It was bad enough when I was just a 'wasteland girl' and now that I'm formally known as 'Mr. Winthrope's wasteland girl' everyone wants to be my friend or in my business."

"Quite honestly, they're probably doing both at the same time, looking for a scandalous bit of gossip to spread," he said. "It's all right to feel that way – it comes with the territory. No matter what or where, those types will always be there, more as you gain popularity, or finances, or anything covetable. Over time you'll learn to be less nervous about it. I bet within another month it won't even bother you. Besides, above all that you have me, remember? I'll always be by your side and easy to take the blows… whether they're dished from them or given by you…"

"Speaking of remembering," she said, trying not to blush too badly at what he'd just said, "I'd almost forgotten why we're here."

She looked around the office and shuddered. It was like Jesse's, yet with a veneer of gloom that seemed to pervade the whole space, seeping into every leather surface, wooden panel, and metal flourish. Even the portraits were gloomy, unknown people staring down at them and unknown places that, despite being painted sunny, were washed out and gray.

"Mayor Webber granted us an hour to look for anything the recovery officials hadn't already returned to Winthrope Limited. I wanted to check for any special documents that Frost might have liberated but kept closer to the cuff. I can't help but think there's more, especially since he mentioned my father and his plans."

"Okay," she replied, looking around the room at the multitude of places documents could be hidden, from desk drawers to bookshelves to furniture, those just being the obvious locations where they could be laid out. "An hour…" she continued, sputtering, "yeah let's hope we're lucky."

AFTERSHOCK STOOD alone on the roof of Winthrope Limited, staring out at the strange, new vista. It was wonderful sight, which happened to be frightening at the same time.

"There you are," said a voice as someone walked up beside him.

Very much alive, it was Aero, his body repaired with lighter alloys courtesy of the production work Frost had started, though there were still panels missing along both arms and his chest.

"Yeah, just needed a minute to decompress. There have been so many damn meetings; is that all you city dwellers do? Have meetings to discuss plans for more meetings?"

"Yes," Aero replied. "I think I heard one of the officials call it job security."

"He should be killed… or fired, however you all do that in here." Aftershock sighed. "How's anything get done? We'd have been finished days ago had this been out there in the wastes…"

"You really aren't liking it in here, are you?"

"That obvious?" Aftershock asked sarcastically.

"Only a little bit," Aero replied equally so.

Aftershock looked back at the city but his hand was thrumming restlessly on his pistol.

"Don't get me wrong," he said, guilt creeping in, "I appreciate everything Jesse's done to get the officials to let me stay, even with opportunities for the future. But, I don't know, something…"

"It's not who you are and despite it being something that you wanted, there's more to you than you first expected," Aero replied with understanding. He looked across to Aftershock, who felt his gaze and returned it. "Seems like you and I have a lot of self-discovery ahead of us."

"I could appreciate the company," Aftershock replied, pointing at Aero's missing chest plate. "What's all this about?"

"Oh," Aero said with surprise, lifting his arms as he considered the missing pieces. "I was planning to head over to the laboratory at Frost Enterprises later and retrieve some of my spare exo-plates."

"They not have any at the place you got the rest of your repairs done?"

"Oh, they did," he said while nodding nimbly. "I just didn't want those... cheaper things making up my entire body. I thought it would be a good idea to keep a few components from my original model integrated, if nothing other than to remind myself that I'm still the original A3R0 unit."

Aftershock, lifted his arm, where a grouping of bracelets adorned with accessories jangled.

"Sort of like these trinkets remind me of places I've been; I add one every time I learn a valuable life lesson. Last one was from Pitchfork; casing of one of the bullets that killed ol' Dante. Have it to remind me not to be arrogant during battle and, of course, help is always nearby."

"Fascinating," Aero replied while admiring the different items. There were other casings, vehicle parts, and clock hands all affixed to his wrist.

"So, you need any help with those ecso-plates?"

"EXO-plates," Aero corrected, "and what you meant to ask was would I like your company?"

"Well... yeah," Aftershock shrugged.

"I'd like that," he replied, though his face became serious as he looked him over. "However, I am going to need you to trim your beard up to be more presentable."

"Excuse me?" Aftershock asked, almost offended. "You want me to trim all of this manliness off my face to better fit in?"

"Yes."

"With those people down there?" asked Aftershock, looking bewildered.

"Indeed," Aero said, holding a pretty stern look, broken at the end with the slightest upturn of his lips.

"Think again, bot boy," Aftershock scoffed loudly. "So, full of jokes now, are we? Well, I'm going as is. Are you ready to go now?"

"We can't," Aero replied. "Which is why I suggested later."

"Why the hell not?"

"Because, I came up here to bring you to another meeting."

Aftershock's jaw fell sort of half open and he glanced toward the edge of the roof, never readier to leap toward meeting-free salvation than at that moment.

APPROACHING A GOOD three-quarters of an hour of searching, Jesse and Jenny were still empty handed, unable to find any documents or other items of interest in Frost's office.

"Maybe there isn't anything else?" Jenny said as she started rifling through the papers in and on the large desk one more time.

Jesse was over by the bookshelves, having rifled through nearly all the books that were there in his search for any loose-leafed notes or plans. There was nothing.

"Maybe you're right," Jesse said discouragingly, holding a book titled *Beyond Steam: Alternative Power Explained* in both hands as he tapped himself on the forehead with it. "I'm not even sure what we are looking for is here."

"I'll admit, that would be helpful to know," Jenny said lightheartedly. "Nothing that a bit of divine intervention wouldn't solve, right?"

Jesse laughed saying, "That could have helped us from the very begin…"

He trailed off, noticing one of the larger portraits on the wall was that of an old clergyman, dressed in a black cassock trimmed in gold.

"Divine intervention… I wonder," Jesse mumbled as he made his way for the painting. Lifting it slightly at the edge, he peered behind to look at the wall and noticed a series of faint of lines. "Jenny, I'm not sure but I think I found something. Can you help me with this?"

Jenny dashed over and grabbed the other side of the frame and gently, the two lifted the heavy thing off its hanger and set it leaning against a sofa. Sure enough, there was a rectangular outline on the wall that had been hidden by the portrait.

Walking up to it, Jesse gave it a quick knock and the resulting sound was somewhat hollow. Applying pressure to the area, he felt it give and when released, the rectangle popped off and fell to the carpet. Inside was a dank niche and a small lock box sitting in it. Decorated with fluted silver edges, the safe was secured by a sliding, four-digit numerical lock.

"It certainly looks like we are on the right track," Jesse said confidently.

"But do you know the combination?" Jenny asked, totally blank herself other than the current year.

Jesse gave it a try, sliding each of the numbers into position to match the year. Attempting to open the box, nothing happened other than sounding a loud *clang*.

"Would have been amazing to get it on the first try," he said, tongue peeking out from his mouth as he mulled over other possibilities.

"Nothing's ever that easy," Jenny replied, noting the time. "Hey, Jess, security will be by soon to collect us; our time's nearly up."

"Okay let me give these a try," he replied.

Sliding the lock to 1687 (the founding year of Winthrope Limited) …

Clang!

Sliding the lock to 1777 (the founding year of Frost Enterprises) …

Clang!

"Argh!" Jesse shouted. "If Aero were here I would have him rip this damn thing out of the wall."

"Well, we don't have that option and we are out of time…"

The clock chimed and Jesse had a sudden chill, a flash of his father leaving through the secret passage all those years ago.

"Surely not," he whispered, trying one final combination before giving up.

1785… the year his father was taken from him.

Trying to open the door and expecting another unfeeling *clang*, the safe yielded instead, light from the room shining on a set of cream parchment sheets that had been tucked away inside. Quickly Jesse snatched them all and slammed the safe shut.

"Jenny! We have them!" he exclaimed, flipping through them.

Jesse saw plans for Aero's so called 'battery' but there were indications a lot more was going on. The plans showed the energy cells screwing into other units, creating longer tubes.

"Do you have any idea what they're for?" Jenny asked inquisitively, looking at each page trying to figure out how it all fit together.

Jesse continued to study them as well, but grew more puzzled the more he looked.

"I'm pretty sure there are some pieces missing," he said, pointing toward several arrows that shot off the edges of the page, yet didn't reconnect on any of the others.

"Great," Jenny said with spurious excitement. "I sense more searching in our future."

"I've always been up for a bit of traveling," he replied, still scrutinizing.

There was a loud knock at the office door, wrenching them both out of their concentration.

"Mr. Winthrope," said a guard on the other side. "Your allotted time is up."

"Thank you, sir," Jesse replied. "We are wrapping up now and will be out shortly."

As Jesse packed up the documents he noticed a faint pattern appear when struck by the light from the window, like a watermark. Holding it up, the pattern appeared in earnest as a symbol across the page.

"You ever seen that before?" he asked Jenny, tilting it so she could get a better view.

She shook her head.

"I'm from a place named the Gulch, Jesse. You're lucky I know what a hammer is."

Laughing, Jesse thought about the missing pieces as he folded the documents up and put the packet inside a suit pocket.

Didn't Father mention something about plans being in Lagos, and that he was on his way to Barro with these?

"Hey Jen," Jesse said with a mischievous gleam in his eye. "You know I love you right?"

"Oh gosh, where are we headed?" she asked tensely.

und up Bolts and Buccaneer. I'll ready an ornithopter.
business to tend to with Duncan."

Vhere's he?"

"In Lagos…"

THE END

Made in the USA
Middletown, DE
08 May 2017